Blue Sun

TRACY ABREY

ISBN: 1490961100
ISBN-13: 9781490961101
Library of Congress Control Number: 2013912594
CreateSpace Independent Publishing Platform
North Charleston, South Carolina

For Tommy and Sophie

"'Twas thus and thus
They lived"; and, as the time-flood onward rolls,
Secure an anchor for their Keltic souls.

Fo'c's'le Yarns—T.E. Brown

PROLOGUE

The stone felt surprisingly smooth and warm under my face, comforting; I wondered if it was only in comparison to the metal just coming into contact with the back of my neck. Like a mouse being toyed with by a cat, I felt the first sharp, almost playful scratch. *Am I bleeding yet?* I imagined a trickle of crimson blazing a trail down the side of my neck that may or may not actually have been there. *Wasn't this destined to happen?* In a way, everything since my flight to the Isle of Man was leading up to this. Somewhere along the way, I lost my hold on logic, because if I had been paying attention, I would have realized that this was always the logical conclusion.

My eyes began watering from the sting. I didn't want to cry. I couldn't let them see me cry. I had to be brave. *This isn't the end*, I assured myself. *It's a new beginning.*

The Comeover

I watched the condensation beading on the outside of the airplane window. The mist adhered almost magnetically to the...*not glass*, I thought as I tapped it with the knuckles of my right hand. *Polycarbonate? Hmm...250 times stronger than glass, but scratches too easily.* I leaned my head against the window, investigating the material while trying to ignore the delicate drops melding into each other until, too engorged to cling to the slick pane, they shot like meteors to the edge. *Triple-layer acrylic.* I rolled my eyes at obsessing over the obvious. But then, I had to find something to divert my attention from the man on my left.

I needed only to flick my eyes in his direction and I could hardly suppress the swell of resentment. I understood the move was logical for him. Even necessary. What options were there for a scientist if a station is built specifically for him? To run your own lab would be a dream come true. Still, to rip your daughter out of her school right before her senior year? That was pretty heartless. I had not just been taken from my home and my country; I had also lost my status in the academic world.

Even though I had already been accepted into the nuclear science and engineering program at MIT, the drop from being top of the class at North East Kansas High School of Science and Mathematics to being an anonymous foreigner at Ramsey Grammar School could only be rivaled by the fall of Icarus, in my estimation. Imagining Icarus dropping like a stone into the ocean made me remember the Irish Sea below. I swallowed hard and tried to forget that once again today, I was hanging in the air over yet another large body of water.

The plane banked hard to the left, and I instinctively grabbed for my drink, momentarily distracted from my resentment. The cup sat snugly in a well in the seat-back tray, but the water inside had tilted to a disconcerting slant. The other passengers stirred and murmured in frightened whispers. I looked out the window to see angry waves where clouds should be. I tried to steady my racing heart. If we crashed over the sea, the impact of the plane on the water's surface would be about the same as smashing against solid ground. Personally, I would have preferred looking out at cold, hard concrete hurtling toward me. There could be no worse fate than water as your grave. I pulled my inhaler out of my pocket and took a deep breath.

A flight attendant, who was standing at the same angle as my water, had stopped to steady herself nearby. Her placid face was reassuring, and the plane leveled back out as quickly as it had banked. My body went limp with relief as sky replaced sea in my window.

"What was that all about?" my dad asked the flight attendant. His English accent would blend in much better than my American twang would. Fear of death was quickly replaced by my next biggest fear: fitting in at a new high school.

"Oh, nothing at all to worry about, sir. The wind had blown us a bit too far north. Some of our pilots prefer to avoid a certain area just off the coast of Douglas." She smiled.

"Why just *some* of the pilots?" he posed, as though he were collecting scientific data.

"Just our pilots native to the island, sir. And sir," she added, eyeing his lap, "we've already made an announcement. You'll need to stow your briefcase now for landing." He fidgeted with the worn leather briefcase in a show of obedience. The flight attendant smiled her passenger-soothing smile again and began making her way to the front of the small plane to secure herself for landing. Another passenger caught her attention, and she dutifully stopped. My dad, seeing she was distracted, kept his briefcase on his lap.

"Native to the island? Probably some old superstition," he harrumphed to himself. "Typical island mentality." He drummed his fingers on the briefcase that he had not opened since our departure from Kansas City. He could have stowed it in the overhead, but he chose instead to slide it under the seat in front of him for takeoffs and landings and clutch it to himself the rest of the time. That briefcase was the closest thing I had seen to an adult security blanket. He seemed always to have it within his reach. *I wonder if he sleeps with it?* I thought and rolled my eyes.

Just as I was beginning to relax, I was jolted as though I had slammed into a wall. The cabin went dark around me, and all I could see was a blindingly bright blue, dense as a twelve-inch-thick pane of stained glass, rippling like tentacles and engulfing my brain. At the same time, the airplane jerked as though it had hit something. The force snapped me out of my momentary hallucination. I slammed into my dad, and his briefcase flew from his grasp and sailed through the cabin. As all of the passengers' upper bodies were thrown into what looked like a sickening, choreographed routine, the flight attendant, untethered by a seatbelt, was tossed like a rag doll, slamming into the ceiling. The plane jerked again, and my head smacked against the crack-proof acrylic window. My temple pulsed. I tried to reach up to cradle my head, but the tumult made it impossible to control my hand. I shut my eyes. I didn't want to see anymore. *God, please don't let me drown. God, please don't let me drown.*

The vibrations stopped rattling through my body, replaced by the thuds of the landing gear descending. Groans. Quick footsteps. Someone vomiting. I opened my eyes. Flight attendants knelt in the aisle next to our seats. I could just see their unfortunate colleague's feet. She had landed in the walkway in front of us. She was moving, so she was alive. The ground bounced beneath us as the plane landed, and I wondered how I would ever be able to stand. My bones felt rattled to powder.

"My briefcase! Does anyone see my briefcase?" my dad shouted over the stewardess as her co-workers helped her off the floor. *Unbelievable*, I thought. Even more unbelievable to me was that a man near the front who had been hit in the head by the briefcase passed it to the person behind him, and passenger by passenger, they handed it back to my dad. He hugged it like a long-lost child. He never asked me if I was OK.

We slowly filed out of the plane. I felt as if I were ninety years old as I held my violin and laptop case in one shaking hand and clung to the railing of the metal stairs with the other, afraid my foot wouldn't land on the next step down. When I finally stood on the tarmac, I looked around. A sign over the entrance read "Ronaldsway Airport. Welcome to the Isle of Man." I didn't care where I was, as long as I was on land. Inside, medics checked each of us over before allowing us to pick up our checked luggage and go through customs. The flight attendant was carried past us on a stretcher.

Dad and I wheeled our worldly possessions out into the reception area of the airport, where a stranger waited for us with a handwritten sign: "Hazard." If I hadn't known my own last name, I would have considered it a warning. The driver took our things except, of course, for Dad's precious briefcase and my violin and laptop. Not wanting a violin to be thrown into the trunk was understandable, but my dad's briefcase obsession was getting ridiculous. What was so fragile and precious in that briefcase that couldn't go in the trunk? The driver led us to the little car he passed off as a limo, and my dad slid into the backseat and cradled his briefcase in his lap.

Before climbing in, I recognized a large sculpture that dominated the front of the terminal. It was a modern interpretation of the symbol on the Manx flag: three legs coming out of a center point, forming a wheel. It was supposed to look modern, but it was too harsh, robotic, almost skeletal. Something about the symbol was more familiar to me than just seeing it on the Internet should have made it. It felt like it was from my childhood. Trying to remember where I had seen it originally made my stomach knot, and I realized that wherever it was, it was not attached to a pleasant memory.

"That's the triskelion there, missy," the driver pointed out. "The Three Legs of Man. You know what that means, don't ya?"

"Um, no. I'm afraid I don't."

"Whichever way you throw us," he said, slamming the trunk shut, "we will stand."

"That's interesting," I said stupidly. "I mean, cool…" I gave up and lumbered into the backseat next to my dad, wondering why *he* couldn't contribute to the conversation and take a little pressure off me.

"Bloody comeovers," the driver muttered before opening his own door. "Like the English aren't bad enough. Sodding Yanks are invading now."

A lot of good Dad's accent did us. My uncomfortable gaze lingered on the sculpture as we pulled away from the curb. As he drove, I gawked at the palm trees that punctuated the airport landscaping. I reminded myself that the Gulf Stream bathed the shores of the island and could support the tropical vegetation that would normally never grow in a latitude so far north. Knowing the reason didn't make the sight any less bizarre. The flowerbeds were lush and bright and such a contrast to the dismal gray that hung overhead. It was an odd mix of tropics and the stereotypical British scenery that I had endured for more than a few childhood summers. But once we left the airport property, the palm trees disappeared.

We passed the ride in an uncomfortable silence as our taxi wound its way down the twisting, tree-lined roads. They were more than tree-lined, actually. So dense were the woods around us, I couldn't see sky much of the time. It was as if we were driving through a fairy-tale picture book. I half-expected Goldilocks to run into the road, fleeing the three bears.

As we approached Douglas, the trees thinned, and a most bizarre building dominated the landscape. A building that looked like an intricately folded origami swan stood in the middle of a large field. Not quite believing my eyes, I pressed my face to the window to study it. Architecture fascinated me, so I was surprised I had never heard of this building before. *Surely, with this unique design, the building should be famous in architecture circles.*

"Interested in the light bulb factory, missy?" the driver asked, eyeing me in the rearview mirror.

"Light bulb factory? I've never seen anything like it," I confessed. At that point even my dad was interested enough to glance over at the building.

"We manufacture light bulbs for most of Britain," the driver bragged.

"Why don't they just manufacture them in England?" my dad asked, irritated that the silence had been interrupted. "Save on shipping."

"Don't know, don't care," the driver snapped.

"It's beautiful," I said, trying to smooth the tension. "Anywhere would be proud to have that building. It's world-class."

"Waste of money, if you ask me," my dad muttered. "You could make light bulbs in a box."

I shut my eyes, trying to will my dad to be civil. To be predictable.

"We take pride in our island and take any opportunity to pay her back by beautifying her," the driver said, making eye contact with me in the mirror. "And nobody asked you," he muttered to my dad once he was looking back at the road.

My dad was back to scrolling through e-mails on his phone and didn't hear him.

I was relieved when we finally passed a sign that read "Douglas—Population 26,218" and palm trees began popping up again. Our taxi began sputtering as we climbed a steep hill, and my heart leaped a little at the thought that we might be near our stopping point. Fortunately, my dad had a business meeting that evening in Douglas, so this leg of the wretched trip was over and done with. We would have to wait another day to reach our new home in Ramsey.

At the top of the hill, we turned up a drive that led to a decrepit, three-story hotel. I felt for the inhaler in my pocket when I imagined the mold that would be growing in a building that old. As soon as the car stopped, I grabbed my violin and laptop and hopped out. The driver got out right after, slamming the door behind him. Apparently, he didn't want to spend any more time with my dad than I did. He put our bags down on the gravel drive, too put out with my dad to take them into the lobby, I assumed. Trying to distance myself from the inevitable bickering over the fare, I walked up the steps to the lobby.

I heard a woman's voice inside. "*Shamyr as yn oaie eck er y baie. Dy ve shickyr.*" She quickly put the phone down when she saw me.

"May I help you, miss?" the woman asked from behind an aged, wooden desk. I was speechless for a moment, a little shocked at the strange language I heard her speaking on the phone.

"Um…" I wondered briefly if I should wait for my dad. *But why should being in a foreign place change the way we do things?*

"We're checking in," I said, pulling my wallet out and handing her my dad's credit card. I had been responsible for the bills, shopping, and everything else for years. I wasn't sure Dad even knew how to write a check. She smiled and began checking us in.

While she tapped on her keyboard, I wandered away from the desk to look around the tiny lobby. There was a pretty curio cabinet at the entrance of the small hotel restaurant. On closer inspection, I saw that the delicate layer of veneer was beginning to peel away from the cabinet's cherry-colored wood, as it was on the front desk. On the glass shelves inside were miniature figurines, many of which looked antique: china fairies in all different colors and poses; a castle surrounded by delicate blown-glass water; a creepy elf caught mid step while tiptoeing; a weird mutant pig-like creature covered in little crystalline quills.

"Those are all for sale, miss," the woman informed me.

"Thanks. I'll keep that in mind," I lied, still studying the collection. I sighed quietly in disgust. Nothing irritated me more than fantasy and fable. I understood the people of the island thrived on tourism, and maybe mysticism was part of their shtick, but I rolled my eyes. I knew real life; I had lived it. And magic didn't figure into the equation.

My dad finally blustered into the lobby, fumbling with the suitcases and his beloved briefcase.

"You're in room 307, miss," the woman said to me, looking askance at my father, whose crazed hair and messy clothes made him look more like a vagabond than a scientist. I wouldn't have wanted to talk to him either. I crossed in front of him to take back the credit card. "I'm terribly sorry, but the elevator is out. You'll have to take the stairs."

I told her thank you and without a word to my dad, I took one of the suitcases, along with my violin and laptop, and began trudging up the three flights of stairs, not looking back to see where he was. Once at the top, I dropped the suitcase onto the floor in front of 307 while I unlocked the rickety door. After bringing in my half of the baggage, I left the door ajar for my dad and threw myself onto a bed.

It felt good to be horizontal. I stretched out and delighted in feeling every muscle in my arms and legs. It was blissfully quiet after a day of airport bustle and airplane droning. I was just beginning to relax when my dad pushed the door open. I didn't want to talk to him, so I pretended to be asleep. I heard his footsteps coming toward me and stop at the edge of the bed. He sighed and when I heard him turn, I peeked to see him pull the blanket off his bed. I quickly shut my eyes again and felt him laying the blanket over me, gently tucking it under my chin. I must have drifted off then, because the next thing I knew, I awoke gasping for breath from a dream in which I was drowning. That was the way I usually woke up.

What time is it? I looked around me. I could hear the toilet flush in the bathroom, so I knew my dad was still there. I sat up in bed, deciding if I wanted to turn on my laptop and look busy so he wouldn't talk to me when he came out. He had changed in the last year. Even after Mom died, he had held it together, but something was different recently. He had become distracted. And angry. The closer we had come to moving, the more detached from me he had become. As much as I was sure he was looking forward to his work on the Isle of Man, something about it seemed to make him anxious.

Maybe I'm being too critical, I thought. I knew how nervous I was in anticipation of going to a new school. As abandoned as I sometimes felt and as resentful as I was that he had moved us, I sat in the soulless hotel room needing my dad. He was all I had. I left my laptop where it was.

"I'm heading out to my meeting," he said, walking into the room. Then, as if he remembered he was my sole caregiver, he added, "Are you sure you'll be fine here on your own?"

That's it? I thought. I wanted him to initiate a hug or tell me he loved me or do *something* paternal! I suddenly remembered his smile from a lifetime ago. It was like looking at a snapshot. He was pushing me on a swing, and I was laughing as he tickled me each time I would swing back toward him. We were buddies then. But the lifeless face in front of me now only vaguely resembled that man. His empty stare burned the memory away in a flash, like a spark to dry grass in the summer. My defenses flew back up, and I decided to give as little as I got.

"Yeah. Won't be any different than usual."

"Right." He picked up his briefcase and headed toward the door.

"Is that what you're wearing?" I couldn't help but ask. He looked worse than he had in the lobby, if that was possible. He looked like…I don't know…his normal disheveled self, intensified by a day of international travel. He didn't appear to have even taken a shower.

"I'm not going to a photo shoot. I'm meeting with some local nut jobs who are up in arms that I'm going to 'ruin the island.'" He waved his hand in the air to stress the "up in arms" part.

"Why should anyone think that? You're working on an alternative power source. That could only help the environment," I stated as fact. *Never underestimate the stupidity of the general public*, I thought to myself, but knew better than to say it out loud. It would only egg my dad on.

"We've been very explicit to the press," he said with an edge to his voice. "I have better things to do right now than deal with a bunch of fanatics." There it was again. That bitter tone I had grown to recognize that signaled he was pulling away from me.

"You're not going to meet with them by yourself, are you? Don't you need backup if you're talking to a bunch of crazies?" I hadn't known about this militant group on the island. *Great. One more thing to occupy my mind.*

"Darius will be there," he said dismissively and walked to the door as though we weren't in the middle of a conversation.

"Who's Darius?"

"My assistant. Enough questions, Genny. I'll be late."

"Whatever," I snapped and went back to my computer.

He came over, kissed me on my head, and walked away. The door clicked shut.

What was the difference between sitting alone in a hotel on the Isle of Man or at home—I mean, in Kansas City? And really, what should Kansas City mean to me? We had only lived there for a couple of years. We had moved around so much that I had never had time to fit in anywhere. So, as much as I had worried about fitting in on the island, what difference was it? If you're too geeky for a science and math high school in Kansas, you won't fit in at Ramsey Grammar School on the tiny Isle of Man either.

I slapped the laptop shut and started mashing buttons on the TV remote. Nothing. "All I need is my violin, anyway," I said to the black-screened TV. I took my violin out of its case. *It's all I've ever needed.*

As I drew the bow across the strings, all the tension, all the dread, all the uncertainty of this unexpected turn in life ebbed from my mind and swirled into the sequence of notes that now danced in the air. I paced a trail in the room, gently swaying, as all was made right in my soul. But peace was short-lived. A sudden wind blew through the open window, making the curtains snap and spasm. I sighed as I put down my violin and reached to crank the window shut. As I stretched for the handle, something outside caught my attention.

Despite the storm that was about to lay siege to the island, a lone man stood across the street from the hotel, near the cliff, eyeing the horizon. Lightning cracked overhead, and I jumped back from the window. Once my heart had calmed back down, I edged back to look out.

The man below still hadn't taken cover, and I found myself worrying for his safety. There had to be something wrong with him. Maybe he had just suffered a stroke and didn't realize what was happening. Nobody in his right mind would stand so dangerously close to a cliff in this maelstrom, watching it as calmly as he would fireworks on the Fourth of July. Without thinking, I grabbed my room key and ran out the door, slinging my heavy cardigan on as I went.

Once outside, it was hard to stand in the gusts that blew in off the sea. I hugged my sweater tighter around me, defying the wind to turn me back. Truth is, nothing could turn me back. I was drawn to the man on the cliffside like a magnet. Someone had to help him, and if no one else saw him, then I had to be the hero by default. He was so engrossed in something out in the sea that he didn't seem to notice me approaching.

"Sir? Sir?" The wind carried my words away, and he didn't answer.

It was difficult to see as the wind whipped my hair in front of my face. Not wanting to startle him, I reached out to touch his shoulder, but just before I did, I realized that everything about the man was deathly still. His body. His clothes. It was a statue. His bronze hands clenched his coat tightly around his neck; the bottom of the coat motionlessly billowed around him. He stared out over the bay, watching. I slowly circled him and ended standing right behind him, looking in the same direction he so intently gazed.

Ominous clouds roiled overhead as the wind churned the sea rolling into the bay. Curiously, in the heart of the dark water below, a small, blue light glowed. *It couldn't be a buoy*, I thought, since the light didn't move as the tumult continued around it. As I stared, I made out the dim shape of a castle highlighted by the light that shone within. *Just a weird lighthouse*, I thought, and began walking back to the hotel.

But as I walked, I couldn't help but turn back to look at the strange blue light. I had never heard of a lighthouse built offshore. In the middle of a bay. It was blue, but clearly not from a color gel like the ones they use for colored lighting in a theater production. And an incandescent bulb wasn't emitting that light. There was an almost indiscernible movement within the light, giving it an organic quality. Despite the light seeming almost alive, its glow made me feel colder than the biting Manx wind.

I held my collar tight against my neck, unintentionally mirroring the statue that had lured me out, and ran back to the warmth and safety of the hotel.

Once back in the room, I quickly shut the window and pulled the curtains closed, averting my eyes from the statue outside. I knew I couldn't see it without thinking of the castle lighthouse with the eerie blue glow, and I wanted to forget about it. Something about the castle made my stomach twist.

I went straight to the bathroom, turned the shower on hot, and peeled the wet, dirty clothes off my body. The steam felt good, and I hoped that after a few minutes of steeping in the hot water, I could feel alive again. I washed the icky airplane film out of my hair and scrubbed it off my skin. By the time I was out, I was so exhausted that I could barely move. My legs felt so leaden that I struggled to dress for bed. When I finally did, I collapsed onto the bed and fell fast asleep again, this time with my wet hair soaking the cheap hotel pillow.

"Imogen?" a woman whispered, her voice sounding like wind chimes or trickling water. I didn't know who had spoken. Only that it was not my mother.

I heard a flutter, like the wings of a butterfly.

"My name is Genny," I tried to say, but my mouth felt as if it were full of marbles. I was helpless to speak, helpless to move, and a slithering blue web circled around me.

"*Cha nel fys aym c'raad ta mee,*" I heard myself say.

"*T'ou balley,*" she responded. The blue faded away, and my usual dream of drowning took its place.

On the tiny tram platform the next morning, my dad stood far enough away that we couldn't talk. It wasn't on purpose. He was checking his e-mails on his phone and he rarely noticed where he was or where I was in proximity to him lately. There wasn't much to say, anyway. I was asleep by the time he got back to the room the night before, and I really didn't feel like trying to explain what I had seen. I was just glad to be on the last leg of our journey.

A man in the little station house called out that our tram would be five minutes late. I glanced up at the Manx Electric Railway sign, wondering how anything could possibly be delayed on an island this small. I considered telling my dad about the delay, since his mind was clearly elsewhere, but I figured it wouldn't matter. He'd be busy reading e-mails until the tram pulled up, regardless of how late it was. At least he had a distraction. I paced on the platform. The man I neared prattled endlessly on his cell phone in a language that clearly was not English.

"*Shoh hooin ee,*" he said, glancing quickly at me. "*Ish t'ayn.*"

He must be speaking Manx, I realized, thinking back to the woman at the hotel. It also sounded like the language from my dream.

I turned my attention back to the station house. It was one of the most curious buildings I'd ever seen. It resembled a tiny log cabin that had been painted glossy red, only the logs weren't straight: they were crooked and placed haphazardly, like a bag of giant, misshapen macaroni noodles had been poured over the building.

I was finding fewer things to keep my interest, so out of boredom, I took the tram ticket out of my pocket to recheck the time printed there. As I did, it slipped from my fingers. I instantly panicked, imagining it blowing into the bay and my dad blustering as he bought me another ticket.

Before the wind had a chance to carry it away, the strange-speaking man appeared beside me, and dropping his black leather case on the ground, snatched the ticket up. His shaved head shone in the sun as he stooped over, and before he was upright again, a red mark on his neck caught my eye. It was just behind his right ear. For a second I thought it was a strange birthmark but I quickly realized it was a tattoo. It was the Manx triskelion. *What a bunch of fanatics*, I thought. I swallowed the lump that had formed in my throat.

"Here you go, miss," he said, smiling as he stood upright. His words were weighted down with a thick, Gaelic-sounding accent, and even though he was speaking English, it took me a moment to decipher what he'd said. "Heading up to Ramsey, are you?" he asked without looking at my ticket.

"Yes, me and my *dad*," I said, nodding in my dad's direction to indicate I was not alone and was too young to be a prospective pickup.

He seemed undeterred. "Oh! You're American! We don't see too many Americans on the island. A few come over during the TT."

I hated to be lured into a conversation, but my curiosity always got the better of me, despite the obvious consequences. "What's the TT?"

"Motorcycle race. The course goes all over the island. Happens every summer."

"Ah," I said, becoming disinterested as soon as I got my information.

"Not the motorcycle type?"

"No. Can I have my ticket back, please?"

"Oh, sorry. Forgot I had it." He handed me the ticket, smiling. I noticed that his rough, calloused hands looked strong enough and big enough to crush my skull. I shuddered as I imagined that happening right there on the platform. "So what are you doing on the Isle of Man?" I couldn't place exactly what changed in his expression. It was like he shifted gears from "pleasure" to "down to business." His aqua-blue eyes narrowed as though he were calculating his next move.

"I didn't catch your name," he said, reaching out toward my arm.

My chest tightened, and I lurched backward to avoid him.

"I—I have to let my dad know the tram's delayed," I stammered. "Thanks for the ticket."

"I think you misunderstood," he called after me as I walked briskly back toward my dad. "I didn't mean anything…"

I didn't look back, but I could tell the man didn't move. I could feel him watching me. I picked up my pace. I had always heard you should trust your instincts. If you have a bad feeling about someone, there's probably a good reason. I definitely had a bad feeling about him.

I couldn't get that tattoo out of my mind. It was like it had been branded there, blood red. It reminded me of the metal triskelion sculpture at the airport that left me feeling as cold as the metal from which it was sculpted. Why would anyone want to make that horrible symbol a part of his body? To etch it onto his neck was even stranger. Everything about that man frightened me to my core, from the tattoo to the calculating conversation. I tried to convince myself that the jet lag was getting to me and making me paranoid, but I couldn't help but feel that the man had been waiting there for me.

Thankfully, the tram pulled up.

It was only two cars long. I should have suspected as much from the old-world station, but I still could barely believe my eyes. The rear car was open and so old-fashioned that it looked like horses should pull it. *Why should I expect any different? I'm literally in the middle of nowhere.* With the tram being so small, though, I had little chance of escaping the creepy tattooed man.

Dad and I put our baggage at the end of the covered front car and sat next to each other. I kept my eyes on the door of the carriage to see if Tattoo Man would sit near us, but he didn't. Once the doors were shut, I scanned the platform. He wasn't there either.

He must have gotten the hint and sat in the other carriage. He was probably just being friendly to a "comeover." Nothing sinister on his part, just jet lag on mine, I tried to convince myself.

As the tram pulled out, the sunlight glinted off the shiny red paint of the station house, catching my eye. It no longer looked like it was covered in macaroni. The bright red shapes resembled rudimentary fragments of the legs of the triskelion, just like on the man's tattoo. The station house shrank into the distance, but it seemed I could see the glint of red much longer than should have been possible.

Almost in unison, Dad and I heaved our laptops onto our laps, and I relaxed a little at the subtle whirring noises they produced. It was an unspoken signal that we didn't have to talk. There was no question as to my first priority on the Internet. I searched "isle of man Douglas castle."

The castle was called the Tower of Refuge and was completed in 1832, thanks to a man named William Hillary. A photo showed a bronze statue of Hillary, windswept and looking down into the bay at the Tower of Refuge. I was a little too familiar with that statue.

After too many shipwrecks on the deadly rocks at the bottom of Douglas Bay, Hillary ordered the Tower of Refuge to be built as a place for sailors to await rescue. He believed in this project so fervently that he himself provided half the money needed. He ensured that it was continually stocked with bread and fresh water for the remainder of his lifetime. I was curious as to the year it had been converted into a lighthouse, but after scanning several different sites and finding nothing, I gave up.

The next thing I remembered was jumping when my dad nudged me. A string of drool dripped down the window where I had slumped against it. I wiped my chin and rubbed my forehead, hoping there wasn't an imprint on it.

There was no telling how long I had been asleep, but I was pretty sure the trip wouldn't have lasted more than a couple hours. I slapped my laptop shut and slid it into my bag. By the time my dad and I had collected our things, we were the last ones off the tram.

I may have been groggy, but even in my woozy state, only one thing was on my mind. As we were disembarking, I looked for the tattooed man from the Douglas station, but I didn't see him. *It's time to let it go*, I chided myself. *He didn't follow you. You're just going crazy.* I decided that being crazy was a more appealing option than being stalked.

I looked around the little station decorated with hanging baskets brimming with red and purple pansies. I could tell it would be a quiet year ahead. The Isle of Man wasn't exactly a center of hustle and bustle. Even the tram stations were fairly quiet. I noticed a woman standing next to the station house. She wasn't hard to miss. She was the only person waiting. It's not like we were in Grand Central Station, but even in a crowd, I would have spotted her. Her hair was a fiery red mess of tight curls springing out uncontrollably in all directions. Her face was a stark contrast to the madness that was her hair. Her porcelain skin looked soft, perhaps because of her plumpness and the natural loss of elasticity that comes with middle age. Soft lines were etched around her mouth and eyes from a lifetime of smiling and laughing. I couldn't imagine being that happy.

I quickly realized those green eyes were focused solely on me. She let go of a pendant she was clutching and looked at her wristwatch, buried deep beneath layers of clothes topped by a woolly brown sweater, and then looked around the platform. The pendant swung gently on its long silver chain around her neck, finally resting low on her chest. She took a quick second glance at me and left. Her floor-length, mottled brown and moss-green skirt billowed around her as she walked, making her appear to float away.

My dad had almost made his way off the platform to a taxi by the time I looked around, once again unaware of my whereabouts. Back home I would have called after him but here I didn't want my loud American accent to draw attention to me. Instead, I ran as fast as I could while dragging my suitcase behind me with one hand and clutching my violin case and laptop to my chest with the other.

The people who contracted my dad had secured a furnished home for us. It was one in a row of about ten Victorian townhouses. It was strange to walk into my new home sight unseen. Most people deliberate over what house to buy; this one doesn't have enough bedrooms, that one doesn't have a big enough kitchen…not my dad. He was content to let them choose a house for us. And the furniture looked nothing like us, not that we had "a look." But if we did, it wouldn't have been cottage style.

The front door opened into a living room filled by an overstuffed, yellow, floral-print sofa. The coordinating throw pillows and framed nature prints hanging on the wall made me feel like I was intruding into someone's home while she was out. It was as if the house had been suddenly abandoned, furniture and all. I guess it shouldn't have bothered me. Why should someone feel uncomfortable over her home being so comfortable? Maybe it was because with just my dad and me, no one had thought of decorating our home. I had become too accustomed to a Spartan existence.

And even if the home situation was slightly creepy, it wasn't like I was going to be there for long. One more year of high school, and I was off to MIT. So what was one year of living in someone else's house? With that in mind, I left my dad, who was standing like a lost puppy next to the sofa, and headed up the stairs to look for my bedroom.

I put my things down gently on the wooden floor of my bedroom and closed the door behind me. I knew it was mine because there were only two bedrooms and this one had a twin bed. An old, white, wooden dresser stood under a window, and a little white nightstand was pushed against the bed. The walls were lavender, and the curtains and bedspread were cream with lavender flowers. A worn lavender rug was in the middle of the floor. I hated lavender. And at that moment, I hated lavender more than anything in the whole world. It made me want to throw up.

I realized this year would be the longest of my life. I fell onto the bed and cried into someone else's lavender pillow.

The Visible Girl

I heard a conversation once between a group of boys. Back when I could understand what people were saying without concentrating. When I wasn't surrounded by people with weird accents.

The topic was "If you could have any superpower, what would it be?" Super-strength and flying were the favorites among the group. One little boy said invisibility. But the group quickly dismissed invisibility as inferior to strength and flying. I wasn't sure how I felt, since I was as good as invisible. I was not ugly, just plain. I was not hated, just ignored. I think that if asked, my former classmates wouldn't remember me at all. I *was* intelligent, but quiet. I never spoke in class. I seriously doubted that any of my teachers could pick me out of a crowd. To them I was the sum of my test results. I existed only on paper.

Shower. Slick damp hair into ponytail. Eat bread roll (removed from airline meal and shoved into pocket for such an occasion as this, since no groceries had been bought). *Jeans. Brown, long-sleeved T-shirt. Jacket.* My near-empty backpack hung deflated off my shoulder. I was about to cup my hands under the kitchen faucet to get a quick drink before leaving when something told me to look in the cabinet. Sure enough, there were glasses, plates…I quickly opened all the kitchen cabinets, not willing to allow curiosity to eat at me the whole day. Cans of soup, pasta and a jar of sauce, cereal…and in the refrigerator, milk. Yesterday's airline roll didn't seem like such a culinary treat all of the sudden. They, whoever *they* were, had thought of everything. I grabbed a granola bar and shoved it into my backpack.

On the table next to the front door, there was a little snapshot of familiarity. "Won't be home for dinner," Dad had written.

I'll be dining alone tonight. Again. I didn't mind. I thought I had seen an Indian Takeout nearby.

I had used Google Earth to locate Ramsey Grammar School, and it was only a couple of blocks away from my house. My dad had already left for who knows where, so I set off alone, looking forward to stretching my legs after more than twenty-four hours of sitting in airplanes and trams the days before. It was a little brisk outside, but some fresh air was just what I needed before a day of weirdness. It was Thursday, and the school term had started on Monday, so not only was I a foreigner, but I was also about to be a foreigner who had to find an unclaimed desk in a sea of unfamiliar faces who had already nestled in.

Up the road I noticed two girls about my age. They were laughing and talking with each other. One had long, black, wavy hair; the other had reddish-auburn hair that hung like a curtain and reflected the sunlight like a piece of polished amber. I tucked the mousy-brown clump of hair that had escaped my ponytail behind my ear. Occasionally, their long hair would swing to the side when they looked back at me. *They're not looking at you. It's just your imagination*, I told myself. Besides, they were obviously their own little clique. Dressed alike. *How lame,* I thought. *Oh no. No, no, no, no...* pleated green skirts, white shirts, green tartan ties, and matching blazers with crests on the pockets... At that horrifying moment, I realized they were wearing uniforms.

They continued to giggle and kept walking, me following behind, slower and less sure of myself with every step. *That company of Dad's thought of a house, furniture, and food, but they didn't bother with my school uniform? Very selective thoughtfulness.*

I would have thought jeans and a brown shirt would have rendered me all but invisible, but I was wrong. I was the opposite of invisible. I was an orange neon sign in a tea parlor and I wanted to die. I was hoping they wouldn't allow me to stay in school for the day without a uniform, but the office staff was too kind and said it wouldn't be a problem, as long as I had one for the next day. The secretary felt sorry for me, assuring me as I left that the other students would probably not even notice I was wearing street clothes. She was wrong. The walk to my locker was excruciating, with students parting around me like the Red Sea.

I put my jacket in my locker and after briefly considering hiding inside until the other students left at the end of the day, I shut the door. *At least I won't forget my combination. Numbers are the least of my problems.*

"You didn't get the memo about uniforms?" a tall, dark-haired boy said, leaning against the other lockers.

"There was a memo?" I gasped, horrified that I had missed some important piece of mail that could have saved me from this embarrassment.

"Um, no. It was a joke. Just not a very good one apparently." His tie was loose and off-center, his collar unbuttoned. "The uniform's not so bad. You can personalize your look just a little." He wore a crooked little smile as off-center as his tie. He stuck his hand out. "I'm Ken."

"I'm American," I bumbled as my hand touched his. I squeezed my eyes shut to avoid seeing his reaction.

"Of course you are. But do your friends call you Imogen?" he asked with a laugh.

"Genny, actually." *No one calls me Imogen but my mom, and she's not here.* "How did you know my name?"

"I'm the new-student greeter. Between us, I'm trying to come up with a...less officious title."

"It *is* a little dorky."

"To put it mildly. Anyway, the secretary told me you were coming. I'm supposed to show new students around, so as you might imagine, my job doesn't keep me terribly busy."

"I can imagine."

"I have a copy of your schedule. A bit heavy on the maths and sciences, isn't it?" he mused aloud as he studied the paper.

"That's kind of my thing, I guess."

"Well, everyone has issues," he said. "Actually, we have English together at the end of the day...come on. We have a few minutes before class starts, so I can show you around." With me in tow, he wove through the students milling around their lockers and went upstairs.

"This," he said, leading me through a heavy, unmarked door at the end of the hallway, "is the lounge for final-year students." There were a few tables and chairs, and an old tattered sofa, and along one wall were some vending machines. "The coolest part is..." Ken rounded a corner, and the room opened out onto a rooftop patio.

"There's no door to the outside? It's got to get pretty chilly in here in the winter."

"Admittedly, you won't find a lot of students in here in the winter months, but it's so fantastic the rest of the year that the school has never closed it off."

"This is really cool." *Decidedly too cool for me*, I noted to myself. *Won't be coming back here again.*

He quickly showed me both buildings and the indoor swimming pool. He mentioned he was on the swim team, so I suppose that made the pool an integral part of a tour. His casual walk around the circumference of the pool was agony to me. I stayed as far away from the edge as I could without it being noticeable. The light danced on the surface of the water. I supposed that to anyone else, the water looked like gently rippling silk, soft and inviting. But all I could see was the heavy stillness that was lying underneath, thick as wet cement.

"It seems like it's kind of a chilly climate to have a swim team," I observed.

"When you swim as much as we do, you get used to the weather." He looked at his waterproof swimmer's watch. "Whoa. Time flies when you're having fun. We'd better get going."

He was walking me to my first class, physics, when a tall, older man in a suit motioned us over. His suit was gently worn with age but had been well cared for. It probably would have been in shreds in anyone else's care. He had a gray, grizzled beard and leaned to the left on a knobbled, hand-carved stick. I wondered what had happened to him, because he didn't look old enough to need a cane. He just looked worn, like his suit.

"Imogen Hazard?" he asked in a baritone voice.

"Genny," I corrected him. "Yes?"

"I'm Mr. Moore, the headmaster, or principal, as I believe you Americans call it." His hand engulfed mine as he greeted me. "I trust Ken has been making you feel at home?" His voice was so deep, and he spoke so slowly and purposefully that I almost felt sleepy. He was like a lullaby.

"Yes, sir."

He smiled warmly at me. "Do let me know if there's anything I can do to help you."

"Thank you," I said.

As Ken led me off, Mr. Moore called after us, "Good job, Kendreague."

"Thank you, Mr. Moore," Ken called back. "He's pure Gandalf, isn't he?" Ken whispered to me with a grin.

"Who's Gandalf?"

"Oh dear. No Tolkien? What else don't they teach you in America?"

"I've never really been into reading. Well, I like reading, just not fiction...fantasy..." My cheeks burned bright red.

"Oh...well, here we are. Physics. Hopefully, this is more to your liking...but I can't imagine how." He laughed out loud.

I tried to join in but only felt stupid. "Maybe I'll see you later," I said to him at the classroom door and instantly regretted it. It was unlike me to be chatty to a boy. To anyone, really. He was just so friendly and the surroundings so foreign, I wanted to cling to him like a life preserver in the ocean.

"Yeah," he said, smiling. "See you later."

While I didn't want to lose the one familiar face on the island, the thought of a science class warmed the cockles of my heart a little. The teacher gave me my textbook and showed me an empty desk. Of course, it was in the front row. I think I was the only student in the world who *liked* sitting in the front row, so I never had to worry about fighting people off to get my coveted seat. My whole body relaxed as the smell of old pages wafted up from the textbook. It reminded me of sitting in my mom's lap while she read to me from an old copy of *The Three Bears*. That seemed like a lifetime ago.

The physics lesson was basic but still felt comforting. The rest of the morning was in large part a replay of the first class. Textbook, front-row seat.

I looked for Ken at lunch, but realized how ridiculous that was. He was probably at the lounge for final-year students that he didn't need to mention was exclusively for the cooler set. If I had seen him in the lunchroom, would I have been bold enough to sit with him? Never, and I knew it. But my lack of bravery didn't matter; he was nowhere to be seen.

I saw an empty chair at a table of girls who were *not* the ones who had laughed at me on the way to school that morning. This was my chance. I could reinvent myself. I had really psyched myself up to be the charming American girl after the move. I wanted to end my high school years on a social high. They didn't know I had always been the quiet, nerdy one with her head stuck in a book at lunch. Surely if I was as smart as the tests said I was, I could pretend to be social for one year.

But I couldn't even make it a day. After concentrating on what the teachers had been saying all morning, I completely zoned out. Picking out the meaning through the alien cadence of a foreign accent was doing my head in. I knew we were speaking the same language, but it was difficult to hear what they were saying over the strange sounds coming out of their mouths. I guess I sounded as strange to them. But then, they had all probably grown up watching American movies and the occasional American television show. I hadn't exactly been raised on a diet of Manx entertainment.

The girls at my lunch table must have thought I was crazy, but I didn't pay enough attention to them to notice their reaction. I allowed their words to waft past me like a river of babble. I may as well have eaten my lunch while an orchestra was tuning before a concert. I could only assume they waited until after lunch to discuss my clothing faux pas.

Walking out, I saw the two girls who had laughed at me all the way to school that morning. Just as I passed their chairs, my foot caught on something, and I stumbled forward, catching myself just before I hit the floor. The girls couldn't contain themselves, busting out in cackles. I looked back in time to see the red-haired girl pull her foot back under the table. *She tripped me? What did I do to deserve that?* I hated them. I hated our stupid house, and I hated the stupid island that I'd had trouble finding on a map. And I wanted to hate my dad for making us move. The only thing that stopped me was that I would have made the same decision if I were him.

One year. It will only be for one year.

I shook it off and went by my locker before my last class to get my backpack and jacket. A quick getaway after school would prevent awkward locker chitchat. I had survived lunchtime chitchat, barely, but I could dodge that bullet for just so long. A homelife of silence had stilted my ability to make small talk, and I avoided it at all costs. Besides, I had never had much in common with people my own age. I'd been waiting to get into college since kindergarten, in the belief that finally everyone my age would catch up to me. It's like I was born old. My mom used to say I was an old soul.

When I walked into English class, Ken was sitting in the front row next to an empty desk I could only presume was mine. Trying to avoid eye contact with the other students until I had on the proper attire, I returned his smile. Much friendlier than the other teachers, Mr. Creer smiled too and handed me a tome entitled *Great Literature of Great Britain, Isle of Man Edition*. I heaved it onto my desk and sat down.

"How's your day been going, Miss Hazard?" Ken whispered.

"I've had better."

"Good. Then tomorrow can only be better."

English class was by far the liveliest part of my day. I could tell that Mr. Creer awoke every day with a smile on his face and a spring in his step, eager to impart his passion for Manx literature to young minds. He bounced as he spoke, barely containing his enthusiasm. There was a teacher like that at every school, but what surprised me was Ken. I would have thought it was out of character for someone like Ken to dominate classroom discussion, but truth was, I didn't really know anything about him. Ken seemed so relaxed and self-confident outside of class that I would have guessed he was a slacker at school, but in class, he sounded as intelligent as…me.

But English was definitely not my forte. Everything is so subjective in literature. Nebulous fluff. Math and science held everything I loved. Unbending, unchanging, cold, hard fact. Black and white. So as I listened to Ken and the teacher banter back and forth, expounding on the subtle nuances of blah, blah, blah, I closed my eyes and imagined I was in a lab, white and pristine. I opened my eyes to discover the other students were as bored as I was and doodled in their books or passed notes back and forth, accustomed to the English class diversion that was Ken. I found myself lazily scribbling chemical equations for polymers in the margin of the text.

My stomach knotted as I shoved my *Great Literature of Great Britain* book into my backpack after class.

My knowledge of American literature would be wasted—not that it wasn't already, in my opinion, but at least it served its purpose to earn my A in English. I would have to start all over in English now. The thought of losing math and science study time to little-known Manx writers made me wince. A waste of brain cells. At least I wouldn't have much work in my other classes. High school science and math was child's play to me.

"How much money do you have on you?" Ken asked me, swinging his backpack onto his shoulder.

"Umm…," I stammered, taken aback. "None. I spent what I had on lunch."

"That's too bad," he said thoughtfully. "I was going to take you by the shop where you can buy a uniform."

"Oh wait. Don't tell anyone, but I have a credit card."

"You were holding out on me," he teased. "You *are* an American girl! A credit card!"

"No, it's not like that!" I pleaded, chasing after him. "I have my dad's credit card in case of emergency. After today I would say that getting a uniform before tomorrow is definitely an emergency."

"I've heard that one before…no, actually, I haven't heard that one before. But you're right. I think wearing a uniform to school tomorrow will make a big difference in your day. A definite state of emergency. Let's go to the high street."

I soon remembered that "high street" was British for main street when Ken took me to a street of shops in the middle of town. Sure enough, one of the peeling, thirty-year-old mannequins in the front window of an old-fashioned shop wore the uniform I'd been looking at on the other girls all day. Apparently, the school uniform in the window was all the storeowner felt he needed to get business, because he certainly hadn't bothered to make any improvements to the store. The carpet looked as old as the mannequins. It was small inside and mostly a sea of identical uniform components, save for a smattering of secondhand clothes hanging against one wall.

I trolled through the racks of blazers until I found one in my size and pulled it on over my shirt. It was so tight, I couldn't button it. My face turned bright red, and Ken suddenly pretended to be looking at a text on his phone. I was mortified. Either I had gained thirty pounds overnight or the sizing was different here. Clothes shopping, my least favorite activity, had just become even more of a chore, and I didn't think that was possible. I knew I wasn't fat, but instantly going up two sizes didn't do much for my self-esteem. After finally finding a blazer that buttoned, I took a whole uniform in the corresponding size into the small, dingy dressing room that was little more than a closet with a brown curtain pinned on either side of the door opening for privacy.

"Ken, you don't have to stay," I hinted through the curtain as I dressed. "You've done enough. I mean, really. You've completely fulfilled your role as new-student greeter."

"Don't worry about it."

"But don't you have homework, or something?" I pleaded, pulling on the skirt.

"Not much."

I knew I had been beaten, so I put my blazer back on, this time over a starched, white shirt.

"Fine," I sighed, pulling back the chintzy curtain. "How does this thing work?" I asked Ken, holding an untied necktie as I walked barefoot out of the dressing room.

"You should…wear your, um, knee socks with that," he said, gesturing at my bare legs.

"Well, I didn't see how my feet could have gotten fatter too. I'm willing to take a chance that the socks will fit."

"Right," he said, roughly running his hand through his hair and dragging his gaze up to my face, "but you'll need to try on some shoes too. Now, as for the tie." He took it from me. "All right. Pay close attention, because I won't be there tomorrow morning to do it for you."

He took the tie and stood close behind me, sliding it around my neck. I felt his warm breath on my ear and silently cursed myself for shivering, hoping he didn't notice. His fingers, occasionally brushing against my neck, began to work at the tie.

"The rabbit hops over the log. The rabbit crawls under the log. The rabbit runs around the log, twice, because he's trying to outwit the fox. Finally, the rabbit dives, safe and sound, into his rabbit hole. *Et voila*." He was about to pull the necktie tight, but stopped. "I think it looks better a little disheveled, though." He carefully unbuttoned my top button, and I could feel my cheeks grow hot again, this time for a different reason. He gently pulled the tie tighter, but left it a little loose against my neck. Just like his.

"There," he said smugly. "I think that's a look you and I can pull off. Not literally, of course," he added, a bit flustered.

"Thanks," I said, quickly disappearing behind the curtain before my face turned into a supernova.

Back on the street, I looked like a down-and-out trust fund baby, with arms loaded down with shopping bags, but of the brandless and cheap plastic variety.

"Do you need help getting all that home?"

"No, I'm fine," I lied, trying not to look overloaded.

"You sure? Because it wouldn't be any trouble…"

"No. Really. My house isn't too far from here. Besides, it's getting late. I wouldn't want you to be late for dinner."

"Right." He ruffled his hair again. "Wouldn't want to make Mum mad," he joked.

"See you tomorrow."

"All right, then. See you."

As soon as Ken was out of sight, I dropped the packages on the ground and rubbed the indentations the heavy bags had left on my wrists. I heaved them back up, trying to keep the weight on each arm equal, and started toward the Indian Takeout.

The sidewalk was a maze of cracks on the less traveled side-road I took. I watched the ground beneath me to keep from catching my foot on a loose bit of pavement. I set the bags down again to rest my aching wrists. Salty air blew down the road from the sea and filled my lungs. It tasted clean and pure, and I stood there just to appreciate breathing it in.

The breeze made the overcast sky swirl above me, like a mother's hand running through her child's hair. I smiled to no one in particular, and remembering the Indian Takeout wasn't too much farther, I picked up my bags again. Although I knew it was just my imagination, my load felt lighter.

It wasn't until after I sized up the large naan in foil alongside the containers of chicken curry and biryani rice on the counter of the Indian Takeout that I realized I should have taken Ken up on his offer. I hadn't wanted him to know that my dad had deserted me for dinner on our second night in Ramsey, but I also wasn't taking into account adding food to my load. I unzipped my backpack and started wedging the containers against my lit book to keep them upright and to provide a barrier between the piping hot food and my back. My fingers burned as I carefully poked them into position.

"I'm not sure I would do that if I were you," the Indian lady behind the counter warned.

"It'll be fine," I replied optimistically. "The food won't spill."

The lady shrugged and disappeared into the kitchen.

I was right. When I got home, the food was upright and perfectly nestled beside my textbook. I ate on the couch while I tried to read that night's lit assignment. The passage was hard going; it was Chaucer, and I felt like I might as well be reading a foreign language, or listening to Manx chatter at lunch. I hated literature that was so old that it used English words that were extinct. I closed the book halfway through my reading and hoped Mr. Creer wouldn't direct any questions my way. I wasn't too worried. Ken seemed to take up most of his time.

Surfing the web was much more inspirational for my science study than my physics textbook. High school science curriculum was so basic for me, it was like sending a high school student to kindergarten to learn to read, but this was a hoop through which I had to jump. My own studies were what kept me motivated. New findings in the field of science always spurred me on to new theories of my own, and then came the excitement of hypothesizing and researching. I never doubted what my future held—life in a laboratory— and I couldn't imagine anything more fulfilling.

I found myself that night lingering on websites about alternative power sources, what my dad had been commissioned to study on the Isle of Man. Maybe if I just looked at this year as my personal sacrifice for his scientific discovery, I could justify it all. Including my personal embarrassment about the whole uniform thing. That was it. This was my sacrifice for a greater good. I finally closed my laptop in favor of my violin, a little smug with my epiphany. I was halfway through Tartini's "The Devil's Trill" when the door lock jiggled, almost making me jump out of my skin.

"Dad?" I called.

Seconds later, my dad trudged into the room. His clothes were crumpled, and his permanent five o'clock shadow was looking closer to six thirty.

"Sorry I'm late. You ate, right?"

"Sure, Dad." *Five hours ago*, I thought. "I have plenty of leftovers if you're hungry."

"No thanks. I think I'll just go straight to bed." He was laying his briefcase down on the counter, but almost as if thinking better of it, he clutched it to his chest and carried it into his bedroom.

"How's your work coming along?" I asked after him.

He came back and leaned wearily against the doorway.

"Fine." He blew the word out, too tired to exert the energy to speak.

"I was just researching alternative energy tonight. It's really fascinating!" I gushed. I envied him so much for getting to spend all his time in a lab rather than in stupid classes all day. *One day that will be me*, I thought, barely able to contain my excitement. "What exactly are you working on in your lab?"

"Alternative energy," he droned.

"Well, yeah, but what kind of experiments are you doing? I've been reading some papers online about wind farms."

"Sure, Genny. Wind farms."

"Maybe I can come out with you one day. I wouldn't be in the way." *Please say yes. Please say yes.*

"We'll talk about it later. I'm too tired right now. And put that violin away. I need to try to sleep."

"OK, Dad," I said, deflated. "Good night."

"'Night," he said as the door shut behind him. A moment later the door creaked open again. "How was school?"

"It was fine, Dad. Go get some sleep. I love you."

The corners of his mouth twitched up into a weary smile.

"Love you too." He couldn't hold the smile on his face any longer and added, after a second of thought, "Genny, I'm sorry." His recent angry exterior melted enough for me to see the dad from my childhood.

"For what?"

He looked down at the floor. "I…I just am." He closed the door.

I stood alone in a house that was not mine. With all I had to think about, being in a new home, a new school, a new country, I should not have had to occupy my thoughts with my father, but how could I not? In a way, I lost him the same day I lost my mother. In a way, I understood why he withdrew. She was the sun in his universe, and when she died, his world became night. All he had left were his equations. Black and white.

Despite the crushing impact her death had on me, part of me felt sorry for him. But a much larger part of me resented him for what he had become. My sun had been snuffed out too. Her death was an accident, but *he* was the one who orphaned me. He had been pulling away from me so much in the last year that I didn't feel like I had any parents anymore.

I interred my violin in its case. My concerto was over for the night.

The Tree

Life goes a lot more smoothly when you don't stick out in the crowd. Wearing street clothes the first day is the equivalent of wearing a clown suit to public school; all eyes are on you for the wrong reason. In retrospect, I would have thought that jeans, compared to a tartan skirt, would have lent me some coolness. Turns out, it's not always about what you wear; it's about fitting the mold, no matter how embarrassing the mold is. Despite wearing what I thought was a ridiculous green outfit, I felt deliciously invisible the second day, like a fish in the midst of a school of its species. It wasn't until I opened my mouth that I exposed my alienness, so I tried to keep that to a minimum.

When I got to school, I threw my backpack into the bottom of my locker. My lit book remained inside. I wouldn't worry about that until the end of the day. Out of sight, out of mind. I had bigger fish to fry. Lunchtime.

Considering the fiasco that was lunch the day before, my plan was to sit alone at a table. It wouldn't exactly be viewed as social, but at least people wouldn't gawk at me like a sideshow freak every time I tried to say something. That plan was crushed as soon as I walked into the cafeteria. Not one table was empty. I sighed and got in line to buy a peanut butter sandwich. Apparently, peanut butter wasn't the staple in the Isle of Man that it was in America, so the closest I could get was egg salad. One more thing to remember: bring lunch from home.

The pressure was on once I had lunch in my hands. I had to sit down somewhere. I had to go to Plan B, which was to avoid the table with the girls who tripped me the day before. And the other girls I sat with the previous day. I had totally ruined any chances I had with them. I realized if I kept this up, I was going to run out of tables. Thankfully, I spied a group of boys who looked, well, a little geeky. If I had a shot anywhere, it was with them.

"Is anyone sitting here?" I asked. They looked at one another like I was crazy.

"No," one of them said, giggling. I suddenly wasn't convinced any of them had ever spoken to a girl. I sat down. We might speak with different accents, but these were my kind. Relaxed a little by the high geek-level of the table, I decided to talk, which was a stretch for me even back on my home turf.

"I'm Reg," the giggler said and formally shook my hand.

"I'm Genny." They all nodded like they already knew. *I guess word travels fast about an American in town.*

"You're in our physics class," Reg reminded me.

"Oh yeah," I bumbled. "Of course. I remember." I clearly didn't remember.

"I'm Jim."

"I'm Ted. Sooo…you're American."

"Yup," I said, taking a bite of my sandwich. "My dad's a scientist, and we moved here for some research he's doing." They were all keenly interested when they heard the word *scientist.*

Reg was pudgy, and his uniform didn't fit him quite right. He wore the obligatory black plastic nerd glasses. Jim and Ted were both tall and gangly and had blond, shaggy hair. They looked enough alike that I knew I wouldn't be able to remember who was whom the next day.

"You've certainly caught the attention of the in crowd," Jim or Ted said, casually nodding to the table of mean girls I had been trying my best to avoid. I looked over to catch them looking at us and rollicking in laughter.

"Oh yeah." I nodded. "Not in a good way. I guess they don't forgive uniform infractions."

"More likely, Celine and Karyn just don't like you," Reg interjected, lightly slapping the back of Jim or Ted's head.

"Really?" I said sarcastically. "I wouldn't have guessed."

"They probably don't appreciate the spotlight being taken from them. They've never had competition in that department before. Celine is local royalty." I looked quizzically at him. "Figuratively speaking," he added.

"Believe me, I wouldn't know how to steal a spotlight if you gave me a screwdriver and a getaway car."

"I think they would beg to differ. Don't worry about them. They're morons." Somehow, I didn't think Reg, Jim, and Ted's opinions mattered much in the social circles of the school. I didn't want to fit in with the likes of those snooty girls anyway, but I sure didn't want to be ridiculed on a daily basis.

"Wait a minute," I said. "They're last year like us, right?" The boys nodded. "Why aren't they eating in the lounge for final-year students? Why aren't you, for that matter?"

The boys all snorted a laugh.

"We clearly don't make the cut," Reg said. "I think it's understood that geeks aren't allowed."

I knew it, I thought smugly.

"As for Celine and Karyn," he continued, "I don't know. They're exactly the type who would love the exclusivity of it. Come to think of it, I don't remember seeing them in the lunchroom until this week. They must have been eating in the lounge the first few days. Maybe they're just staying in here now to keep an eye on you."

He laughed as he said it, but I wondered how much truth was in his joke. Celine and Karyn seemed to be the type of girls who would have been waiting all those years of high school to bask in the glory of eating in the lounge. Why would they forsake it? *Surely they don't care that much about me. Why would they? I'm a nobody they just met.*

"We were just talking about the film *Hot Rod*," Reg said, graciously changing the subject. "Have you seen it yet?"

"No." *Oh no. I'm striking out at the nerd table.* "I haven't been to a movie for a while. Is it good?"

"Um, yeah," Jim or Ted answered, turning slightly toward the other two to continue their conversation. "So, I'm still not sure about the feasibility of the time-travel technology they used."

"Of course it's not possible," Ted or Jim replied, annoyed at his friend's stupidity.

"What kind of time-travel tech?" I asked. They looked at me, dubious.

"Two kids convert a hot rod into a time-travel machine."

"Really, I think the important thing about sci-fi is not that the tech can be proved possible, but that it can't be proved impossible," I said. They nodded thoughtfully. That comment definitely earned me some nerd points.

"I'm fairly sure that driving a hot rod into a wormhole could be proved impossible," Ted or Jim continued.

I burst out laughing. "OK, you've got me on the car part of the scenario!" All three of them started laughing too.

"Have you seen *Blackout*?" Reg asked me, his eyes widening in excitement. "What do you think about that?"

I was starting to think that the whole "bloody comeover" mentality might not extend completely to the younger generation on the island. I was more of a curiosity than a threat to my classmates now that I looked more like them. This attitude did not extend to Celine and Karyn, of course. I had never understood why it was necessary for popular girls and nerdy girls to be at odds with each other. But I was beginning to wonder if they disliked me because I was a science geek, or because they were threatened by my uniqueness.

Ken walked into the cafeteria after I had already finished my lunch. He seemed to be looking for someone, and when our eyes met, he smiled. He sat down at Celine and Karyn's table, though. Karyn unconsciously combed her fingers through her dark hair. Celine seemed more at ease with him.

As they chatted, she looked briefly over her shoulder at me. I hated to admit it, but she was beautiful. Her silky auburn hair wasn't all she had going for her. It only served to frame her flawless, porcelain skin. Before her emerald eyes flicked away from me and back to Ken, I looked away and pretended to be enthralled by my nerd conversation. I was ready to go home, but unfortunately going home was not possible until I waded through my English class. As if social torture wasn't enough to endure.

The bell sounded, and everyone stood up and began shuffling out the door. I kept my eyes trained on the floor, prepared for Celine to trip me again.

"See you in physics tomorrow," Reg said, snapping me out of my trance.

"Sure. See you tomorrow." I walked to my locker and grabbed my backpack and my jacket so I could leave immediately after class to avoid awkward, after-school locker chitchat.

As soon as I walked into the classroom and saw Mr. Creer, guilt washed over me for not reading the English assignment. He smiled at me, making me feel even worse, and I forced a smile back. Great. We had already made eye contact before class even started. He was sure to call on me. I sat at my desk and forced myself not to slouch down in my seat. I *was* sitting in the front row. Did I really think I could hide from the teacher? And yet I couldn't stop myself from sliding down as low as I could without falling onto the floor.

Suddenly, the lights flickered. A buzz of excited chatter rose from the class. *If the lights go out, they'll be forced to dismiss school early! Please, lights, go out. Please, lights, go out,* I hoped so fiercely that I thought I might just will it to happen. For just a moment, I reveled in darkness interrupted only by a little sunlight struggling through the one small window. The lights came back on, though, seeming much brighter than they were before our plunge into darkness, and the students moaned in unison. Ken rushed into class with his usual confident smile planted on his face, completely unfazed by the excitement.

"Green suits you," he whispered out of the side of his mouth.

He made me blush. I unzipped my backpack and pulled out my lit book.

"Ugh. Why does your textbook smell like curry?" he asked, pulling a face. Like waves radiating out from a pebble thrown into a pond, one by one everyone in class began sniffing, their noses scrunched in disgust. Then everyone looked at me. Ken was right. The room suddenly smelled like an Indian restaurant. The steam from my chicken curry had permeated my textbook. I instantly kicked myself for not realizing that was going to happen. Last night I couldn't tell the book reeked because I had been desensitized by the curry I was eating. I decided I could blame jet lag for at least a week of mental short circuits.

"I had Indian last night," I muttered to Ken.

He sniffed. "I can tell. You can take your text out in the hall, if you want. You can look off mine."

If I could have soldier-crawled out of class with the book, I would have. Every eye was on the weird American as I slinked out of class and propped my rank book against the wall in the hallway. The bell rang while I was outside. So much for being invisible.

Mr. Creer began the lecture after I scooted my desk next to Ken's. In a bizarre way, I think the curried textbook worked in my favor. Mr. Creer was merciful and didn't bring any more shame on me by asking me a question. As he lectured, I couldn't take my eyes off Ken's book. Every bit of white space was filled with notes he had made; word meanings, symbolism, metaphors…It was enlightening. The dry words I had tried to read the previous night sprang to life before me. I didn't hear a word Mr. Creer said, but I appreciated the previous night's assignment much more after that class.

The final bell rang, and the classroom began to empty.

"How do you know all that?" I asked Ken accusingly, pointing to his book.

"I read it. Didn't you?"

"Yes…well, not all of it. But even if I had, I wouldn't have that much to say about it," I said, pointing to his scribbles.

"I don't know. Runs in the family, I guess. Have trouble with literature, do you?" he asked.

"I don't have trouble with anything. Not in school, anyway." At that moment, all of my frustrations about the class, about moving, about life in general came flooding out in an ugly torrent. "And *I* don't enjoy literature. In any form. And now most of the literature I've studied over the years is completely useless to me, because at least half this course is literature from the Isle of Man. I mean, why does the curriculum put so much emphasis on Manx writers? Don't you think it's a little jingoistic to only leave half the year for the rest of Western civilization's literature?"

Ken looked quizzically at me while I tried to slow down my frustrated breathing.

"You shouldn't forget where you are, Genny," he said calmly. "We don't. And if we don't lift up our own, who will? The works of Manx writers will be washed away, forgotten. Do you think anyone off this island thinks about the Isle of Man? Gives us one moment of consideration? We're as good as invisible to the rest of the world. We can't afford to ignore our own."

I pushed my desk back into its place, thinking more about protecting my GPA than the legacy of Manx literature.

"Would it help you if we studied together?" he asked.

"I don't need help," I snapped.

He sighed. "Would you *like* to study with me? It would just be the three of us. You. Me. Your ego…" My jaw dropped. "I have Friday after school free."

"This has *nothing* to do with my ego!"

"Right." He smirked at me. "Then we're on for Friday?"

"Fine."

"Good." He left, and I could have sworn he snickered as he tried to avoid the stench surrounding my textbook.

I dragged my backpack out into the hallway and stood for a moment, staring at my textbook and wondering if I could find a plastic bag to wrap it in before I stuffed it into my backpack. After considering my options, I decided that the backpack wouldn't suffer any more now from the stench than when I carried the book in it that morning. As I was dropping the book into my backpack, the principal and the janitor strode into the hallway.

"I checked the fuse box, Mr. Moore, but I didn't see any reason we should have had a power fluctuation."

"Strange," Mr. Moore replied, stroking his grizzled beard. "Well, as long as it doesn't happen again, we'll just consider it an aberration, Mr. Tills."

"But it's not the only time it's happened, sir," he said, breaking out into a light jog to keep up with the long-legged Mr. Moore. "Two days ago after school, the power went out for almost a full minute."

"Genny." Mr. Moore nodded at me as he passed.

"Mr. Moore," I greeted him in return.

"That is strange, Mr. Tills," Mr. Moore said more quietly. "Very strange, indeed."

I hate to admit it, but I looked forward to my tutoring session with Ken all week. I didn't want to like the Isle of Man, but it was becoming more difficult to stay unattached. The brooding, overcast island spoke to me on a level I couldn't quite grasp. It was like the island was alive and knew my emptiness, could feel it. Like a nurturing mother, it seemed to ache with me, and that empathy was like a healing balm to my soul.

Ken was a different story. He was exasperating, but all he had to do was flash that smile, and I would melt a little. His enthusiasm about everything was contagious. Being around him made me want to feel again. I had tried to shut down my emotions so long ago that his intensity and passion were an enigma to me, and I desperately wanted to unravel the mystery. He seemed to be passionate about everything: life, literature, his home…I was surprised to feel my heart beat a little faster, wishing I could be on that list.

"Are you ready to delve into the beauty of Manx literature?" he asked as he walked me back to my locker on Friday afternoon, an ironic half grin on his face. I sighed.

"Ready as I'll ever be," I said, shoving the unwieldy anthology into my backpack. "Are we going to the library?"

"No."

I waited for the rest of the answer, but when none came, I panicked. "I don't think it would be a good idea to go to my house." There was always a slim chance my dad could show up.

I followed Ken out the doors of the school and squinted in the sunlight. I could feel the heat of the sun on my skin despite the chilly wind.

"We're not going to your house. Although I *would* appreciate an invitation one day." My heart fluttered a little. "And we're not going to my house either."

"The library?"

"You've already guessed that. Keep trying."

"What's left?"

"Are you telling me that in your wildest imagination, there is nowhere on this island to go other than the library and your house?" he asked, not bothering to hide the astonishment in his voice.

"I don't know…Do they have Starbucks here?"

"Only in Douglas," he said, sighing.

I silently mourned missing my last chance for a latte before heading on to Ramsey after we arrived.

"We're going to a place my mum used to take me when I was little. She used to tell me it was the spirit of the island. I think it will help you understand the Isle of Man. And your literature book!" he said, laughing.

As we walked through the town, I thought about Ken's "spirit of the island" and found myself questioning it. Part of me couldn't see past the kitschy, seaside resort and retirement destination, but there was no denying this place had something else. In a way, I wanted to know what made the Isle of Man feel…alive. We turned and walked through a wrought-iron entryway into a little park.

"*This* is what I wanted to show you." He waved his arm grandly in front of him and grinned. I darted my eyes in both directions to make sure I wasn't missing something obvious.

"The...tree?"

Ken's eyebrows knitted together. "Yes, the tree!" he said indignantly.

I was assuming it was a tree, but could only guess that because of the foliage. From where I stood, there was no evidence of a trunk. It seemed to be a mass of reeds. I guessed it was a willow.

"I hate to tell you this, but we have trees in America."

"Not like this, you don't." He grabbed my wrist and began to pull me through the thick curtain of willowy branches. I closed my eyes to protect them as soft, flexible tendrils and leaves brushed past my face. When my eyes opened, I was startled by the size of what I could only consider a room. The sun shone through the fine branches like twinkling stars in the night sky. It was like being in a miniature observatory, only in the middle of the room hulked the trunk of a tree. It was twisted and gnarled.

"This is...beautiful," I whispered.

"I know." He dropped to the ground to sit, his legs folding around him. "My mum used to read me fairy tales here. Sometimes I almost thought I could see fairies rustling in the branches." His dark eyes looked black in the dim light, and I noticed our breathing became synchronized. His eyes were so beautiful that my chest ached. *Why on earth did he bring* me, *of all people, here?* He drew closer. "Let's get started, shall we?" My heart skipped a beat.

"Hmm?" I stammered. He opened his backpack and pulled out his lit book and a flashlight.

"We're here to study, right?"

"Right," I said, sitting. I couldn't tell for sure in the darkness, but I thought I saw him smirking to himself.

The verdant air filled my lungs. It smelled like damp moss, like budding life itself. Then, another smell overwhelmed us as I unzipped my backpack.

"Why is it that whenever I discuss literature with you, I crave Indian food?"

"Very funny." I sighed.

He gestured toward my book. "May I?"

I handed it to him and watched, bewildered, as he stood and walked to the wall of branches in front of us. With a slightly sinister smile, he dropped the book onto the ground outside our little dome of secrecy with a heavy thud.

"Hey!"

"Hopefully, it'll air out some. And you, lucky girl, can look off my book." I didn't mind. I understood everything so much more clearly when I read out of his book. "So, our reading assignment is some poetry by T.E. Brown. Have you heard of him before?"

"You're joking, right?"

"Yes," he said dryly. "Brown is the most famous Manx writer of all time, and have you heard of him? No. He is a prime example of just what we were talking about the other day. If the Manx don't study him, no one will."

I was sure Ken didn't intend to, but something about the tone of his voice shamed me. Maybe it was because he spoke these words in such a dark and intimate place this time, instead of a noisy school.

"Oh," he said, scanning a page, "I think you'll like this first one. It's one of my favorites." He couldn't hide the excitement in his voice. "It's the 'Dedication' in the second series of *Fo'c's'le Yarns*." He whispered the poem aloud.

Dear Countrymen, whate'er is left to us
    Of ancient heritage—
    Of manners, speech, of humours, polity
    The limited horizon of our stage—

Old love, hope, fear,
All this I fain would fix upon the page;
That so the coming age
Lost in the empire's mass,
Yet haply longing for their fathers, here
May see, as in a glass,
What they held dear—

May say, "Twas thus and thus
They lived"; and, as the time-flood onward rolls,
Secure an anchor for their Keltic souls.

"Beautiful, isn't it?" he asked at full volume, which startled me and made me jump. "Genny?"

"Oh yeah," I stammered, realizing how stupid I sounded. He breathed life into words and made them dance.

Still reeling from the music I heard when he read, I was jarred back into the present by a pain in the tip of my index finger. I had been so distracted while he was reading that I hadn't realized I had been clawing into the ground. Fresh dirt forced the edge of my fingernail uncomfortably away from my finger, and I quickly picked the dirt out. In the dim light, I saw a circular pattern in the soft soil next to me.

I panicked, imagining how Ken would think I had defiled the "spirit of the island." I pretended to study the poem as he spoke, all the while casually raking the area with my palm until the circle had been rubbed out.

"You see, this poem is echoing what I've been telling you: looking back, respecting the past and the traditions of the island. What do *you* think about the poem?" I looked at the page and tried to see beyond the words, beyond the black and white.

"I think it's interesting that he's writing about an island and there's water imagery," I said thoughtfully.

"Yes! That's great! Literature is like a tapestry, Genny. There are so many different threads that enrich the whole picture."

I was quietly proud of myself.

We took turns reading aloud the poems that were in our assignment, but I never sounded as eloquent as Ken. As the sun outside set, the stars in our private night sky faded. The cold seeped under our cocooning branches, making me shiver.

"I guess we'd better be getting back," Ken said, looking at his watch. "I can't believe how I let the time get away from me. Have you got other homework to do for Monday?"

"Yeah. I completely forgot about it." I couldn't believe English homework had distracted me from science.

"Well, it looks like we're making strides then," he said, patting me on the back. I shivered again, but not from the cold. "I have a confession to make," he added.

I gulped as I considered all the horrid, or at least disappointing, things for him to confess. Girlfriend was at the top of the list.

"You don't know my last name, do you?" he asked.

It didn't sound like he was about to confess that he had a girlfriend, but I was mortified for another reason. *How could I sit under a tree with a boy and admit to him that I didn't even know his last name?*

"No," I admitted, feeling my cheeks flush with embarrassment.

"It's Creer," he said with a little smile on his face.

"You're the English teacher's son?" I laughed and punched him on the arm. "Why didn't you tell me?"

"Ow!" he said, laughing and rubbing his arm. "You never asked! It's not my fault you didn't bother to find out my last name."

"Well, that explains why you're so good in literature," I said, rolling my eyes.

"And I guess your dad being a scientist explains why you're so good at science," he countered.

"No, it does not!" I said, the joking quickly disappearing from my voice. He raised an eyebrow at me, and I realized he had me. "Touché."

"The reason I know so much is, well, it's complicated," he said, laying back on the grass and staring up into the dark branches. "Let's just say I didn't have a normal childhood."

"Who does?" I mused. He glanced over at me and then resumed staring into the canopy above.

"My parents expected a lot from me," he divulged.

"Unrealistic expectations?"

"Well, I don't know. My childhood wasn't normal. It was like I was born into training. Like my mum had a list of things I had to master and things I had to become. My parents wanted me to be this Manx authority at sixteen. I suppose their expectations were realistic to them. I'm just not entirely sure they were realistic to me. Then, last year, I got into a relationship that"—he sighed—"was wrong for me."

I tried not to look upset. Of course someone like Ken had had a girlfriend. Probably tons of them. And there was no chance that we had a future anyway. A freethinking competitive swimmer with a logic-ruled hydrophobe?

"Why was it wrong?" I wanted to know, and I didn't want to know.

"Oh wow, this is going to sound so stupid," he said with a smirk, roughly bristling his hair with both hands. He sighed and said, "Because my parents wanted me to stay pure."

Am I hearing this right? I wondered, but desperately tried not to let my face show it. *Does anyone even say that anymore?* "You mean—"

"Yes." He cut me off, rolling his head in embarrassment. "I can't believe I'm talking about this." He wasn't making eye contact with me. *Do I dare ask him if he still is?* He couldn't take the silence anymore and continued. "I was so desperate to make my own decisions for once and not just follow along with everything my parents had planned."

"Are you a rebel, Ken Creer?" I asked playfully, trying to make him relax, but his tone remained quiet and thoughtful.

"A girlfriend was just a quick and easy way to break out of the mold they had me in. But duty stopped me from... going too far. I've probably told you way too much. So, anyway, I tried to be a rebel for a few months," he said with a laugh, and then rolling onto his side to face me, added, "but I've given up on it."

"What changed?"

He paused for a moment and looking out of the corner of his eye into the branches above, finally said with a smile, "Everything." He looked at me.

I had never had a boy look at me that way, so instead of feeling giddy and not being able to wait until I could tell my friends, it only made me vaguely uneasy. I wished it didn't. I wished I could just throw myself into his arms as he lay under the tree, but I couldn't. It wasn't logical.

"I'll walk you back home," he said as he pulled himself up to stand.

"You can just walk me to the corner of my street," I answered quickly.

"It's not a problem. Really."

"No," I stated firmly. I could tell Ken ran a lot deeper than I had thought. He had things he didn't want to divulge, and God knows I did too. I didn't want him to see that I pretty much lived alone, and on the off chance that my dad *was* home, I really didn't want my dad and Ken to meet. He thought his life was weird? Meeting my dad would be a whole new level of weirdness.

It was eerily quiet that night as we wound our way through the streets of Ramsey; it made me a little nervous.

It felt like a night when animals sense a storm and take cover. On the corner of my street, a man was rummaging through the trunk of his car. Just as I was about to breathe a sigh of relief at seeing another person and say my good-byes to Ken, I noticed a tattoo on the man's neck, behind his right ear. It was the same red triskelion tattoo worn by the strange man at the tram station who disappeared somewhere between Douglas and Ramsey.

"OK, then. See you on Monday," Ken said, about to continue on alone.

"Would you mind walking me to my door after all?" I whispered.

He tried to hide his shocked expression.

"Um, yeah...no." He nervously ran his hand through his hair.

"I don't mean...anything. I'm just a little...Forget it."

"No. Don't worry about it. It'll only be a minute difference for me," he added, letting me know he hadn't misunderstood my motivation, even though I was pretty sure he originally had. We were both embarrassed as he followed me up to the door of my house.

"Thanks," I said, looking past Ken at the man with the tattoo. The man looked up from the trunk of his car, and we made eye contact for a brief moment before he shut the trunk and slid into the passenger seat of the car, quietly closing the door behind him. The car started up, and as it passed, I strained to see if they were watching us, but the windows were darkened. Ken, noticing I was distracted, turned to look at what held my attention as the car drove out of sight.

"Everything all right?" he asked.

"Sure," I replied, unable to control the shaking in my voice. I fumbled until I opened the door and quickly stepped in, leaving the door ajar only enough to peek through the crack. "Good night," I said, looking past him and down the street. "See you Monday."

I shut the door, leaving him bewildered on the doorstep.

Physics and Other Stuff

"We are going to begin work on our science projects today," Mr. Quirk announced as the bell rang. "As always, projects will be done with a partner, so choose wisely whom you'll be working with, especially as this project is worth 30 percent of your final grade. You can switch seats just for today and begin brainstorming."

Nightmare, I thought. I hated teamwork. Especially in science. *Other people only slow me down.* Jim and Ted sped over to Reg, no doubt to battle it out over him as a partner. I looked over the rest of the class and sighed. *How could I ever work with any of them?* I supposed my best option would be the Jim or Ted who didn't end up with Reg. I stood and walked over to the three of them before another student approached me.

"So, what's the plan over here?" I asked them. They always looked genuinely surprised when I spoke to them. I assumed it was because they still weren't used to being spoken to by a girl.

"We were just talking about it," Reg said, still seated at his desk and obviously reveling in the small gathering fighting over him, "and we thought Jim and Ted could work together, and if you'd like, you and I can be partners. If you'd like," he repeated, hastening not to sound too presumptuous.

Thank goodness. Reg was probably the one person I knew who could actually contribute rather than just let me do all the work.

"Yeah, that sounds fine to me."

Jim and Ted shuffled off and pushed their desks together. I pushed the desk next to Reg's over and sat down, relieved.

"So," Reg said, rubbing his hands together in excitement he couldn't control, "what are your ideas?"

"I don't know…"

"Didn't you say your dad is a scientist? What's he working on?"

"He's working on alternative power, but—"

"I refuse to power a Manx light bulb with a Manx potato," he joked.

"I know, right? I've seen that done a thousand times, well, except for the Manx part. My dad's research is on experimental new aspects of wind farms."

"We could build a wind-powered generator," he pondered.

"No way. I don't want to do something my dad is doing."

"But we'd have an expert in the field we could go to—"

"No," I said, cutting him off.

Reg wasn't sure why I was so vehemently against grabbing a good idea from my dad, and I wasn't in any mood to explain the rising tensions between Dad and me concerning his work. Tentatively, he tried to change the subject.

"So, where's the wind farm?" he asked.

"Hmm?"

"Where's your dad hiding a wind farm on an island this small? I haven't heard of one, and news travels fast here, you know."

I hadn't thought of that. It is a small island. Surely a wind farm would be noticed. Maybe even talked about in the papers. My mind raced.

"Maybe he hasn't constructed an actual wind farm. Maybe he's just working on some technology that would make them more efficient."

"It's not really any of my business, but how could you not know what kind of work your dad is doing that brought you to another country?" he asked, laughing. "Do you and your dad even talk?"

"You're right. It's not any of your business," I snapped. "And who sits around and chats with their dad about his work?"

"Sorry," he sputtered. "Sorry. I didn't mean anything." Reg wasn't sure what he had said, but he definitely wished he hadn't said it. I felt sorry for him. He didn't know why I exploded like that, and truth was, neither did I, exactly.

Something had been nagging me about my dad's job here—his evasiveness, the ambiguity of it all. For once there was something I *didn't* want to think about: the possibility that my dad was not being truthful with me. I had been sweeping my intuition under the rug, but Reg had unwittingly made me think about what little my dad had told me, and his story didn't add up.

"Don't worry about it, Reg. I was just being sensitive." I patted him on the arm, and a visible shiver went through him. Poor Reg. It didn't take much to keep him happy. We were quiet for a minute in thought. He tapped his pencil while I leaned back in the chair and looked at the periodic table next to the board.

"Still," Reg thought aloud, "we could make a wind-powered generator without too much trouble."

"I'm pretty sure you and I can handle something a little more meaty." I couldn't help but smile. He was determined. I'd give him that.

"We could probably even get the parts fairly easily," Reg countered. I scowled at him this time. "Look, we're only in high school, Genny."

"But I thought you were like me." The shocked look on Reg's face told me I had hit the nerve I was aiming for, so I continued. "This is the one time in the whole school year you or I can shine. And we're graduating in only a few months. It's our last chance. Our last chance to do something great," I pleaded.

Reg looked longingly over at Jim and Ted, who were already busy scribbling in their notebooks. "OK," he sighed, "what's your idea?"

"I don't really know," I admitted. "I just want to break new ground. I want to make a discovery." The hairs on my arms bristled at the thought.

"I'm all for thinking big, but I'm also all for an easy A, and between the two of us, I think we can do something a little less lofty than 'making discoveries' and still get an A. And," he added, "you don't have any ideas, do you?"

"No. But let's not be hasty. If we haven't decided on something better in a few days, then we'll make a wind-powered generator." The bell sounded, and everyone began packing up to go to the next class. "Deal?"

"Deal." Reg began stacking his books. "Hey," he whispered. I leaned closer. "I was tired of working with Jim or Ted every year. I'm glad you're my partner. Even if you don't like wind-powered generators."

"I'm glad you're my partner too, even if you *do* like wind-powered generators."

"How about meeting up tonight? You know, for some more brainstorming?" he quickly clarified.

"Um, sure. Where should I meet you?"

"The library? After dinner, around six?"

"Sure."

Since Ken was nowhere to be seen at lunch, I sat with the guys and was careful not to bring up the subjects of wind, power, or generators. I had just taken a bite of my sandwich when I heard a commotion right behind me. I turned just in time to watch Karyn stumble toward me and throw warm chicken soup onto my head. I gasped for a breath through the soup dripping down my face.

"Oh, I'm so sorry," Karyn said, barely able to conceal a smile. Uproarious laughter pealed from the table where she had supposedly been making her way with the soup, but since her table was close to the lunch line and mine was on the other side of the cafeteria, it was obvious she had gone far out of her way to "deliver" the soup.

I wiped the wet mess from my eyes and looked toward the commotion. Celine had laid her head down on her table. She was shaking with laughter, and her friends were all wiping tears of glee from their cheeks. I was determined I wouldn't cry. Not in front of them. I wouldn't give them that pleasure. With all of the dignity I could muster, I stood and began calmly walking to the bathroom.

"I'll bring your things," Reg called after me.

Once in the bathroom, I looked in the mirror. Tears streamed down my face, damming up against the noodles stuck to my skin. *I am not going home,* I thought. I was not going to let Celine run me away from school.

I ran the water warm and put my whole head under, hoping I could get the majority of the soup out of my hair.

I had seen the way Celine looked at Ken. There was no doubt in my mind they had dated at some point. Obviously, she was not as over him as he was over her. Still, I couldn't help but notice he was a little too cozy with her for my comfort. It may be officially over between them, but there was still some kind of relationship there.

"Reg?" I called out as I squeezed the excess water out of my hair. The sink had a handful of noodles stuck in the drain.

"Yes, Genny?" I heard from outside. I poked my head out the door.

"Could you hand me my backpack, please?"

"Sure." He juggled our things and handed my backpack over. "I can't believe she did that."

"I'm sure it was an accident." I couldn't admit out loud that I could be hated that much.

"Yeah," Reg said, not wanting to upset me further. "Probably."

I combed through my hair and picked the noodles off my uniform. Tugging down on my jacket, I looked into the mirror with resolve. *I am not going home.*

I heard the door swing open behind me.

"Reg?" I asked. I turned to see a pretty girl with long, flaxen hair.

"Your hair's wet," she observed.

"Weren't you in the cafeteria?" I asked the stranger. *Surely everyone saw what happened.*

"No, I was in swim practice." *Swim practice! Ken's not in the lounge! He's at swim practice every day at lunchtime! Maybe he's not too cool for me.* This was such an exciting revelation that I forgot for a second how upset I was.

"I have a hair dryer in my locker," she added. "I'll go get it for you, if you like."

"That would be great," I told her, breathing a sigh of relief.

"I'll be right back." She jogged out, her beautiful hair swaying as she bounced.

I popped my head back out the door to find Reg waiting patiently, like a worried puppy that wasn't sure his master was returning.

"Are you going to be OK?" he asked.

"Yeah. That girl has a hair dryer she's going to bring to me. You don't have to wait here, Reg. It's sweet of you, but I'll be fine." He frowned a little, and I wondered if I was robbing him of his knight-in-shining-armor moment.

"OK. I'll go finish my lunch. They're jerks, Genny. Don't let them get to you."

"Easier said than done, but I'll try," I said and patted Reg on the shoulder. "Thanks for being such a good friend."

He looked even more wounded at the word *friend*.

"That's what friends are for," he said with a forced smile and walked back toward the cafeteria.

The blonde girl jogged toward me from the opposite direction.

"Here you go," she said and handed me the hair dryer. "If you don't mind, I'll just wait until you're done so I can put it back in my locker. I'm a bit lost without it."

"Sure," I said, and she followed me in. I plugged it in and flipped my head upside down. "I can't thank you enough for this," I yelled over the dryer.

"No problem," she yelled back. "How did you end up with wet hair, anyway?"

"Someone…accidentally spilled soup on me."

"On your head?"

I nodded as best as I could while upside down.

"That's bad luck."

"Yeah. Terrible," I agreed as I flipped my head right side up. I ran the hair dryer over my clothes for a minute or two, drying up the majority of the dampness. I switched it off and unplugged it.

"Was that your boyfriend waiting for you outside?" she asked.

"No!" I answered a little too quickly. "No. He's just a friend."

"Oh. Your 'friend' looked pretty moon-eyed over you," she said, smiling.

"Yeah, I was afraid of that. Anyway, thanks again for the hair dryer," I said, handing it back to her. "It would have been an uncomfortable afternoon if it weren't for you."

"Don't worry about it," she said. "Glad to help."

I couldn't help but notice how beautiful she was. She wasn't wearing any makeup on her tan face, and she didn't need any. She looked like a Malibu Barbie dressed up in a silly school uniform that she couldn't wear quite right, as if she were only comfortable in a swimsuit. It made sense she was on the swim team.

"I'm Jocelyn," she introduced herself.

"I'm Genny."

"I'd better go. I've got to grab a bite before class. See you around, Genny."

"See you, Jocelyn." She smiled and jogged back out the door.

I stood for a moment, motionless. Although I refused to be bullied into leaving school for the day, there was no way I was ready to go back to the cafeteria right then. I would return to the cafeteria the next day and prove to Celine she could not frighten me, but as for today, I just needed to be alone.

Afraid I'd be heard by a hidden minion of Celine's, I quietly padded down the deserted hallways to my locker. I found the granola bar that I had thrown into my backpack on the first day of school and sat down on the floor with my treasure. Footsteps echoed at the other end of the hall, so I kept my eyes down. I'd had plenty of practice in my life at being invisible. I only hoped whomever it was would either not notice me or not care. I pretended to read the nutritional information on the package while I listened to the footsteps come closer and closer. Finally, a pair of worn, black leather shoes stopped next to me.

"Why are you out here?"

I looked up to see it was Ken, but I had recognized him instantly by his voice. His hair was still wet from swim practice, and he smelled faintly of chlorine.

"I…I just wanted to have some alone time."

"Too bad," he said, plopping down next to me.

I smiled.

"Can I ask you something?" I was so tired and upset and embarrassed that I didn't have the strength to keep my guard up, and I couldn't hold in the question that had begun plaguing me.

"Sure," he replied innocently.

"Why do you hang out with someone like me?"

He blinked in what appeared to be shock.

"What do you mean by someone like you?"

"In case you haven't noticed, I'm a geek. A nerd. And you're"—I stumbled, motioning to his perfect swimmer's physique—"obviously not."

"I don't think you're a geek. Or a nerd. You're just you. You don't give yourself enough credit."

"Really," I said flatly.

"You're not just smart, Genny. I'm beginning to think that's all you can see in yourself. "

I didn't reply since that truly was all there was to me, and I didn't feel like arguing the point.

"There's a lot more to you than you realize," he said.

"Like what?"

"You have no idea how strong you are."

"And you do? How long have we known each other?"

"I apparently know better than you," he countered, raising his eyebrows as though he had trumped me.

"For your information, if I tried to do a pull-up, the most I could do is hang from the bar for a few seconds before I dropped onto the floor."

"Not *physically* strong, no offense," he said while gently squeezing my flaccid bicep. "You're strong inside. You're purposeful. I can tell. And you're pretty," he added quickly while letting go of my arm to rub the back of his head. I could still feel the warmth of his hand long after he withdrew it from my arm. "Where did the sudden crisis of confidence come from anyway?"

"It's not sudden, Ken! I've felt like this since forever. You seem to be the only person in my entire life who hasn't realized I'm a nerd. Well, you're one of two." A picture of my mom flashed into my mind. "But still, being one of only two people in the history of man indicates you're definitely in the minority." I shook my head in disappointment. I had let Celine and Karyn get to me. I was right to try to be by myself and cool down. It was just misfortune that brought Ken along at the wrong time to stir up my emotions.

"Hey, you've got a lot going on, with moving here for your last year of high school. It's probably just got you down today. Don't worry. Things will look better tomorrow." *If only*, I thought. "I have an idea. I have a swim meet tonight here at the school. Why don't you come? It'll get your mind off things."

He had no idea how right he was. Staring into enough water to drown in would certainly make me forget any other problems in my life. I didn't respond to him as I imagined watching, white-knuckled, as people willingly dove into what I could only think of as a deathtrap. I didn't know if I could subject myself to that.

"Come on," he said with a wicked little grin and cocking an eyebrow. "You know you want to cheer me on."

I knew one thing: If he thought I was so strong and "purposeful," I certainly couldn't let him know my fear of water.

I relented. "OK. I'll come. What time?"

Ken smiled triumphantly. "The meet starts at six." The bell sounded to end lunch, and Ken hopped up as students began filtering into the hallway. "I'd say you could sit with my parents, but they've got a meeting tonight and won't be there."

"Don't worry. I'll be fine." I was more accustomed to sitting alone than Ken could possibly fathom. I had spent a lifetime sitting alone. Solitude was one thing that wasn't a problem for me.

"I'll see you in English class," Ken said over his shoulder as he trotted off.

"See you." As soon as Ken was out of sight, I stuffed the rest of my granola bar into my mouth.

I went home after school to eat, but despite the TV blaring, it was too quiet. Another table for one at the Indian restaurant, I decided. I changed out of my uniform and into what I was beginning to call "human clothes": jeans and a sweater. I was about to walk out the door when thoughts of red-triskelion-tattooed men stopped me. I would be out past dark and walking alone. Normally, I wasn't afraid of being by myself, but I couldn't get the tattoo out of my mind.

I needed a way to protect myself. I walked into the kitchen and spied the butcher block that had been there when we moved in. I couldn't exactly walk around with a steak knife in my pocket. For lack of a more effective, concealable weapon, I settled on the nail clippers that rested on the top of a junk pile I had begun in a pretty little basket that had also come with the house. *I could always clip someone to death.* I rotated the tiny file out of its housing and skimmed my thumb across the edge. *Dull.* I had a better chance of shaping an attacker's nails than inflicting damage on him. *It has to be better than nothing,* I thought, and headed out to the Indian Takeaway, armed and ready.

The woman behind the counter smiled when I walked through the door. I was coming in so often that she asked if I wanted "the usual." A little embarrassed by my predictability, I said yes and paid with exact change. I had memorized the amount and shoved it into my pocket at home. I wondered what it would be like to be normal. To not think about everything. To not remember how much my dinner will cost. I wondered if normal people were bothered by all the surprises in life that they could have anticipated if their brains worked like mine did. I wondered if they felt free, or if they never considered how free their normally functioning brains made them.

By the time I had set out my giant English textbook and notebook on one of the little, two-seater tables near the counter, she brought my food out. Carefully, I balanced my chicken curry and naan in my lap. I had learned my lesson about smelling like my dinner, so I was careful not to spill any on my clothes.

She looked at me and smiled with what I could only imagine was pity. She knew I ate alone every night. I never brought friends and I never brought family. I smiled back, trying to reassure her that my state was not as sad as she was imagining, but my gaze couldn't hold hers, and my eyes flicked down to the floor. She went back to the counter to her crossword puzzle, compassionate enough not to look back.

"The Rime of the Ancient Mariner," I read on my assignment sheet. *At least it's not Manx*, I sighed to myself as I flipped through the pages of my textbook and stuffed a bite of curry into my mouth. *Ancient is right*, I thought as my eyes settled on the first page of the poem. *I hate poems. I hate rhymes. No one rhymes when she talks. It's unnatural.* I took out a sheet of grid paper and allowed my pencil free rein to doodle on the paper as I began to read.

Against my will, I felt myself being sucked into the story of the sailor who killed the friendly albatross. So much so that I forgot about the food in my lap and the swim meet. I was lost in another world, out on the sea with the sailor, watching a skeleton ship approach in the mist.

My eyes skimmed back and rested on a line of the poem. *"Alone, alone, all, all alone,"* I read and suddenly jerked my hand up, the pencil I held dropping to the floor.

"Ouch," I moaned to no one in particular. It wasn't until my hand cramped up that I realized that as I continued to read, my unconscious doodling had become more furious, causing my muscles to seize. I looked up at the clock. It was six. I was late for the swim meet. I shoved my books into my backpack and crumpled up the grid paper, wedging it into the bottom. Mournfully, I threw my uneaten food into the garbage and headed out. I was not going to risk carrying Indian food with me again.

As I approached the swim building, the hollow sound of crowd murmur bounced off the surface of the pool, giving me goose bumps. The light played off the water within and flickered like flames through the windows and into the dark night. I pulled the heavy metal door open and squinted as the sickly fluorescent light hit me. When I stepped in, that heavy, damp air seemed to lie on my face and chest like a wet wool blanket, suffocating me. I stumbled over to the edge of the blue benches and sat, closing my eyes, trying to steady the room that rocked like a little boat on the sea. I was out on the sea again, with the sailor, killing an albatross.

Ken. I can't let Ken see me like this.

I pulled the nail clippers out of my pocket and opened them, rubbing the tiny, rough nail file within until the tip of my thumb began to tingle. I willed myself to open my eyes, and I eventually steadied the room. The pool took up 85 percent of the floor space, and I was grateful that I'd sat at the end of the bench, near the door, instead of in the middle, where I would fear the rippling water would jump out of the pool to engulf me. I was grateful for the comforting strip of tile bordering the pool, which stretched out in front of me.

Alone, alone, all, all alone,
Alone on a wide wide sea!
And never a saint took pity on
My soul in agony.

The words of "The Rime of the Ancient Mariner" bubbled up in my head, tormenting me.

"Genny!" I heard a voice call out. It was Ken, standing at the far end of the pool with the other male swimmers. I'd never seen him without a shirt on. I had always imagined that he had a good body under his school uniform. But at that moment, I had all the evidence I needed. He was Poseidon, his chiseled body glistening with water. I waved halfheartedly, hoping that waving wouldn't be the thing that pushed me over the edge and made me fall off the bench or vomit on the shiny, clean tiles. His face lit up, and I wished I could look equally as happy, but it was all I could do not to pass out.

A voice crackled over a loudspeaker announcing the next race, and a group of boys began pulling on their swim caps and taking their positions at the edge of the pool; Ken stood in what would be the middle lane. Each in his own idiosyncratic way positioned his goggles, in what looked like a ritualistic act. Poised to launch, they wrapped their toes around the edge of the pool. At the buzzer, the boys shot into the water like missiles.

My chest tightened until they began surfacing, but that wasn't until they were almost midway across the pool. *Could I hold my breath that long?* I wondered. They moved through the water like creatures of the deep, much more gracefully than I could walk through town. It was as though they were mistakenly consigned to dwelling on land and only in the water were they truly free. Momentarily, I forgot to fear the water as I marveled at the beauty of these elegant creatures in their element.

Then, as though waking from a dream, I saw past the beauty and remembered water for what it really was. *Water is a grave. Water is a grave. Water is a grave.*

The many men, so beautiful!
And they all dead did lie;
And a thousand thousand slimy things
Lived on; and so did I.

Fear and desperation, mixed with shame that I felt those emotions, merged together to form a living thing, like a slug, that swelled in my throat and chest. It wriggled inside me and stretched to fill my airways. *It's not real*, I assured myself. I dropped the nail clippers in my lap and fumbled for my inhaler. Pump. *Breathe it in slowly. The slower, the better.* Pump. *Slowly.* I felt the slug I imagined inside me die and shrivel, and the damp, chlorine-infused air tasted cool and sweet, filling the void it had left. I replaced the inhaler with the cool feel of the clippers again. Despite the buzz of the albuterol that had already begun to zip through me, electrifying me along the way, I felt relaxed and suddenly engaged in my surroundings.

Although it felt like hours had passed, the race was still underway. When the swimmers reached the edge of the pool and flip-turned to make their way back across for yet another length, Ken had easily pulled away from the rest. I wondered if Ken felt about swimming like I felt about thinking. *If it's so easy for me, why isn't it for everyone? Why can't they keep up with me?*

The crowd cheered as Ken's fingers were the first to touch the edge for the last time. He pulled the goggles up onto his forehead and wiped the water from his face, squinting up at the time board, and then across the building at me. A wave of warmth washed over me, and I felt a blush spread across my face with my smile. The boys pulled themselves up onto the edge of the pool, and Ken, distracted, followed after.

A stab of pain seized my right hand again. I raised my hand to massage the inside of my palm and saw the nail clippers still clenched between my thumb and forefinger. Peels of blue paint curled off the end of the nail file. Confused, I looked down next to where I sat. Etched into the paint of the bench next to me was a complex design, as precise as if it were drawn with the use of a compass. Within the outer circle of the design, there were layers upon layers of intricately crossing lines—like the most complex knot I could imagine. It looked familiar to me, but at first I couldn't place where I'd seen it.

Then I remembered; it was the same design I had dug into the soil under the tree. When I was with Ken. I looked around at the people nearest me, and they were all staring with rapt attention at the next race that was already under-way. I gently brushed the tiny bits of paint off the bench and quickly pocketed the nail clippers.

"Fancy meeting you here," a voice said. I jumped.

"Ken!" I gasped, clamping my hand over my deface-ment of public property.

"I've only got a minute before I have to be back over there, but I wanted to say hi." He stood, still moist from the pool, at the end of the bench. He wore track pants and a towel around his neck. I slid over, hiding the strange knot design underneath me.

"Thanks for inviting me. I've never been to a swim meet. It was amazing to watch you…everyone, I mean." As socially awkward as I was, no one could unintentionally make me feel more awkward than Ken. Having a shirtless Ken that close to me was more than I could ignore.

"I'm really glad you came," he said. "I'd better be going, though. My next race starts in fifteen minutes. Sorry I can't stay with you longer."

"No problem. Thanks for coming over. I'll see you tomorrow in class." I added, "You really were amazing. I mean, your swimming." I felt my face get hot.

"Thanks." Ken started to walk away but turned back. Rubbing the wet hair at the back of his head, he asked, "You wouldn't want to go out after, would you?"

As a thrill of excitement ran through me, the starting buzzer sounded, and I turned just in time to see beautiful Jocelyn diving into the pool, along with a row of other athletic-looking girls. *What am I thinking? He's not interested in me when he's surrounded by girls who look like that! The whole swim team is probably going out, anyway. Don't be stupid. He's just including me to be polite.*

"I'd really better be getting home. I don't want my dad to be worried about me." I quietly wondered if my dad would even come home that night.

"Sure." He nodded. "I'll see you tomorrow." He padded back to his side of the pool and sat on the team bench with the other boys, several of whom were staring curiously at me. I knew the girls would have been even more intrigued by me if they weren't in the pool.

I slipped out the door after Ken's next race, which he won by almost a full length. Trusty clippers in hand, I made my way back home through the quiet streets of Ramsey. Although I was still fearful of tattooed men lurking in the shadows, my mind raced much faster than my feet when burdened with the weight of an English textbook in my backpack.

The design carved into the bench glowed in my mind as though it were burning in the darkness in front of me as I walked. *Of course!* I realized. *There probably wasn't a design on the bench at all. It was no more real than the one I was imagining at that moment. It must have been a hallucination from the inhaler, or the asthma attack itself!* With that load off my mind, I couldn't suppress a smile. I obviously didn't carve it.

With the mystery of the design put to rest, my thoughts drifted back to Ken. I was no expert, but I thought he should definitely pursue swimming after high school. He had to be good enough to get a scholarship to college, maybe even go to the Olympics. No one was even nearly as fast as he was in the pool that night. By the time I revisited the memory of the swim team boys staring in disbelief at me, and again tried in vain to understand why Ken was talking to me in the first place, I was jogging up the front steps of our house.

With the door locked behind me, I let my backpack slip off my shoulders onto the couch, and I dropped down next to it, tossing the nail clippers onto the coffee table. I closed my eyes and rubbed the soreness from my shoulders. I was the only student at Ramsey Grammar School who, for all intents and purposes, had her own place. I came and went as I pleased, without the overseeing eye of a parent. Ironically, I was also probably one of the most responsible students at Ramsey Grammar School, so there was no mischief going on at my bachelorette pad. I came home like a forty-year-old coming home from work, caught up on housework and laundry, messed around on the computer, and went to bed at a reasonable hour.

I trudged up the stairs and, too tired to get ready for bed, I left my clothes on the floor and climbed into bed in my underwear. The sheets felt comfortingly cool on my skin, and I fell asleep happy and relaxed for the first time since we had moved, thinking of the rhythmic stroke of Ken's strong arms pulling through the water. Normally, the thought of water was terrifying, but there was something about Ken that diffused the fear for me. And I needed that.

Day Trip

I never thought I'd say it, but the bright spot of every day was becoming English class; as I floated into physics class the next morning, my thoughts were much more on the physical attributes of a certain godlike swimmer in my English class than on physical science. I sat down at my desk and turned to my friend, but before the words "Hi, Reg" could escape my lips, I remembered.

When I was at the swim meet, I was supposed to be at the library working on the science project with Reg. Reg kept his eyes trained on the front of the classroom. I could feel Jim and Ted glaring at me from behind, radiating smugness. They had known it all along. That I had been leading Reg on. That Reg had been the last thing on my mind. And it seemed he was.

"Reg," I blurted out, "I'm so sorry. I completely forgot—"

"Yeah, don't worry about it," he said curtly, still not looking away from the empty blackboard ahead.

"I'll make it up to you, Reg. I promise. We can even do the stupid wind-powered generator for the project."

He looked briefly at me and then back at the board. "Fine," was all he said.

"Great. Let's walk over to the library together right after school. Would that work for you?" The word *together* seemed to soften him. In a way I couldn't believe I was pleading for Reg's forgiveness, but whether or not he realized it, he was probably my best friend, and I didn't want to lose him.

"Sure. I'll meet you at your locker after school," he said. Instantly I cringed, remembering that Ken often followed me to my locker after English class at the end of the day. I was beginning to think that a social life wasn't all it was cracked up to be.

That afternoon, when the final bell sounded, Ken took up pace at my side as I left English. Imagining Reg on one side of my locker and Ken on the other was too much. Ken and I began discussing "The Rime of the Ancient Mariner," which I never in my life thought I would do, when I started planning how to shake Ken—something else I never in my life thought I would do—before arriving at my locker.

He touched my arm.

"I've been thinking," he started tentatively. "How would you like to go—"

"Genny!" Reg's voice rang out. It was too late. Reg was standing down the hallway, right where Ken always propped against the locker next to mine. I felt awkward with Reg being in Ken's spot, and apparently, Ken felt that way too.

"Um, I'll talk to you later, Genny," he said and left, running his hand through his hair. I felt my cheeks get hot. *What was he going to ask me? At least tomorrow is Friday,* I consoled myself. *If it's important, he can ask me when we study under the tree. Oh, please be important...*

"I've got some great ideas, Genny," Reg bubbled. All had been forgiven. So much so that Reg seemed unfazed by Ken's brief appearance near the locker. I wasn't even sure he noticed that Ken was with me at all. While we walked to the library, Reg chattered on, oblivious to the fact that my mind was elsewhere, thinking only of my dark-haired Poseidon.

"I thought we could get together again today after school," Ken began the next afternoon, "but something came up with my family." He was propped against the lockers—his, not Reg's, rightful place.

"Oh," I said, trying not to sound too disappointed. "Don't worry about it." The shining light at the end of every week was Friday afternoon, when Ken and I would study under the tree. Ken had certainly helped me make lemons into lemonade in English. But I still wasn't sure about our relationship. Not that we had one, really. In truth, he tutored me once a week, and he had invited me to a swim meet. *Both of which could possibly be out of pity*, I thought.

"But I was thinking tomorrow, if you're free, maybe we could go to Douglas for the day?"

"Really?" I asked, trying not to sound too excited. This sounded almost like a—dare I say it—date. My heart pounded. *Don't make any assumptions*, I thought. I had to test the waters very, very carefully. "Who all's going?" *Genius*, I flattered myself.

"Um, just…us. I thought. But if you'd like to get a group together…" He scruffed up his hair as he spoke, which I was beginning to realize was a sign of his being flustered.

"No," I jumped in. "I just…no. That'll be great. Fun, I mean. Um, yeah."

"All right." It had to be my imagination, but it looked like his whole body relaxed. "I thought it would be nice to show you around our biggest city. Get some more of the Manx experience into you. Like you said, you've only got one year until you graduate, and then you plan to take off."

So, I thought, *it wasn't a date. It's another mercy mission. Another "let's Manxify the American girl" expedition.* I supposed hanging out with my hot tutor was better than staring at a computer screen alone in my house all day Saturday.

"Why not? Only one year." All of a sudden, "only one year" had changed from a chant that made the Isle of Man tolerable to a thought that made my stomach knot. But I had to focus on the moment. And at that moment, for whatever reason, Ken was planning to spend Saturday with me.

"Let's get an early start. I'll come by your house at ten o'clock. Does that work for you?"

"Yeah, great."

I began my walk home and kept repeating to myself, *it's not a date, it's not a date,* but it didn't work. All the convincing in the world couldn't dispel the butterflies and completely illogical giddiness that painted a goofy grin on my face. I was so lost in my thoughts that I ran right into someone.

"Oh! I'm so sorry," I stammered and looked up into the face of Celine.

"You should be," she spat. I looked around for Karyn, but for once, she was not standing at Celine's side. I looked down and tried to walk around her, but she sidestepped, blocking my path. "No. You don't get to walk away from me. All I ever hear about is you, and now you're going to hear what I have to say. Look at me," she said, grabbing my face and forcing me to look her in the eyes. Her face was trembling in anger, and hot tears were streaming down her cheeks, which usually looked porcelain but at that moment were splotched and pink.

"You think you can just prance onto this island and act like the queen of everything? Well, I've got news for you. I may be the only one, but I don't care who you are. You are ruining my life."

"I'm sorry," I muttered, diverting my eyes, even though I couldn't loosen my face from her viselike grip. I was embarrassed that tears escaped from my eyes as well, because her tears were from rage and mine were birthed from fear.

"Stay away from Ken," she said, shoving me away. She strode past me, brushing me with her shoulder and knocking me onto the ground. I scrambled up and looked to see if anyone had seen us. The street was empty. I stood behind one of the little saplings that lined the street until I couldn't hear her footsteps anymore, and then I ran home, hoping all the way that I could contain the flood of tears until I shut the door behind me and burst into a sob on the sofa.

The doorbell rang at ten o'clock sharp that Saturday. I peered sideways out the window to make sure it was Ken and not Celine. The previous afternoon had left me jumpy. Her hate was so deep that every time the house creaked or a dog barked that night, I wondered if it was Celine trying to break in to kill me. I knew it was ridiculous and kept banishing the thought, but minutes later, I would find myself peeking out the window again, looking for Celine. All night long, I saw nothing but shadows.

When I looked out the window that morning, I wasn't sure what warmed me more, the sun beaming in a cloudless, blue sky or the sight of Ken in jeans. It was still strange to me to see him in something other than his uniform or a swimsuit.

"We'll be taking the tram today," he said, a little too chipper.

"Yay?" I said sarcastically.

"You know, mostly it's just the tourists who take the electric tram," Ken mused as we began to walk. "Tourists and teenagers desperate for a day of excitement in Douglas."

"I'm so glad we fulfill one of the criteria for tram riders. Would they not let us on if we didn't?" I asked in mock seriousness.

"Absolutely not. They card passengers to ensure there are no Manx-born adults with fulfilling lives who board."

"Understandably. Only the unknowledgeable and inexperienced could handle the thrill of the tram trundling along at ten miles per hour," I said with a smile, elbowing him. "And come to think of it, Douglas itself seems like a real hotbed of activity."

"There's *lots* to do in Douglas. There's the Manx Real Dairy Ice Cream Parlor. Horse-drawn trams. Can't forget them. Very exciting. The horses are named Ian and Mark, I believe."

I burst out laughing. "There's a horse named Ian?"

"Don't laugh, Genny. Horses are very sensitive." He was incredibly attractive when he joked. He was incredibly attractive all the time.

"Well, I'll be sure to get all the laughing out of my system by the time I get there. I'll only have about an hour, though, right?"

"Hour and a half by electric tram, fifteen minutes by car," he said, gently elbowing me back.

I hadn't been to the electric tram station since the day I arrived in Ramsey, and I realized walking up that I hadn't underestimated the size of it. A little brick building nearby sold tickets, but the tram actually stopped next to a graffiti-covered shack, where the tracks dead-ended. The electric tram pulled up, and we hoisted ourselves up the old, overly steep stairs to board.

I must have been so jet-lagged when I first arrived on the island that I didn't even notice the inside of the covered car of the tram. It looked like something out of a Sherlock Holmes story, with dark wood interior walls and seats upholstered in burgundy velvet. As the tram started to pull out, the large windows clattered loudly, making it sound like the passengers were all applauding that the tram was moving at all. Without a word, Ken and I burst out laughing.

The tram route I had missed on my earlier ride to Ramsey was unbelievably beautiful. Much of the time we were tunneling through dense, green forest. Some tram stops that we sped by were nothing more than a sign in the middle of what seemed to be nowhere. Occasionally, a tiny town would blink past the window. And the tram was moving slowly enough that for a town to shoot by that quickly, it was very small indeed. When the trees broke, we were overlooking a valley filled with little houses and punctuated by the occasional steeple.

"We're in Laxey. And that's the Laxey Wheel." Ken reached past me to point out a huge, red waterwheel nestled against a hill as we approached the center of town. He smelled clean, like chlorine and soap. I inhaled deeply. I had never thought of chlorine as an attractive smell before.

The tram stopped, and a few tourists got off to see what a sign proudly called the "World's Biggest Waterwheel."

"It was built back in the mining days. Now it's just a tourist attraction. There's another tramline that leaves from

Laxey and goes up to Snaefell Summit. It usually runs April through October, but it's been closed this season."

"That's too bad. Why is it closed?"

"Line work, they say. The roads to Snaefell are closed too. Pity. You'd have loved the view. It's the highest point on the island. They say on a clear day you can see seven kingdoms: Isle of Man, England, Ireland, Scotland, Wales, Heaven, and Manannan."

"Heaven and Manannan?" I asked.

"The sky and the sea."

"Well, I'm sure they'll get the Snaefell tram up and running. We'll have time to see all seven kingdoms at once before I leave." I instantly kicked myself for saying "we" and not "I," and my stomach knotted again at the word *leave*.

"You never know."

For the rest of the journey, the tram wound along the edges of rocky cliffs that dropped into the ever-churning Irish Sea. We finally pulled up to the last stop, and sure enough, a horse-drawn tram waited nearby.

"Oh, you really have to ride the horse tram. You wouldn't have really experienced Douglas without it," Ken teased, pushing me toward the tram.

"Wait," I said, going up to the horse. "Is this Ian or Mark?" I laughed even harder when I saw the nameplate on the horse's neck. "His name's Ken! Who's a good boy, Ken?" I asked the horse while stroking his nose. "You are! Yes, you are!"

"Must be a very intelligent horse," Ken said and sniffed.

Douglas had seemed small when I arrived on the island, but after a few months of living in even smaller Ramsey, Douglas seemed a lot more bustling than I remembered. Ken insisted I shop some, and even though I hated clothes shopping, I felt like I'd be disappointing him if I didn't at least leave him waiting outside while I pretended to try things on. After an hour of trolling up and down the cobblestoned high street, popping into the occasional clothes shop, he felt like he had filled my shopping needs and led me up a steep climb in the middle of town.

"I think you'll find this more enlightening," he said. The cracked sidewalk ran alongside a tall, concrete wall that was being attacked by climbing vines. The vines were winning. That was one of the beautiful things about the Isle of Man. In the battle of man versus nature, nature was winning, and man didn't mind. As the sidewalk went higher up the hill, the wall became shorter, until I could see it was the bulwark for a building atop the hill.

"This is the Manx Museum," Ken said proudly. "Beyond these auspicious brick walls lie the answers to all of your questions. At least, your Manx-related questions," he added, smiling. "Or most of them, anyway."

I couldn't help but giggle. He really was adorable.

Judging by the dearth of cars in the parking lot, I wasn't expecting much, but once inside I saw that Ken was right, as usual. The national pride of the Manx people shone through in this celebration of Manx history. The museum was divided into different categories. We began in "The History of the Isle of Man" at "The Hunter-Gatherers of the Mesolithic Age" and made our way to the Celts and the Vikings. I hadn't realized how diverse the history was on this little island.

While Ken was engrossed in the Viking swords exhibit, I wandered away, alone. Around the corner, I stumbled upon the "First Christians" exhibit. In the center of the room was a grouping of stone carvings, most of which were grave markers. I wondered if the museum curators had intended to replicate a small graveyard, because the dim lighting in this particular room paired with the silence of the empty museum gave me goose bumps.

Some of the grave markers were simple, incised crosses, while others had more elaborate, ring-headed crosses. Then, there were the different types of crosses: the dragon cross, platted to trap dragons; Gaut's Cross with its intricate ring-chain design that was still used on the island to that day; and Thorlief Hnakki's Cross, again with dragons ensnared in the interlace. I wondered how long it took to carve the designs in the unyielding stone, given the primitive tools available.

I lingered longest at a slab that also must have been a gravestone, but its simplicity made it difficult to tell. It was a roughly hewn slab with a rudimentary cross scratched into the middle. When I looked closely, I noticed there were small crosses scratched randomly around the rest of the stone. Among the more elaborate stones, it seemed lonely to me.

"Genny?"

I jumped. "Ken," I gasped.

"It's a bit spooky in here, isn't it?"

"I thought so at first," I replied. "It just feels peaceful now."

"You're not like anyone I've ever known, Genny," Ken said softly. "You have a beautiful soul."

I didn't know how to respond. No one had ever said anything like that to me before. *Thank you? So do you? I know?* I looked down, speechless.

"Come on," he said. "We've got more ground to cover."

Papier-mâché tree trunks dotted the walls of the "Manx Legends and Folklore" exhibit, and branches hung overhead, creating a manmade bower. In the center of the room, a carved fairy sat on a giant toadstool. She looked out from under her thick lashes sideways and wore a coy little smile. Orange, curly hair was piled carelessly on her head. She definitely had been the centerpiece of this section of the museum since the nineteen sixties. She was all but wearing fairy bell-bottoms. I couldn't help but compare the sweet refuge under Ken's tree in Ramsey to this gaudy man-made version.

Out of respect for Ken, I forced myself to read as many of the legends as I could stomach. They were printed on leaf-shaped plaques and mounted on the walls as though they were leaves falling from the branches of the tree. The leaves told of good fairies with healing powers, bad fairies who stole babies, giants who hurled the mud that eventually became the island, ogres who stomped angrily around the countryside, pigs with magic quills. Blah, blah, blah…

I felt Ken slide up close beside me, and then his breath on the side of my neck.

"You liked the history section more than the legends and folklore," Ken stated, not asked, in a near whisper.

"This exhibit's a little...hokey. Besides, I like things I can see. I can feel," I replied, a little out of breath feeling him so close. "Legends are nothing but mirages. They're what we want to be true taking shape in the mist of the unknown."

"You can't see history," he whispered. I wondered how he could be talking about something as innocuous as history, but make heat wash over me like a Pacific island's hot breeze.

"No, but I can see the results of it," I said a little too stiffly, trying to snap out of my trance.

"How do you know what you see *isn't* the result of folklore and legends?" He too suddenly adopted his "debate" voice.

"So you think the island was actually formed by giants who were literally mudslinging?"

"Why not?"

I groaned out of necessity, but in a way, I loved the way he riled me.

"You can be so exasperating."

"Yes, but in a dashing kind of way," he said with a smirk.

"Maybe." I giggled.

"Oh, before we leave, are you sure you don't want a genuine, silver-effect, fairy necklace? You seem the type to be into that sort of thing."

I laughed and lightly elbowed him. "I'm good, thanks." He took me by the hand, and we exited through the gift shop. I spent the walk back down the hill feeling only the warmth of his hand encasing mine.

As the sun was beginning to set, he took me to get ice cream at the ice-cream shop on the boardwalk, as he promised. He got two scoops of Banoffee fudge, and I got one sweet cream. We took our cones across the street to the beach and sat on the edge of one of three large concrete blocks that jutted out onto the little rocks that were too big to be considered sand.

"This is actually an outlet pipe from back when they would pump raw sewage into the bay," Ken said, patting the makeshift bench affectionately like he would an old car.

"Classy. Do you always bring girls here?" I hid my smile behind my ice-cream cone.

"Only the American ones."

Closer to the water's edge, the rocks disappeared under a blanket of inky seaweed. Beyond that, the Tower of Refuge was silhouetted against the dusky sky. On the south side of the bay, the shore had been built up with giant, macaroni-shaped objects that from a distance looked like they were made of rubber. *The ticket office!* I remembered. The builder of the ticket office must have been mirroring the unique feature of the bay. The pieces were identical in shape and looked to be of the same material as those affixed to the sides of the ticket office, only the ones used to barricade the bay were ten times larger. *Giant, hacked-up legs of the triskelion*, I thought while looking at the crooked shapes. I wanted to ask Ken about it, but I really had to stop acting like a nerd. Being logical, I imagined the barrier must have been built to prevent erosion, so I tried to push all the other questions out of my mind.

I kicked my feet, letting the heels of my rubber soles bounce off the concrete behind them, and finished my ice cream too quickly. I couldn't believe I had spent the day alone with Ken. My heart rate sped up, but not because we sat a little too close on the beach; I was staring out once again at the strange castle that appeared to float out in the bay.

"When do they turn the light on in the lighthouse?" I asked.

"What?"

"In the castle? The Tower of Refuge?"

"It's not a lighthouse," he corrected me. "It was a shelter for shipwrecked sailors. Sir William Hillary had it built to save sailors—"

"Yeah, right, but it has a light too."

"No, it doesn't. How do you think they'd get electricity out there?"

I hadn't thought about that. I hated to be stumped, but at least it didn't happen often. "A generator? I don't know, but I've seen a light in the castle."

"You couldn't have," he stated.

"But I saw one. There was a light in the ca—the Tower of Refuge the first night I was on the island."

"You saw a light?" he asked in shock now, not disbelief.

"Yes," I stumbled, beginning to doubt myself. "There was a blue light inside the Tower of Refuge. I saw it. I know I did."

"Do you see it now?" he asked, looking back out at the castle.

"No, of course not. I'm not crazy. Ken, what's going on?"

"She was right," he whispered to himself, still staring at the castle. He quickly took both my hands in his; his wild, excited eyes meeting mine.

"Who's right?" My mind raced, trying to put a puzzle together without all the pieces. I could feel my bronchioles contracting in spasms, and I yanked my hands from his, searching desperately for my inhaler.

"Genny? Genny, are you all right?" Panic replaced excitement in Ken's eyes. I took a puff and held my breath, feeling the medication ease the tightness in my chest. I closed my eyes so I couldn't see him. So I couldn't see the castle.

"One thing at a time." I exhaled. "What's out there? What's the light I saw? What's inside the Tower of Refuge?"

"There's an old Manx legend." He hesitated. "It's not supposed to be talked about with…comeovers. But I guess I can make an exception." He smiled, but for the first time, Ken looked unsure of himself. "The legend says there is a man in the Tower of Refuge. He must never leave and no one must ever enter. He must stay there alone until his destiny is fulfilled."

"What's his destiny?"

"He is our savior."

"Like…Jesus?"

"No." He chuckled, and the mood lightened for only a moment. "He's not here to save our souls. He's here to save our lives. He's the savior of the Isle of Man."

"What's he supposed to be saving the island from?"

"I don't know, exactly. Only one person each generation is allowed to read the original prophecy. That person lets others know what they need to do." Romance fled as logic regained control of my mind. As much as I liked Ken, I was furious with him. It was one thing to admire legends in a museum. It was entirely another to actually live by them.

"And no one needs to know exactly what catastrophic event is going to happen to the island," I said, trying not to sound sarcastic.

"Well…no, I guess not."

"So, let me get this straight. Only one person on the island can read these prophecies, and he doles out important information as he sees fit, *and* there's some poor person out there in that castle—"

"Tower of Refuge," he interrupted.

"Tower of Refuge, who is not allowed to come out, not allowed to be seen, not allowed to be visited…How does he get food?" I sputtered.

Ken looked shocked at my line of questioning. "I don't know."

"You do realize that story is fantasy, right?"

"It's legend."

"Legend is fantasy."

"Not here," he said.

I buried my head in my hands. "How can you believe all this?"

"How can you not? You're the one who saw the light."

"So what? There was a light on inside a lighthouse. Stranger things have happened."

"It's not a lighthouse! No one has seen a light in the Tower of Refuge in over a hundred years."

"So, what? Are you saying I'm the only one who can see it?"

"Maybe. Was there anyone else around when you saw it?"

"No. It was during an awful storm. I can't imagine there were too many people running around outside that night."

"Then, maybe it's not just you. Maybe you were just lucky enough to see it."

"Lucky me." I rolled my eyes. "Look, all I'm saying is, if there *is* someone out there, someone should help him. He's been trapped out there since when, the eighteen hundreds? I bet he's pretty sick of it. Surely he could save the island just as easily if he were living in an apartment in Douglas."

"You are mocking the legend our lives are built on," he snapped.

I knew I had crossed the line. I liked Ken so much. *Why can't I be one of those girls who bats her eyes at whatever a boy says and wins his heart?* But I wasn't like that. I couldn't blindly accept everything someone said, no matter how much I liked him. I wanted Ken to like me, but I couldn't change to make that happen.

"OK, maybe I was being a little too flippant." I repented as best I could. "But do you see my point? If you truly believe this, as an intelligent person, don't you see the injustice being done to this person who has been quarantined in a tiny castle out in the sea? Tower of Refuge," I corrected myself.

He looked at me like I was crazy. Maybe I was.

"Then let's go for a visit," he replied.

"What?"

"Let's go to the Tower of Refuge." It didn't look like he was joking. His eyes were unflinching, and despite the odd conversation, I could feel myself go wobbly.

"N-n-now? We'd have to rent a boat, right?"

"Haven't you noticed that you never see anyone out there? No boats are allowed in Douglas Bay or twenty miles past the Tower of Refuge into the sea. Actually, no one is even allowed to swim in the bay. At least with swimming, though, we'd be less detectable."

I had never heard of a bay with no swimmers and no boats, but Ken was right. My stomach twisted as I noticed there was no one in sight. That would be a difficult swim for anyone, especially in the water moiling in from the sea. How could I tell him I couldn't swim? Worse than that, that I had hydrophobia.

"Why isn't anyone allowed in the bay?" I suddenly was not so concerned that Ken was willing to do something that would seem to violate his Manx ethics. I was petrified that I was physically unable to follow through in his cockamamie scheme with him.

"There are no boats so no one can get to him. No one can interfere with his purpose."

"So, as serious as you are about your legends and rules, why are you willing to break Manx code *and* the law?"

"Because…" He hesitated, and after finding resolve, looked into my eyes. "Because I want you to believe."

"That shouldn't be more important to you than being true to what *you* believe in."

"I know. But right now, it is." He leaned toward me and gently kissed me. Everything we had talked about, weird legends and creepy castles that appear to float out in the sea, evaporated in the heat of his lips on mine.

Rational Fears

We were the only passengers on the tram back to Ramsey. We sat close to each other this time. It was strange to be friends on the way there and "more than friends" on the way back. It was all so new to me. My arm brushing his arm, my hand resting in his instead of alone at my side. Just a few inches made all the difference in the world.

"Let's come back next weekend," he whispered into my ear, and his warm breath on my neck sent tingles up my spine. His lips brushed my ear. My heart was thumping so hard that I was afraid he would feel the vibration. I wanted to be wherever he was. Just like this. But I knew swimming Douglas Bay next weekend was not going to be possible. It would never be possible.

"We need to talk about that, Ken," I said.

"Oh." He gently pulled away from me. "Did I misunderstand?" He ran his hand through his hair. His face looked embarrassed and hurt. "I…I'm so sorry…"

"No!" I said a little too hastily, grabbing his hand and encasing it in both of mine. "It's not about…us. It's just about us coming back to Douglas. I'd love to come with you, but I can't swim out to the Tower of Refuge with you because…" I paused, choking on the words. "I can't swim." It was hard enough for me to talk about swimming, let alone do it.

He threw his head back, laughing, and the dim tram lighting danced off his perfect white teeth. "That's funny."

"It's not a joke," I said, irritated it could be conceived as one.

"I thought you could swim," he said, his eyebrows furrowing.

"What made you think that?"

He looked up, as if the answer he was searching for were hanging from the ceiling of the tram. "I just…assumed. Swimming seems like such an American thing to do." He paused again, and then sputtered, "I could teach you."

"It's not that easy. I have hydrophobia."

"Oh." He seemed confused, like he had mistakenly brought the wrong girl with him and just realized it. "Have you always been afraid of the water?"

"No." Everything around me—the tram, Ken, the island—seemed to dissolve as memories that had visited me too many times before became tangible in my mind. "I was eight years old. My parents were both scientists. My mom was a marine biologist. She was stationed in Hawaii to do research, so she and I moved out there while my dad stayed on the mainland to finish up some work before coming out to meet us. I was out on the boat with her and her research partner one day. Mom had let me go along with them to tag dolphins for a study on their migration patterns. I was sitting on the bench near the front of the boat when my mom left me to get the equipment. Her partner was watching the radar screen.

"The sun was so hot, it felt like my skin was baking, so I went to the other side of the boat, where there was a little shade from the cabin. It was cooler there, and I could feel the ocean breeze, but my clothes were stuck to my skin from the sweat. That was why I took off my safety vest," I said, shaking my head, wishing somehow I could turn back time and undo what never should have happened.

"I waited for what seemed like forever to an eight-year-old. Then something caught my eye in the water. I turned, but I didn't see anything, so I stood on the bench to look over. I'll never forget how big the ocean looked. I mean, that sounds so obvious, but to a child, when the water stretches out as far as you can see with no land in sight, it seems like the whole world is nothing but water.

"I looked down to see if I could find what had caught my eye. At first, all I saw was the hypnotic rippling of the water, but after a minute or so, I saw something moving under the surface. My heart stopped when I saw a dorsal fin. It sped by and then seemed to circle back toward the boat. I was so scared. I thought the shark was coming to kill us all. I turned to scream for my mom, and when I did, I fell over the edge. I was only underwater for a second or two, but when I opened my eyes, I saw it coming toward me. I tried to scream, but salt water flooded into my lungs instead of air. That was when I knew I was going to die. Not because of a shark. Because of the water.

"I clawed at the surface like it was somehow going to become solid and I'd be able to pull myself out, but it didn't take long for my body to go limp and sway with the current. I thought I heard a splash near me, but I was past the point of caring. It wasn't until I felt her hand that I knew I'd be OK. I knew it was my mom because it was the grip of a frightened mother. Like steel. As she was hoisting me up to her partner on the boat, I didn't know I was looking at her for the last time. Even then, she was beautiful. Her eyes were scared, but as she saw me being pulled up, she smiled a little. I passed out right after that.

"I found out later that when her partner tried to help my mom back into the boat, she was already dead. She had an asthma attack in the water. And the shark I was so frightened of was just a dolphin."

Ken hadn't made a sound or a movement the whole time I had spoken. I was a little embarrassed that I had let the most painful time of my life gush out on a tram, but I also knew that at that moment, I had never felt as close to anyone as I did to Ken.

"It wasn't your fault, you know," he said.

"I don't think my dad would agree with you," I said without crying. "Besides, I remember every second of that day, and I can't figure out how it wasn't my fault." I was very practiced at turning off my emotions when I thought of my mother's death. And I thought of it a lot. "Well, that's it," I said, slapping my knees and trying to rally. "That's why I have...problems. I can barely get near the water, much less swim. I thought I was going to pass out at your swim meet. Just the thought of swimming makes me petrified." *But I think it frightens me as much that I could lose you if I don't swim.*

143

"I would never ask you to do something you are uncomfortable doing. Ever."

"I just thought that somehow my not being able to go would be a deal breaker. Things kind of came together for us in Douglas." I felt my cheeks turn hot as it was my turn to be embarrassed.

"Are you joking?" he asked. His eyes looked shocked and confused. "Do you think I started liking you because we were going to swim across Douglas Bay together?"

"Well, that *was* when you first kissed me," I said, looking down.

"We also had an argument out there, remember? But I still kissed you. We won't ever agree on everything, but I really like you. A lot. And it doesn't matter where you are, or what you're doing. I like to be with you." He lifted my chin with his finger to look me in the eyes. "Do you know how long I wanted to kiss you? It took me that long to work up the courage."

"I thought you were just a flirt and weren't really interested."

"How could anyone *not* be interested in you?"

"Are you joking? Have you not noticed that I'm a geek?"

He frowned. "You're intelligent, Genny. And beautiful." He stroked my hair.

"Would you have noticed me if I weren't American?" I asked, enjoying the feel of his hand in my hair too much to care about the answer.

"It didn't matter where you were from, Genny. We were meant to be together," he whispered.

I went quiet for a moment. I wondered if I was allowing my mom's death to define my life. I knew that wasn't what she would have wanted. She used to tell me I was "the best little scientist" in the world. She believed in me. She was so proud I wanted to follow in her and Dad's footsteps. I only realized as I got older how brave she was to go into a field that was male dominated, but I'm not even sure she thought of her career that way. All she wanted was to be a modern-day explorer like Christopher Columbus, discovering the unknowns of the ocean rather than the unknowns of a map. She was so brave and fearless. So brave.

"Then teach me to swim," I whispered back.

"What? There's no way I would allow you to do that. Not for me!"

"I'm not doing it for you. I'm doing it because I'd never forgive myself for giving up a chance to go on a real adventure. It's any scientist's dream to be the first to prove or disprove a theory, much less a legend. That's what science is all about. Exploration. Discovery. I'm doing it for myself. Because I want to see what's out there. I'm doing it because it was meant to be."

"I'll do whatever you ask me to do, Genny."

Our faces drew together, but right before our lips touched, the tram jolted as it braked to a stop. I looked out the window into total darkness.

"Why did we stop?" I asked.

"Somebody must have waved the driver down at a request stop." I watched out the window as Ken spoke. A little flashlight beam bobbed closer to the tram as the carrier walked in the inky blackness. "The little stops are by request only, since so few people use them. There are a few of them out here—usually nature preserves."

I couldn't understand why anyone would be haunting around a nature preserve in the dark. I had the same creepy feeling as if I'd seen someone, flashlight in hand, walking out of a cemetery in the dark.

I turned when I heard footsteps plod up the wooden stairs in the back of the carriage. A bald man lumbered in and sat in the back. He hunched over to put his flashlight into an old, black, leather case he had carried on. He was dressed head to toe in black, which I thought was an odd choice if you were planning to catch the attention of a tram driver in the dead of night.

I turned back to face the front as the tram started off again, but couldn't concentrate on what Ken was saying. There was something so upsetting, but strangely familiar, about the man that I couldn't stop thinking about him. Like metal to a magnet, I finally couldn't resist the pull and turned around to look at him again. He was staring right at me.

When our eyes met, he pretended to look out the window, but all he would have seen was his own reflection against the darkness outside. It was then that I saw a glimmer of red behind his right ear, and I remembered with a twisting stomach where I had seen him before. He was the man in Douglas, at the station, the day after we arrived on the island. The one with the tattoo on his neck. The one who caught my ticket before the wind carried it away.

"I know that man back there, Ken," I whispered, trembling.

"Where from?" he asked, turning around.

"No! Don't let him see you looking at him!" I hissed.

"Okaaaay," he said, a little amused.

"This is serious. I think he's following me."

"How could he be following you? He got on the tram after we did."

"I don't know. But this is the second time I've run into him."

"This is a pretty small island, Genny. Stranger things have happened than running into the same person twice," he said and squeezed my hand in an attempt to reassure me. I realized I must sound like a paranoid weirdo to him. He was right. Of course I'd see people more than once on an island. But it was the tattoo on his neck, the same one I had seen on another man on the street, which was for some unknown reason so upsetting to me.

When we arrived back in Ramsey, my heart was thudding when I turned to disembark the tram. I knew he'd be staring at me, but he wasn't there. I looked frantically out the window, but couldn't find him.

"He's already gone?" Ken asked, knowing what I was looking for. "So he wasn't following you."

"I guess not." I sighed, unconvinced.

Ken walked me to my street in silence.

"Oh," I said, surprised and relieved to see a light in the window of my house. "My dad's home."

"Is he not supposed to be?"

"Well, he's usually just…not. I'll see you Monday."

"Yeah," he mumbled, sounding a little puzzled. "See you Monday." Ken disappeared into the darkness and left me with my uneasiness. Before digging for my key, I tried the doorknob. It was unlocked.

"Where have you been?" my dad demanded before I could get through the door. His voice was fraught with worry or anger; I couldn't tell which. I didn't remember hearing him speak in that tone before, and it scared me.

"I was out with a friend."

His body relaxed, and he rubbed his face. He plopped onto the sofa.

"You've made a friend?"

"Yes, Dad, I have a friend." What a sad commentary on my life that my dad was surprised I had a friend, and that he didn't even imagine it could be a boy.

"I didn't know where you were. I was worried."

I wanted to tell him that it had been awhile since he'd seemed worried about me and that I was even surprised he noticed I wasn't there, but I didn't.

"Sorry," I said instead.

He looked up at me, unsure of what to say, and back down at the floor. "It's my fault," he finally responded. "I should have gotten us cell phones by now. Maybe you can go buy us some. You still have the card, right?"

"Sure. I can do that." There were dark shadows under my dad's eyes, and his skin looked brittle, like a forgotten paper bag rained on and dried out by the next sunny day. He might have been wearing the same clothes from the day before. A mug of noodles sat on the coffee table. Knowing him, it was probably the only meal he'd had that day. At that moment, I held no grudges. I only wanted to be close to my father.

"I'm sorry, Dad. I had no idea you'd be here. You've been working so late. I don't even know where your lab is. I wouldn't know where to find you if I needed you. Maybe I could come out after school sometime? You could pick me up. You know how I love to tinker in a lab. And alternative energy is such an exciting field. The applications are so important for the future of the whole planet. You can show me what you're doing…I could bring takeout for dinner."

"It's a top-secret facility," he interrupted, stirring his noodles. "No one is allowed in but personnel."

That makes sense, I thought. *They couldn't have the locals poking around and getting in the way, potentially disrupting their experiments.*

"Even family?" I tried one last time.

"No. Top secret."

"How top secret can a wind farm be?" I laughed.

"I never said it was a wind farm."

"Oh. I thought you did. I guess I just assumed," I said, remembering how even Reg could figure out that a wind farm wasn't possible on the island. "That was silly of me. You're studying aspects of a wind farm, though, right?"

"Sure. Right. Look, it's complicated."

"My friend and I are going to build a generator for science class. Maybe you could give us some ideas—"

"Leave it, Genny!"

"What exactly *are* you doing, Dad?" I didn't know why, but the hairs on the back of my neck bristled when I asked.

"I told you. I'm researching alternative energy sources," he said, stirring his noodles too intently.

"What then? Solar power?" He didn't answer. "Why would alternative energy sources need a 'secure' area?"

"They're very private."

"Who are *they*?"

"My funders," he said, sighing.

"Who are your—"

"That's enough, Genny," he said, slamming his mug down, weedy noodles spilling onto the table. "There's *my* business and there's *your* business. Stay out of mine, and I'll stay out of yours. You've been accepted to MIT. You're a genius. You'll be the next Marie Curie," he mocked me, shimmying his hands in the air. "Good for you. But you don't know everything. You were so caught up in your little, white-tower world back home, it's probably a good thing you got pulled out of it. Maybe you needed to be taken down a notch."

"W-what?" I stammered. "Don't pretend you moved here for me! Ever since you started looking into this project on the Isle of Man, you couldn't be bothered to do anything for me, even if it was to take me down a notch!" My mind reeled, releasing all the hurt I had buried, which bubbled uncontrollably to the surface.

"You're jealous of me, Dad!" I shouted. "You don't want me in on your little secret project because you're just afraid I might show you up! That's why you keep pushing me away!"

"You don't know what you're talking about," he muttered, sinking back into his usual lethargy.

"Ever since Mom died—"

"Don't you dare bring her into this! She'd still be here if it weren't for you." His eyes blazed with hate. I suddenly felt empty inside, like a hole had been blasted through the middle of my chest. I grabbed onto the chair in front of me to steady myself.

He confirmed what I'd always wondered. He blamed me for her death. I had always felt responsible, but hearing him say it out loud had given life to the skeletons in my closet and made them dance in front of me. Despite the hot tears that began streaming down my face, I was not crying. It was anger, anger that had caused my eyes to spring a leak. Anger at that shell of a man in front of me *not* eating his mug of noodles, and *not* buying cell phones, and *not* loving me. I ran up the stairs, wheezing from the asthma gripping my lungs, and into my bedroom, slamming the door behind me.

I was restless all night, chased in my dreams by the tattooed, bald man with the black leather bag. In every dream, he would corner me and begin to open the bag. He reached in to pull something out. I only caught a glimmer of cold steel each time before I would wake up in a sweat.

Then he was gone, and I was back on the boat with my mom the day she died. I remembered my mom letting go of me as her research partner hauled me up into the boat. She laid me down on the floor.

"*Cadjoor y fadyraght,*" she said, gently wiping my wet hair out of my face. She turned to go back to the edge of the boat, and as she did, I saw the red tattoo of the triskelion partially hidden by her ponytail.

The plunge

I awoke to a new reality. The sun coming through the window offered nothing for me. Everything felt dark. I awoke to a world where my mom hadn't died in a tragic accident, but was murdered. Murdered by people who were now stalking me. And I was alone. At least I finally knew why the triskelion had frightened me from our first day on the island.

I was becoming accustomed to loneliness. For a three-day stretch after our argument, I didn't even see evidence of my dad having been home when I was gone. I found myself worrying about him, like a mother would her child who had run away. I wondered if he was eating properly. Was he sleeping? Then I would dismiss such sentimentality. He didn't care what happened to me. Why should I care what happened to him? I immersed myself into other things that would occupy my mind.

I had officially given in to Reg's idea to make a generator. We spent much of our time together bickering like an old married couple over the details. While he was stuck on wind power, I kept pushing him to think outside the box. Surely we could come up with something less pedestrian than wind or potatoes for power.

Then there was Ken. Despite all I had said about making discoveries and my dedication to science overriding my fear of water, I was relying on the cold autumn and winter months to postpone what appeared to be inevitable: learning to swim. I had flat-out refused to enter the school's swimming pool. I thought it was because having people around would make my nerves even worse, but I wonder if it was a subconscious move to put it off.

To Ken's delight and my chagrin, the forecast for the following Saturday was unseasonably warm. There was no avoiding it. It was time for swimsuit shopping. I wasn't sure what the swimsuit array was usually like in Ramsey, but in November I assumed one couldn't be choosy.

I decided to brave Ramsey's high street alone after school one day. Somehow I had managed to avoid it up until then;

the most adventurous shopping trip I had taken was my weekly excursion to the grocery store. Ken begged to go and be my Ramsey high street guide, but I staunchly refused. He was *not* going to watch me parading around in swimsuits any more than necessary. I said good-bye to him at school and ran by my house first.

The wooden stairs groaned as I jogged up to my bedroom, slamming the door behind me. I threw my backpack onto the bed and stripped off my uniform. The reflection in my closet-door mirror caught my attention just as my body relaxed, free of the stifling uniform. A pasty girl stared back at me, her shoulders slumped and her feet splayed out like a duck's. *He's going to see you in a swimsuit,* I reminded the girl in the mirror and quickly sucked my belly in and threw my shoulders back.

My comfy MIT sweatshirt was calling to me from a drawer, so I covered myself up with it and some jeans. I detested clothes shopping, and I didn't particularly want anyone to see me toting around shopping bags. There was something about advertising for a clothing store by carrying its bag around that drove me nuts. Not to mention the fact that I was afraid that clothes shopping made me look shallow. I would have preferred to inherit clothing and leave the agonizing shopping trips out of my life.

I unzipped my backpack and dumped everything out onto my bed. *My backpack will be perfect for hiding shopping bags, if I actually find anything that looks good. Plus, I'll still look studious!* Even I couldn't believe the lengths to which I would go to avoid appearing girly. I picked up the backpack and raked at the inside to pull out any leftover junk.

A crumpled piece of graph paper tumbled out. Curious, I picked it open and flattened it onto my bed with the side of my hand. A perfectly geometrical symbol was drawn on the paper; it had the same intertwining rings I had imagined etching into the bench at the swim meet. This was the paper I'd had out when I was reading my English assignment at the Indian restaurant that same night. *I didn't imagine it*, I admitted to myself with a sickening twist in my stomach.

I studied the design. As I remembered from the pool, it was as though it had been drawn with tools. I traced my finger around the perfectly drawn curves, lacing through them as though the design were three-dimensional. I didn't have to look. My finger traced it perfectly without even having to think of it. This design was an extension of me. But it hadn't always been. It was not until I came to the Isle of Man that I first drew it. But there was more.

What was the connection to the times I had drawn it? *Ken? No, he wasn't with me in the restaurant.* The Indian restaurant, the swim meet, probably under the tree…It didn't make sense. I knew there had to be a logical explanation for why I had been drawing the knot, but I couldn't come up with one. *Somewhere else,* a thought nagged me. *I've seen it somewhere else too. But where?*

I didn't want to think about it anymore. For once, I didn't want to think. When I shoved the paper into my nightstand drawer to get it out of my sight, I saw the nail clippers pushed to the back of the drawer. I sighed, too curious to resist.

I flipped the lever up and swiveled the file out. Residuals of blue paint were embedded in the grain of the nail file. It was the same blue as the swim building bench. My hands began to tremble. I fumbled and dropped the clippers onto the floor with a clatter, and quickly edged them under my bed with my foot. I didn't want to think about what was happening to me, or what the significance of the design was. I grabbed my backpack and ran down the stairs and out of the house.

The high street was quaint and quiet. I needed that. *Maybe shopping wouldn't be a bad diversion after all,* I thought. I was surprised at some of the unique shops. Across from the town square stood a little store called Infinity Crystals, and I wondered how a small town could support a strange little specialty shop like that. I rolled my eyes at the window display of crystal fairies, Native American dream catchers, and a dark-cloaked wizard statue in the corner.

Right next door stood the obligatory Isle of Man motorcycle shop with the TT race fan's every need, from souvenir T-shirts to bumper stickers. I couldn't begrudge them that. The annual TT motorcycle race was the island's main source of tourism, bringing in a lot of money for the inhabitants. The farther I went down the street, the more I assumed everyone went to Douglas for clothes shopping. Finally, after a smattering of mom-and-pop newsstands and other assorted shops, I found a little department store.

It wasn't as big as most of the department stores I remembered from the States, but it had everything one of the big stores would have, just less of it. The doors opened onto the cosmetics department, definitely not my natural habitat. I felt myself shrinking among a sea of shining bottles of perfume that lined the wall like an ornate, jeweled inlay. The sharp, angle-tipped MAC lipsticks stood in a row on the glass countertop like red-coated British soldiers standing at attention. When a waft of jasmine and primrose tinged air floated up to me, I almost believed in the imitation spring they created and wished I had worn a tank top and shorts instead of a sweatshirt and jeans.

"May I help you find something?" asked a woman with blonde hair stacked up so high on her head that she towered above me, despite my looking down into her eyes.

"Swimsuits?"

She lightly shook her head as though a bee was buzzing around her hive of hair. "It's November. We don't carry swimsuits in November."

"Do you know who might?"

"No. No one sells swimsuits in November."

"Thank you, anyway."

"Wait," she said, eyeing me like a mother bird would her chick. "You're a pretty girl. You don't do much to help yourself, though." Despite what she said, I could tell by her gentle tone she wasn't being critical. Only maternal.

"It's just been me and my dad since I was eight. By the time I needed help with makeup, there was no one to show me how to do it. I never really thought about it, I guess." I felt very vulnerable, all of a sudden.

"I'll show you some tricks. It'll only take a minute," she assured me. She took me by the hand, sat me on a stool, and disappeared behind her counter lined with more soldier-like lipsticks that stood motionless and silent in disapproval of me. Across the walkway, vibrant lines of MAC's tiny circles of eye shadow were on display, like a rainbow Twister board. I couldn't begin to imagine how to use them, but I could envision someone painting a landscape with them. I bet the MAC lady knew how. *I asked for swimsuits at the wrong cosmetics counter*, I lamented.

She returned with several tubes of makeup, patted my hands, and began.

"I'm Susan."

"I'm Genny."

"We don't get many Americans in here," she said. I was afraid to respond at that point, because she was painting on my lip gloss.

It's strange to have someone that close to your face. The experience was much more intimate than I was used to being with anyone. Even when Ken had kissed me, I had closed my eyes. We certainly weren't staring at each other.

She talked me through how to apply lip gloss, concealer, blush, and mascara, and as she predicted, she was finished in only a minute or two. She held the mirror in front of me.

I was shocked. The girl looking back at me was pretty, but was she me?

"See? You were there all along," she said and smiled.

"I think I was already me," I said, "but I will take the concealer and the lip gloss." I handed Susan my dad's credit card. When she returned from the cash register, I had my backpack open. She dropped the little bag into it.

"You're not supposed to save makeup for a special occasion, you know," she reminded me. "You should use it every day."

"Got it." I zipped up my backpack, smiled at her, and wished my mom were still alive.

Outside, the wind had picked up, and I was again glad I had worn a sweatshirt. I went into store after store, and one sales clerk after another looked at me like I was crazy for asking where the swimsuits were at that time of year.

My feet ached and I was becoming discouraged, so I turned to head back the way I had come, toward home. *At least I have an excuse to postpone the swim lesson. You can't swim without a swimsuit,* I thought. Many of the stores had closed by six o'clock, and that end of the high street was as quiet as a cemetery. The darkening street was deserted except for one man, a few storefronts away, who had stopped at a newspaper dispenser. He was on his cell phone and little snatches of what he said floated over to me.

"*Hooar mee ee.*" He shoved the phone into his pocket. He was big, and his leather jacket stretched tightly over his rock-like biceps. I began walking, but as I neared him, I noticed that although his fingers played at the money slot of the newspaper dispenser, he held no money. In vain he pulled at the handle that held fast. He glanced over his shoulder at me, and I slowed. A foot of the red triskelion tattoo peeked out from beneath his jacket collar. Turning, I sped in the other direction. I heard footsteps quickening behind me, and I broke into a run.

"*Bee er dty hwoaie. Gow kiarail!*" He breathed and grabbed my arm roughly, pulling me hard toward the wall of closed stores. I wrenched my arm from his grasp, narrowly avoiding a car door that swung open, half blocking the sidewalk, and ran as fast as I could.

Realizing I couldn't outrun him, I spotted a lone, lit store window just ahead and skidded to a stop at the door, flinging it open with enough force to hurt my shoulder.

By the time the little brass bell on the door finished ringing to announce a customer, I was halfway across the store.

"Hello, love," the sales clerk at the register said, looking up from her paperback book. "In a hurry?"

Since the man didn't follow me in, and I couldn't see the back of her neck, I decided to play it down. "The wind caught the door when I opened it and startled me. Sorry." I looked around and found I had taken refuge in a second-hand charity shop. "I know this is a long shot," I said, panting, "but do you happen to have any swimsuits?"

"Oooo, good question. I remember something coming in a while ago," she said, heading to the other side of the store. "I don't think it's sold. Not much demand for it this time of year, is there?" She chuckled as she ran her hand along hangers of activewear.

"No, I guess not. I'm actually going to try to learn to swim," I confessed, keeping an eye trained on the door.

"Good for you! Never too late. Ah," she said, pulling a hanger from the rack, "here we go. Looks to be about your size too." I forced my gaze to the swimsuit. It was brown and plain. The thought of a secondhand swimsuit was pretty disgusting, and my face must have revealed my thoughts.

"Run it through the wash with a bit of bleach. It'll be good as new," she assured me.

Honestly, I would have bought it even if I were going to take it home and throw it away. I didn't have the heart not to buy her swimsuit. She was so sweet. She was the kind of woman that I wished were my aunt who would come for Sunday dinner every week. I wished I had someone like that in my life. Again, I ached for my mom.

"It looks perfect," I said. She walked me to the register and began to ring me up.

"Ten pounds, love." As I dug through my backpack for my wallet, the lights flickered and then went out completely, leaving us in darkness.

"Oh, not again," she moaned. With the cover the blackout afforded me, I tiptoed toward the window, hoping to see if the man was still outside, but it was only more darkness; the streetlights had gone out too, and I could see nothing.

"Does this happen often?"

"Never seen it happen before a month or two ago. But it's always been around midafternoon. This is the first time the power's gone out in the evening."

"I thought it was just happening at the high school," I said, remembering Mr. Moore's conversation with Mr. Tills, the janitor.

"Seems to be all of Ramsey. No worries, though. I'm sure they'll get it all sorted soon enough."

"Very strange," I said, echoing Mr. Moore's sentiments from before.

The lights came back on, momentarily blindingly me. I blinked as I adjusted and quickly walked back to the counter and paid.

She handed me the bag. "Best of luck to you," she said and came around the counter to give me a hug. I felt stiff in her arms, even though I wanted to hug her back. "I'm sure learning to swim will be no trouble at all for a clever girl like you."

"Fingers crossed." I went back to the front of the store and lingered at the door, trying to see past the glare on the glass and into the street.

"Everything all right, dear?" she asked.

"Sure. Everything's fine." I pushed the door open and stuck my head outside. The street was empty. "Just fine," I repeated, more to reassure myself than her.

By the time the door shut behind me, I was already half-way down the block. I ran as fast as I could all the way home, not taking the time to scan the streets for more of them. It didn't matter if anyone did show up; I was planning to run so fast, he'd never catch me anyway. Once I reached my front door, my hands shook so violently, I didn't know if I could steady my key enough to unlock it. Just as I pushed the door open, I heard a car passing the house slowly behind me. I slammed the door behind me, twisted the bolt, and collapsed on the floor, grabbing for my inhaler.

Pump. *Breathe it in slowly. The slower, the better.* Pump. *Slowly.*

By the time Saturday rolled around, I had thoroughly ruined the swimsuit. Despite following the instructions on the bottle, the bleach had splattered and left markings on it that made me resemble a tie-dyed giraffe. I was just grateful the only thing in the wash was the swimsuit. I would have been really upset if it were my everyday clothes. I considered using the bleach fiasco as an out for my first lesson with Ken, but I forced myself to be brave. I knew if I put if off, I'd give in to the fear and never do it. I layered my clothes over my giraffe skin and hoped Ken would think I bought the swimsuit that way.

When the doorbell rang, swimsuit issues went from my mind, as did my usual excitement over seeing Ken. The doorbell sounded to me like a death knell.

"Hi," I said quietly as I opened the door. His mouth was creased in concern.

"We don't have to do this. We can get our books and go to the tree—"

"Let's just go," I said, swinging my bag over my shoulder and shutting the door behind me.

We walked to Mooragh Park in silence. The big, wrought-iron gate at the entrance opened onto a calm, azure-blue lake where a few people were out splashing. I looked up to notice triskelions lurking in the corners of the gate's arch. He led us off to the left, through a wooded area to a more secluded part of the lake.

"I'll go on in, and you can come in whenever you're ready, OK?" he said, leaning his bag against a tree.

"Sure. I'll just be a minute." I stood frozen a few steps from the water's edge. Just when I didn't think I'd be able to take my eyes off the water, I saw Ken peripherally.

He too was looking out at the lake and was sliding his black T-shirt over his head. He was perfectly built. Lithe and beautiful.

He walked out into the water until he was chest deep. He looked so at ease, raking his outstretched arms back and forth against the surface of the water. I quickly used my inhaler. *He won't let anything happen to me*, I thought. He was a gentleman and continued to face away from me while I undressed down to my swimsuit. I walked to the edge and carefully toed the water. It was warmer than I expected. I slowly waded out until I was waist deep. With every step I could feel panic swelling inside me.

"Ken," I barked, "I don't think I can come out any farther."

He waded as quickly as he could back to me.

"I think we better take things slowly," he said, touching the back of my head. "I just thought we could get used to the water together. We can go back and sit on the edge, if you'd like?"

I couldn't help but smile, either because he had to be the sweetest boy on the planet or because I could see his chest again. I tried to keep my eyes locked on his eyes.

"If you stay with me, I can stay this deep." I was quite proud of being waist high in the lake.

"I'm not going to leave your side, Genny. I'd never do that to you."

We waded around in the water for more than an hour, gradually getting deeper and deeper as time passed. I started to understand why he liked raking his arms through the water. It was liberating, like when the wind blows through your hair when you're riding a bike.

"Are you ready to go?" he asked suddenly.

"Already? I haven't learned to swim yet."

"Rome wasn't built in a day. I wasn't expecting you to learn to swim today. You need to get over your fears first. Baby steps, Genny. Baby steps."

"It wasn't as bad as I thought it would be," I confessed.

He smiled as he took my hand, and we started walking back to the shore.

"Good. Do you mind if we go by my mom's store? She called before I left to see if I could bring the house key to her. She forgot it at home."

"No, of course not. You never told me your mom had a store." I was glad my hair hadn't gotten wet. I would have been mortified to meet Ken's mom for the first time looking like a wet dog.

"You never asked," he chided, and I remembered him saying the same thing when I realized Mr. Creer was his dad. "It's just a little store on the high street."

We walked to the changing rooms at the main entrance of the park and slipped back into our street clothes. I checked myself in the mirror. *Why couldn't I have worn something nicer? Ken's mom will think I'm a slob.* I sighed. I wondered if she was the nice lady in the secondhand shop. She had dark hair like Ken, and she seemed to like me already. *That would be very handy,* I hoped.

"My mom's been wanting to meet you," Ken said, taking my hand. As we walked, wafts of algae floated past my nose when the breeze changed direction. *Great. I smell like lake water.* My only hope was that she would remember me from when I bought the swimsuit and that would explain my dank smell. *Oh, I hope she doesn't ask about how the bleach rinse went,* I thought in panic. I calmed down, recalling that Ken didn't seem to notice the bizarre pattern on the swimsuit, so he probably wouldn't even think to mention it to her.

"You're awfully quiet," Ken commented, snapping me out of my reverie. "I didn't push you too fast today, did I?"

"No. You were great, Ken. I couldn't have asked for a better teacher. Or a better friend." I mustered a smile. "If you want to know the truth, I'm a little nervous about meeting your mom."

"Don't be. She's probably more nervous about meeting you." He paused, as if he were rethinking his last statement. "You know, you're an American. You're exotic." Neither of us could suppress a giggle at the thought of my being "exotic."

I had been so wrapped up in my own thoughts that I suddenly noticed where we were.

"Isn't this the store?" I asked, seeing we were about to pass the secondhand shop. The woman who had helped me with the swimsuit was hanging a top in the window display as we passed by. We caught her eye, and she smiled at me before we disappeared out of view.

"No," he said, cocking his eyebrow quizzically. "If you've never been there, how did you think you knew where it was?"

"I don't know," I admitted. I considered telling him about the nice store lady, but thought against it. He probably already thought I was a little odd. *No need to fuel the fire*, I thought.

"Well, here we are," Ken announced. I looked up at a window full of fairies. "Infinity Crystals."

"Oh, your mom works here?" I asked, trying to hide my skepticism.

"She doesn't just work here. She owns it," he said, taking my hand and leading me through the door.

Chimes tinkled as the door swung shut behind us. It was as little inside as it appeared it to be from the street.

"My mum must be upstairs in the storeroom. Have a look around, and I'll go get her," he said and jogged up a stairway in the back of the store.

I rolled my eyes while looking around the room. I never thought I'd be caught dead in one of those weirdo stores. One wall was ceiling-to-floor books, ranging in topic from "Crystals and Their Powers" to "Manx Folklore." The "Fairies and Other Mythical Creatures" collection was sizable, if the window display was any indication. A long table stretched across the store from front to back, where all sorts of crystals and stones were on display. I ran my fingers over a bowl of smooth, fiery-red stones, telling myself they didn't really feel warm to the touch; it was just my mind playing tricks on me.

The Plunge

The most bizarre thing about the store was the wizened, leafless tree that seemed to grow up through the center of the table and almost touch the ceiling. Hanging from the tree were crystal ornaments: fairies of all shapes and sizes, rainbow-tinted butterflies, delicate spun sugar-like strings that twirled and caught the light like tiny icicles. I was stifling a giggle over a green, winged seahorse when something else caught my eye. A hand-carved face made of wood was displayed in the center of the tree. His hair was a bower of wooden leaves and resembled a lion's mane. I felt watched by his omnipotent, but benevolent, eyes and it made me embarrassed that I had laughed at the dumb seahorse. I was so transfixed by the wooden tree god that the sound of footsteps coming down the stairs startled me.

Ken bounded into the room, grinning.

"Genny, this is my mom," he said, stepping out of the doorway. From behind him walked a woman who was not unfamiliar to me. She had appeared in my dreams, in my thoughts as I played my violin: sometimes kind, sometimes frightening. She had haunted me from the first time I saw her at the tram station on my first day in Ramsey. I didn't know what to make of her with the untamable red hair tumbling madly past her shoulders. It was difficult at that moment to connect her with Ken, even though they were both standing in front of me.

"Hello, Imogen," she said with a tentative smile, holding out her hand. The bracelets stacked on her wrist clanked together as she did so, breaking me out of my frozen shock.

"Genny," Ken and I corrected her in unison.

"Hi," I said. I shook her hand and mustered a smile, unable to take my eyes off hers. I was so jarred that I didn't even remember that I reeked of lake water.

"I'm Cerdwyn. It truly is a pleasure to meet you," she said while still holding my hand. I couldn't tell if she was nodding her head as she spoke, or bowing slightly.

"It's a pleasure to meet you too," I stammered. Ken separated our awkward handshake, taking both our hands in each of his.

"All right, you two. That's enough of…whatever that was."

"You have a very interesting store," I told her, interrupting Ken. "You must be very proud of it."

"Thank you. I am. We're coming up on our twentieth anniversary," she said proudly.

"Congratulations."

"Well," she said, spinning the keys Ken brought on her finger, "I have what I need, so you two go out and have a nice evening on me." She handed Ken some cash she already had in hand. He kissed her on the cheek.

"Thanks, Mum, but you didn't need to do that."

"For services rendered. Oh, and Genny, I wanted to invite you to a picnic we're having with some extended family next Saturday. We're celebrating the autumn equinox. Would you like to come?"

Ken looked sharply at her.

"Sure," I said.

"I'm sure she'll have to check her calendar, Mum," Ken interjected. "Americans are very busy people." Ken gently began pushing me toward the door. "Don't commit," he whispered to me under his breath.

"I'll have to check," I said awkwardly.

"All right, dear. Hopefully, I'll see you next week."

"Right," I said as the door shut behind us. "What was that all about?" I asked as Ken dragged me down the sidewalk. For the first time, I was a little miffed at him for making me look rude.

"I don't know if you're ready for our 'extended family' yet, Genny. You think Mum's store is strange? That's nothing compared to the picnic. Trust me. You'll be hitting a whole new level of strange."

"I admit, the store was…different for me, but it's part of your mom, and your mom's part of you. And anything that's part of you, I want to be a part of. Did that make sense?" I wondered aloud.

He sighed. "I just…I don't want to lose you, Genny," he said, stopping abruptly and turning to look at me. "You're just opening up and beginning to see things through different eyes. I'm afraid the people at the picnic will be too… intense for you. There's no need to rush things. There's no reason to go."

"There is nothing I could see, no one I could meet, that could make you lose me," I said. "I want to go."

Little did Ken know that with every word he had spoken, my desire to go burned hotter. My desire to be closer to him was close to being supplanted by a mystery to unravel. I wanted to see what he was so desperately trying to hide from me. He had opened a Pandora's box—an unknown for me to discover.

The Picnic

"Are you crazy? Put your face mask on."

"What are you—my mother?"

"You'll damage your retinas!"

"I haven't turned it on yet," I said. "You don't have to protect your eyes until right before you start. Besides, I only need goggles with a gas welder." Out of the corner of my eye, I saw Reg cross his arms. "Fine," I sighed, tugging the goggles down over my eyes. "I can't see as well now. I hope you're happy. Now I look like a total dork."

"So? There's nobody else here. Besides, you look cool. Kind of steampunk."

"With welding goggles on. Right."

"You'll thank me when you're still able to see afterward, so keep them on," he scolded from a safe distance. "How did you learn to use that thing anyway?" He gestured toward the welding gun.

"Science isn't only theoretical, you know. I wanted to put theory into practice, so I started taking shop classes back home."

That was the problem with Reg. He had the knowledge, but was afraid to do anything with it. I thought he was going to pass out when I told him that Mr. McCreary, the shop teacher, had given us permission to come in after school to work on our project. Mr. McCreary was sitting in his office doing paperwork, occasionally glancing over his glasses at us through the window into the shop classroom. He had looked a little dubious about my abilities, but when Reg walked in, Mr. McCreary looked out and out concerned. I lowered my voice.

"You're the one who was bent on doing this, remember?"

He began nervously bouncing on the balls of his feet when the welding gun lit.

"Stop talking and just be careful," he said.

The metal melted into a little pool, and using the welding rod like a magic wand, two pieces of metal became one. There was a purity to the process that I loved, like playing my violin. When I finished and turned off the gun, I turned to Reg to see that although he had baby-stepped his way across the room, away from the heat, he was dripping sweat.

"How does it look?" I asked, already knowing the answer.

He cautiously walked back over as though he was afraid the welding gun would light on its own and come after him.

"Perfect," he said, smiling. "Perfect."

"Reg," I started, beginning to put the tools away, "how much do you know about Ken's family?" I didn't make eye contact with him. I didn't want to frighten him away from the subject, like a mouse scampering away from a loud noise. Reg and Ken, though they ran in different circles, had lived on the Isle of Man all their lives. Surely, Reg had to know the dirt on Ken.

"Well, he's Mr. Creer's son."

"I know that." I sighed, reliving my embarrassment with Ken and mentally kicking myself once again for looking so stupid. "Forget it."

"Why do you want to know?" The pitch of his voice rose as he spoke. "You two aren't…," he stammered.

"Kind of," I said, awkward, as if my dad had asked.

"Genny, that is a really bad idea."

Speaking of bad ideas, what was I thinking asking a guy who obviously has a thing for me about a guy I'm kind of dating?

"You're new here. There's a lot you don't understand."

"I understand more than you think, Reg. Like that you have a crush on me, and I shouldn't have asked you about him." I instantly regretted saying that.

"Fine." He swung his backpack over his shoulder and strode to the door. "Find out the hard way."

The next week seemed to last a month, every day drawing out longer than the one before. Ken didn't mention the picnic at all. He probably hoped I would forget about it or decide against going; little did he know I could think of nothing else and nothing would stand in my way of being there. Anything that was so mortifying to him must be worth seeing. I thought it was kind of cute that he didn't want me to see his embarrassing extended family.

I had to tread carefully around the subject, so I decided to confirm a meeting time for Saturday at the last minute, lunchtime on Friday. Fortunately, Ken had moved his swim practice times to before school every morning, so although he was always tired, at least we had started eating our lunches together.

"Hi, guys," I said to Reg, Jim, and Ted on the way past their table. My cheeks flushed in embarrassment that I had forsaken my previous lunch buddies.

"Hi, Genny," Reg said. "Did you want to work with us on physics homework?"

"Oh," I said, slowing, "I already finished it. Sorry. Maybe next time?"

"Sure." I could tell Reg was disappointed. They had lost their token girl.

I sat down at the corner table of the cafeteria, at what had become "our" table, feeling awful. Did the guys understand I didn't forsake them to hang out with somebody popular? It wasn't like that at all. I didn't even see Ken as popular. He was just Ken. And I didn't stop hanging out with them because of who they weren't. I couldn't pull myself away from Ken because of who he was.

Ken walked into the cafeteria and straight to our table.

"Hi," he said, smiling playfully at me and taking a seat across the table. My heart fluttered.

"Hey." *No better time than the present*, I thought. "Are you going to come by and get me tomorrow, or should I meet you at the picnic?"

His brow furrowed.

"I thought we discussed this," he said.

"We did, and I told you I wanted to go."

"I told you I *didn't* want you to go."

"No, you told me you didn't know if I was ready and that there was no reason to go. Well, I say I am ready, and the reason I'm going is because I was invited by your mom and I want to go."

"This is a big mistake," he said, defeated.

Some of history's biggest discoveries were born out of mistakes, I thought, but decided not to say it out loud.

"So, what time did you say you're picking me up tomorrow?" I persisted.

He sighed. "How about three o'clock?"

"I'll be ready."

Ken picked up his uneaten lunch and got up. "Sorry, Genny, I have some things I have to take care of before the end of the day. I'll see you in English."

He hadn't had things to take care of on any of our lunch breaks before, and I wondered if I had pushed him too far.

"Um, yeah. Sure." I felt so helpless. *Why couldn't I just leave well enough alone? Why couldn't I be one of those compliant girls who just kept her mouth shut and made everyone happy?* I knew I could potentially drive Ken away at this rate, but I also knew I had no other option. I wouldn't reprogram myself. I couldn't stop being myself for anyone, including him.

I noticed Ken detour to the mean girls' table on the way out. He didn't stop, but a minute after he was gone, Celine left suddenly too. I knew it had to be paranoia, but it was a little too coincidental that she never came back for the lunch she abandoned on her table. I didn't want to be alone right then, but did I dare go back to sit with Reg and Jim and Ted? I didn't want to use them to fill a void. It wasn't fair to them. If I was going to be their friend, it couldn't be just when it was convenient.

I stared at their table. Reg and Jim or Ted were gabbing about something geeky, no doubt, but Ted or Jim seemed out of sorts, staring into the distance. I followed his gaze and saw what, or whom, he was staring at: the same pretty girl who brought me a hair dryer the day Karyn poured soup on me. *Jocelyn*, I remembered. She was sitting at a table on the opposite side of the cafeteria.

I packed up my things quickly and walked over to the guys' table.

"Hey. I was wondering if you guys were going to a movie this weekend. I'm available on Sunday. If you're all available?" The three of them had frozen in mid-movement.

185

"I don't think we have any plans on Sunday, do we?" Reg asked the other two.

"No…no…," Jim and Ted answered nervously to each other. Reg suddenly lost whatever cool he had as an idea hit him.

"There's a two o'clock showing of a sci-fi movie on Sunday. We could meet at the cinema?" His face became sullen as he looked at the table where I had been eating lunch lately. "Will you be bringing Ken with you?"

"No," I said, "it's just me."

"Great! That'll be…great!" He laughed out loud in excitement.

"OK then. I'll meet you there," I said and hesitatingly added to Ted or Jim, "You should ask her out."

"What?" he asked, flustered.

"Jocelyn. She's cute. You should ask her out."

"Jocelyn? She's out of my league. Anybody that beautiful…she'd never go out with me. Her interests are all different. She goes to the Point in Port Saint Mary just about every weekend to surf. Maybe I should take up surfing…," he said, becoming lost in thought. "It's just physics, really. It shouldn't be any harder than compensating for the torque caused by the hydrodynamic forces—"

"She's really nice. You don't need to do anything to impress her. I think you should be yourself, Ted."

"Jim," he corrected me.

"Sorry, Jim," I apologized, knowing full well I'd forget which was which the next time I saw them. "You want someone to fall in love with *you*, not someone you're pretending to be, because you can't pretend to be someone else forever."

He looked down at the floor, and I knew what he was thinking. That he wasn't good enough for her or anyone else to fall in love with him. I knew what he was thinking because I'd always felt that way too. I wasn't pretty enough for anyone to notice me, let alone fall in love with me. I was just always more willing to be alone than to be untrue to myself.

"So," I said, breaking the silence, "see you Sunday?"

"Sunday," Reg confirmed, grinning. As I left the lunchroom, they were chattering away, giddy as schoolgirls.

Ken smiled politely at me when I walked into English class that afternoon, but aside from that, he didn't make eye contact with me for the rest of class. My stomach churned while I found myself questioning if I had done the right thing in pushing him about the picnic. I knew in my heart that I wouldn't have rested until I went, so I tried to console myself with that.

When the bell rang at the end of class, we picked up our books without a word and walked to my locker.

"OK then, I'll see you tomorrow at three o'clock," Ken finally said with less enthusiasm than I had ever heard him use before. Even though part of me, a big part of me, thought it was stupid for anyone to act this way about a picnic, it pained me to see Ken upset about something. I resolved to stay unwavering.

"OK, Ken. Can I bring anything? Potato salad? Cupcakes?" Not that I could make either of those.

"No, everything's taken care of." He hesitated and kissed me on the forehead. "Bye."

While I was perfectly capable of walking home on my own, it had been so long since I'd done it that a nagging feeling haunted me all the way, like I'd forgotten something. I spent the evening alone as usual, but I was restless. I played my violin in fits. I would play for a few minutes, then become bored and stop, only to pick it up again awhile later. Waves of excitement and nagging dread washed over me and prevented me from concentrating on anything. It was the dread that irritated me. That was all Ken's fault. He had ruined a perfectly fantastic social experiment with all his unnecessary concern.

Promptly at three o'clock the next day, the doorbell rang. I opened the door to find that my slouching, smirky, unintentionally smoldering Ken wasn't there. A stiff, sullen, intentionally cold Ken had replaced him.

"Hi," he said with a sigh.

I had had enough.

"Will you just cut it out? I've never seen anyone act so juvenile about anything. Put your big-boy pants on, and let's go have fun at a picnic," I said, stepping past him and slamming the door behind me. I was striding down the sidewalk in front of him when I realized I had no idea where I was going. I turned to find him right behind me, where I knew he'd be. How could I go so quickly from insecurity in our relationship to a cockiness that would surely push him away? I stopped and took his hand.

"Please don't be like this," I pleaded.

He didn't respond. He simply looked at me.

"I'm sorry. I just let the excitement get the better of me. Don't punish me because I'm excited. I miss you. The real you," I said, gently pushing my finger against his chest.

He gave a small half smile, and I grinned back in return, grabbing him in a bear hug.

"All right. I'll try to relax," he said, hugging me back. "Just don't say I didn't warn you."

"Deal."

I expected to go to Mooragh Park, where we swam, but we were definitely winding the wrong way through town. I was surprised when we stopped at the electric tram station.

"The picnic's in Douglas?"

"No, there are stops between here and Douglas." He helped me into the tram and left me to go talk to the driver. He came back and sat next to me in an uneasy silence. He smiled, and I could tell he was trying to be himself. It just wasn't working very well.

"A request stop?" I deduced.

"Yes." He chuckled. I could tell he was proud I was learning the native ways.

I watched silently out the window as the tram trundled through the lush greenery. It slowed to a stop midway through the trip to Douglas. I felt like we were close to where the strange man had boarded in the darkness that night, but I had no way of knowing for sure. Ken took my hand and stood to leave the tram. It was disconcerting to get off in the middle of nowhere, but I assured myself it wasn't "nowhere." According to the little painted sign next to the tracks, it was Ballaglass Glen.

There was no platform there, only loose gravel at the edge of the dense woods. Once we had stepped away from the tracks, the tram pulled away and left us to a symphony of the whirring and clicking of bugs. Still holding my hand tightly, Ken led me to a path that disappeared into the thickly packed trees. As we descended some makeshift steps down a steep incline, I noticed a brook trailing along below us on the left, curving lazily under a footbridge at the base of the steps.

"Be careful," Ken warned as we were stepping off the footbridge on the other side. "It's easy to trip."

I looked down to see that the ground was covered in a web of tree roots, like veins that had crept to the skin's surface. They almost appeared to pulsate with life.

He veered left toward a little brick bridge twenty feet above us that I hadn't realized our tram had crossed. Golden sunlight spilled out of the circular opening under the bridge, where the brook gurgled out, dancing around large rocks and tripping over little ones, creating miniature waterfalls along the way. I stopped to steady myself on a tree next to the stream, not wanting to miss anything—the cacophony of bugs playing against the babble of the water, the smells of moss and damp earth and spring onions. I wanted every detail to be perfectly steadied in my mind. I did not believe in magic, but if there were such a thing, I thought, it would surely exist here, in this place.

"Are you all right?" Ken asked quietly.

"I don't think I've ever felt more right. This is perfection. It's…ethereal," I whispered, afraid to disturb the sanctity of the glen. I rested my hand on the green coat of moss that crept up the side of the ancient tree next to me.

"Where are your friends?" I asked, breaking momentarily from the distraction. "Where's the picnic?"

"Don't worry," he said, sighing. "They're coming. I brought you early. I wanted you to experience Ballaglass Glen before you experience…them."

"I'm glad. I had no idea what I was in for."

"No, you didn't," he said sadly, and I felt the weight of his double meaning. "Come here." He took my hand, and we walked back past the footbridge, following the edge of the brook. "I want you to see this before they get here." He stopped near a particularly rocky section of the brook. The sound of the water was louder here, but still perfectly serene.

"Watch," he whispered, pointing at nothing in particular on the other side of the brook. "Don't look at the other side," he instructed. "Let your eyes relax."

The sun peeked through the lattice of leaves overhead, channeling narrow beams of light through the darkness. I allowed my gaze to rest, but not focus, there. It didn't take long for me to notice something strange. I blinked my eyes hard and looked again, but it was still happening. The shafts of lights were not straight and steady. I knew it had to be a trick of the lighting, but it looked like the beams of light were very subtly trembling.

"That's not possible," I whispered, as much to myself as to Ken.

"It is here. As far as we can tell, this is the only place on the island this happens."

"Try 'only place in the world,'" I said, not daring to take my eyes off the quivering lights.

"Come on. There are some pretty places this way I'd like you to see before the others get here." Ken started walking, assuming I was following him.

But I didn't. I couldn't. *Can an electromagnetic pull cause this distortion in light frequency?* I wondered, involuntarily stretching my hand out as though I could grasp one of the beams.

Suddenly, what appeared to be an insect darted into the shafts of light. The insect's body was not horizontal, but vertical, and whenever the light hit it, it glowed an iridescent blue. It zipped from place to place, and I struggled to keep track of it. Then, as if as equally curious about me, it appeared about six feet in front of me, hovering in the lights above the water. It was approximately three inches long. Its wings moved so quickly in a figure-eight pattern that it gave the appearance of a slender, spinning top. The wings were positioned about three-quarters of the way up its body, where arms would be on a human. The tail section appeared to split into two near the bottom.

Slowly, contradicting the creature's other sporadic movements, the head of the insect turned to look at me. I instinctively pulled closer and we looked into each other's eyes. She cocked her head. She had eyes, a nose, and a mouth that turned down at the corners as though she were sad. Delicate arms unfurled from her body like ribbons from a spool, and I noticed then that the tail section was actually legs. She cocked her head, studying me, and I stood motionless, not trusting my eyes, but not distrusting them enough to risk scaring her away.

"Imogen?" she asked.

I wondered if I was hearing the gurgling waters below her.

"Imogen?" she repeated, and I forced myself to accept that the voice that sounded like the distant echo of a wind chime was coming from the creature before me.

I tried to say something, but no words came from my mouth. I stood mute before her.

"*Shee dy row hiu,*" she said. "*Nar jarrood. T'ou balley.*" Without a warning, she was inches from my face. Her delicate hand touched my cheek, and a pulse of energy shocked me. "*S'treih mooar lhiam dy jarroo shegin dhyt jean reesht eh, Imogen.*" Her hand slid away from my skin, and she zigzagged through the beams of light and disappeared, leaving me stunned.

Shaking, I crumpled to the ground, tears of shock rolling down my cheeks. *But how did she know my name? I must have imagined it. No*, I corrected myself. *I didn't.*

"Genny?"

I looked up where she had been.

"Genny, what happened?" Ken asked, kneeling next to me.

I tried to look at him, but I couldn't focus.

"I'm so sorry. I thought you were right behind me."

What could I tell him? A little flying person, who knew me, stopped by to say hello? I couldn't. He'd think I was crazy. Or that I had hit my head.

"I fell. I tripped on a tree root. I might have hit my head." I knew that wasn't too far of a stretch. My eyes darted wildly around in the vain hope that I could find the little creature, but she had vanished as quickly as she had appeared.

"Are you hurt?" he asked, wiping the tears from my face.

"I'll be all right. I think it was more…shock."

Ken helped me to my feet, and I dusted myself off. "See, I'm fine." I managed a faint smile. I heard voices and footsteps coming down from the tram stop.

"Great. They're here," Ken hissed. "It couldn't be worse timing. Let me take you back home."

"How? The tram back to Ramsey isn't coming by for another half hour, right? I'm fine," I repeated, this time more convincingly. He took my hand tightly in his, and we headed toward the voices.

In the dark distance, it was hard to distinguish anyone, but I could pick out Cerdwyn and Mr. Creer.

It was hard to miss her hair and unique clothes even in silhouette as she glided through the glen. Mr. Creer followed along behind her, staring at the ground for every step and still managing to trip over tree roots. This was obviously not his element: the outdoors. He seemed terribly out of place.

It was strange to see a teacher out of the context of the classroom. As English teacher, Mr. Creer was quite formidable. Bumbling behind his wife, he was little more than Cerdwyn's husband. Cerdwyn led the group, which appeared to be about thirty people in all, through the glen with all the authority of a queen of the wood nymphs, she was so much at home.

"Ken! Genny!" she called out, waving. After what I had just seen, so much unbridled friendliness seemed a little overwhelming, and I wasn't sure I was ready for it. She walked over to us while the rest of the group congregated near the footbridge.

"Have you two had fun exploring the wonders of Ballaglass Glen?" she asked. She reached out to hug me, but it was one of those awkward ducking and dodging situations where we almost bumped heads several times before we finally coordinated, my head docking on her left shoulder and pressing onto a thick silver chain that disappeared under the layers of her clothes at her neckline. Her echoing laughter put me at ease; she was one of those people whose manner soothed people naturally.

"Yes. It's the most beautiful place I've ever been." She released me but still remained close. What little remaining light that was sifting through the leaves reflected in her green eyes. Her gaze lingered on me a little too long for comfort, and I took a step back, bumping into Ken.

"She just had a fall a few minutes ago," Ken interjected. "I'm not sure she's well."

"Oh dear," she said, patting my cheek. "Maybe some food will help? Let me introduce you to our friends. They have been so looking forward to meeting you."

Ken seemed frustrated when she took me by the hand and led me to the group. Mr. Creer fell in line with Ken, as I was beginning to think he always did.

"Everybody, this is Genny. She's a friend of Ken's," she said, beaming. Everyone smiled and helloed, and I smiled and nodded back. Despite the smiles on their faces, their eyes were a little too wide, like they were looking at an alien and trying to act normal. I hated being the only American around.

"Well, let's eat," Cerdwyn said, breaking the awkward silence.

"I'm the only person here who didn't bring any food," I muttered to Ken as his parents walked over to help the others and to unpack the food Cerdwyn brought. Some pulled out their covered bowls, others spread blankets out on the ground, but periodically I would catch a random person sneaking a peek over his shoulder at me.

"I think you were destined to stick out in the crowd," Ken whispered lightheartedly. "Besides, they would have felt awful if you had brought anything. You're their guest."

All the food was set on one blanket and people helped themselves. We sat with Cerdwyn and Mr. Creer. Judging by the way Ken had been acting, I had half expected everyone to be menacing, or at least, odd. But everyone was chattering and laughing, calling out from one blanket to another to include others in their conversations. Aside from the uncomfortable introduction, they seemed normal enough. I couldn't understand why Ken had been so worried. I wanted to be a part of the group, but like so often in my life, I felt like I was floating. I wanted to be present with Ken and his parents, but in my mind, I was being pulled somewhere else by the little blue creature that somehow knew my name.

"Cerdwyn?" A voice cut through the fog that was clouding my brain. I turned to see a woman kneeling next to our blanket.

"Yes, Aithne," Ken's mom responded with a hug.

"I just wanted to make sure you knew Celine is sitting with our family for dinner?"

Celine? I thought to myself.

"Where else would she be?" Cerdwyn laughed.

"Well, I wanted to make sure it was all right with you since today *is* a special day!"

"Karyn might as well be part of the family, Aithne. Those two are inseparable. Of course, Celine can sit with you."

*Celine and Karyn? Surely not the same...*I scanned the crowd of people until I saw them. They were on a blanket close to the stream. Celine's head was cranked as far as possible to the side, and she was glowering straight at me. Even in the dim light, I could see the scowl on her face. Karyn turned to look too, as if sensing Celine and I had made eye contact. I couldn't believe Ken's ex and her best friend were there to glare at me.

"If you'd rather, the girls can sit with your family—" Aithne started.

"No," Ken interjected. "It's fine with me. Really, Aithne."

"Of course. Pardon me," she said. As she turned to speak to me, I peripherally noticed Ken tense up. "Imogen?"

"I just go by Genny, actually. Yes?"

"I just wanted to tell you what an honor it is that you're here," she gushed. Ken and Cerdwyn exchanged quick glances.

"Thank you. That's very kind."

"I could hardly wait to see you today. All of us feel that way," she said, gesturing to the throng chewing on their sandwiches and now and then stealing glances our way.

"Thank you, Aithne," Cerdwyn interrupted. "You'd best be letting Genny get back to her dinner."

"Oh, of course. Of course. So sorry for intruding," she said, hurrying to her feet.

"Don't be silly, dear. No intrusion at all," Cerdwyn assured her, but her tone suggested otherwise. Aithne made an odd little bow before making her way back to her seat.

"She's a bit…highly strung," Cerdwyn whispered to me. Ken rolled his eyes as if he knew this was going to happen. "Everyone's just a little star struck at the American, I'm sure." She patted me on the leg.

"It's no problem," I told Cerdwyn, more confused than disturbed. People were staring at me more than they should just because I was a foreigner. *Can they see it on my face? What I saw at the creek?*

Ken pulled me close to whisper in my ear, "Sorry about that. You look upset."

I hadn't realized my feelings had betrayed me.

"I just feel a little awkward knowing Celine is here," I whispered back, trying not to let Ken's parents hear. Fortunately, Cerdwyn had already begun a noisy conversation with a family on the blanket next to ours, and Mr. Creer was engrossed in a book, so I felt fairly safe talking to Ken.

Ken pulled back. "Why?"

"You two seem like you've been…pretty close," I stammered.

Ken's eyebrows knitted together. "I'd hardly say that. As sisters go, she can be a bit of a pain."

"Sister?" I repeated. My cheeks flushed in embarrassment.

"You didn't know Celine is my twin sister?" he asked in bemusement.

"How was I supposed to know?" I retorted. "You never mentioned you have a twin sister."

"Well, we have the same last name," he continued in disbelief. "You missed that little fact with my dad too, if memory serves me correctly."

"I knew *Mr. Creer's* last name…I just didn't remember yours at the time," I admitted. "I've gotten some weird vibes from Celine and Karyn," I whispered to him, under-exaggerating what my interaction with Celine had been. "I thought Celine and you had dated."

After he finished laughing at my expense, he whispered, smiling, "Were you jealous?"

I looked away, not wanting to answer. "Maybe," I finally whispered back.

"Even if she weren't my sister, she doesn't hold a candle to you. No one does. I do need to tell you, though…" Ken looked awkward. "It was Karyn and I who dated. That's probably where you detected some weirdness from them."

Karyn! I had never thought of Ken and Karyn. It was one thing wondering if Ken was involved with someone before we met; it was another thing altogether to know who it was. As I imagined Ken touching Karyn, brushing her hair from her cheek, taking her hand in his, pressing his lips against hers, my stomach knotted.

"When did you two break up?" I asked, trying to sound grown-up and casually inquisitive about it, but my voice cracked, and I sounded like a jealous child.

"The day I met you," he answered.

Well, that explains why they hate me. Day one I was at the school, Ken dumped Karyn, Celine's best friend, for me. For me? For me! I wondered why. Why leave your girlfriend for a very average-looking, socially inept stranger? The realization of Ken leaving his girlfriend for no other reason than me made me feel dizzy. I wished I could touch him, but the environment was far from fostering romance. Sister or no, I could still see Celine staring a hole through me.

At least I finally understood their problem with me. Still, though, I thought Celine was overreacting just a little. *The end of a high-school romance is not unheard of. Besides, Karyn should be more upset than Celine, but Karyn wasn't the one who had threatened me.* I wondered if Ken wasn't telling me the whole story.

After we finished eating and packed up the food, everyone instinctively gravitated toward the place where I had seen the quivering lights and the creature. I followed, holding Ken's hand. It was evening, though, so the only lights I saw were the flashlights that everyone carried. With Ken, I joined the others, forming a circle. Cerdwyn stood in the middle.

"Blessed autumn equinox to you, my friends," Cerdwyn formally greeted us.

"Blessings," everyone but me murmured in response.

"The Bible tells us, 'Whoever sows sparingly will also reap sparingly, and whoever sows generously will also reap generously.' Let us take cues from the island, our home, to examine our lives. Let us look to the land that is being harvested and reflect what our lives should produce. Faith. Peace…"

My eyes flitted to where I had seen the blue creature hovering over the brook to see if she had returned, but I saw only darkness. That unearthly visitation an hour earlier and Celine's glare from across the circle made me feel as if my mind was beginning to crack like fragile, November ice on a pond.

Cerdwyn looked meaningfully at the others. "And bravery," she added.

"But tonight we have not only the autumn equinox to celebrate, but also a new spirit joining us."

I stopped breathing again, afraid she was talking about me, but instead, she turned to Ken. "My own son, Kendreague, is now of age. Tonight is the night of his dedication. Tonight, he becomes a Keeper." Cheers rang through the woods as all eyes were on Ken. He looked down, clenching my hand. "Kendreague, I have never known a young soul who believes as wholeheartedly as you, who honors our traditions, upholds our folklore, and so completely lives for this island. It is my honor, both as leader and as your mother, to welcome you as a Keeper."

The crowd fell silent as a man walked out of the group toward Ken and Cerdwyn. He placed the black case he was carrying on the ground and began unbuckling it. Incased in foam inside was a small, handheld device and vials of different colors. Ken gave one last squeeze to my hand before releasing his grip.

He stepped over to a large, flat stone and knelt in front of it. The man removed the device that looked a little like a hot-glue gun, and attached a red vial near the grip at the bottom of the gun.

"*T'eh ny arreyder*," the man proclaimed loudly.

As he bent down to whisper some instructions to Ken, a shriek from the crowd startled the man, and he pulled away to look for the source. A red mark on the man's neck flashed in and out of my view as he searched frantically for the shrieking, injured person. I had no doubt what the red mark was. The triskelion was etched into his neck just behind his right ear.

The scream got louder and louder, and everyone looked around to see who was making this inhuman noise that sounded like a kettle coming to a boil, every second louder and more out of control. Person by person I began noticing the marks on their necks. All the adults I saw bore the tattoo. Ken bolted up from the stone, looking at me through tear-filled eyes.

Cerdwyn grabbed my shoulders. I looked at her and realized her long hair no doubt covered the triskelion that was on her neck as well. I wondered if I was suddenly imagining it glowing through the curtain of her long, red curls.

"Genny! Genny!" she screamed over the ear-piercing noise that filled the glen. I could feel myself vibrating in her grip. "Calm down!" It was only then that I realized the screaming was coming from me. "Genny!"

I looked around wildly, like a trapped animal.

"She's going to have a seizure," a man called out, and thick arms wrapped around me from behind. I thrashed against the hold and looked over my shoulder at my captor. It was the tattooed man from the tram station. He finally had me.

"You need to calm down," he said, holding me as tight as a vise.

The scream slowly dwindled down to nothing, and I went limp in his arms.

"I told you she shouldn't be here," I heard Ken shout.

"I'm sorry," Cerdwyn stammered. "I thought she was supposed to be here. Everything that I've learned—"

"That's just it! You know *about* her. You don't *know* her. Not like I do. I can't believe I let you talk me into this. I could have told you this would happen."

I felt Ken take me from the tattooed man and lift me into his arms. His footfalls crunching through fallen leaves were all I could hear in the silence as we crossed the footbridge and started up the steps.

"Are you awake?" Ken asked once we were at the top. I took in a breath to answer, but the wheeze from my lungs stopped me short. He quickly put me down, and the ground felt like it was moving once my feet were planted. I took out my inhaler and tried to slow my breathing. Not wanting to answer him, I kept my eyes trained on the ground. I wished I could be in Ramsey in my bed, with the covers pulled up over my face. But there was nowhere to go. I was at the mercy of an infrequent tram.

"Are you all right?" he asked quietly, not touching me.

"What do you think?" I asked, looking up at nothing in particular. I just didn't want to look at him. "I guess you're going to say, 'I told you not to come'?"

He reached out to touch my arm.

"Don't touch me!" I screamed. "Murderer!"

"What?" he stammered, stumbling backward in shock.

"Your *people* down there murdered my mother!" I shrieked, willing myself not to crumble to the ground when I said the words.

"You need to calm down, Genny. You're not making sense."

"I remember, Ken. My mom's research partner. The one on the boat. I remember she had your mark on her neck. She was one of you!"

"You need to calm down. Nobody killed your mum, Genny."

I wouldn't look at him. I stared into the impenetrable web of trees instead.

"You're a liar," I whispered. "And I hate you."

He didn't respond.

"I want to go home," I said.

"The tram will be here soon."

"No. I want to go back to America. I want off this island."
I sniffled but refused to allow myself to go into a full sob.

"I don't think you can," he said quietly.

"I know." Tears blazed a trail down my cheeks. "But I
hate it here. Nothing makes sense here. I thought I had you,
but now…" I stopped.

"But now what?"

"You're not who I thought you were. You're just…" I
paused, considering whether I should say what I was thinking. "You're one of them."

"You don't understand who we are—"

"Oh yes, I do. You're a bunch of brainwashed, jingoistic
zealots."

"That's rich, coming from you," he said unflinchingly.
"The girl who doesn't believe in anything. I didn't blindly
adopt the beliefs of anyone, not even my parents. I chose
them and accepted them because I could feel in my gut that
they were right. And if feeling something so much that it
takes over your life makes you a zealot, then fine, I must be a
zealot. But I'd rather be a zealot than someone who believes
in nothing, like you!"

"That's not true," I screamed. "I believe in science.
I believe in making the world a better place…in a tangible

way. A *real* way. Just because I don't go around getting my little cult-club-member tattoo on my neck doesn't mean I don't believe in anything!"

"We aren't a cult, Genny. We are Keepers of everything that is sacred on this island. And *you* don't believe in anything you can't prove. In all of your eighteen years of accumulated knowledge, you must be the world's leading expert in everything, right? Funny how you're so brilliant, but you can't even piece together members of the same family. We have the same last name, Genny. You didn't need to be Sherlock Holmes to figure it out. You don't live in the moment. You live in a textbook. You're so blinded by your equations, you can't even see what's happening around you. It wouldn't surprise me if you couldn't bring yourself to believe in something you saw with your own eyes, just because it *shouldn't* be there, according to you."

My thoughts wandered to revisit the creature I'd seen in the glen. I remembered every detail of her. I knew I always would.

The quiet rumble of the tram approaching interrupted my reverie. I stepped out close to the track to wave my hand in the bright headlights so the driver would see me. It came to a stop, and I climbed on.

"You were wrong, Ken," I said, looking down on him. "I needed to come tonight. I needed to see you for who you are."

"Well, unfortunately, I was all too right about you." He shook his head and walked back toward the stairs.

"I'm sure Celine and Karyn will be happy to hear about this!" I screamed after him. "You shouldn't have any problem going back to Karyn! She'll take you back! Because she's just as crazy as you are! Maybe she'll get a matching tattoo with you!"

The tram pulled away, its door slamming shut. It didn't matter. Ken hadn't stopped walking. He had disappeared back down the steps into the woods while I screamed at him.

I rode back to Ramsey alone.

The Movie

I was lost in a maze of trees so tall that I couldn't see the sky. It was nighttime. At least, I assumed it was, because the darkness had sucked the color out of everything, leaving the claustrophobic landscape a foggy gray. At every turn of the maze, I found myself on an identical path. And midway along every path, the tattooed man from the Douglas tram station stood in the shadows, still as a statue, his triskelion glowing red in the darkness. He never made a move toward me, but I ran as fast as I could to get away from him until I reached the next corner. Then, along the next path, I would see him again, just as before.

Again and again, I would run from him until I finally went down a path and he wasn't there. The shadows were empty. I relaxed a little and noticed a light ahead. I had found the exit! I began running toward the light, but right before I reached it, a pair of thick arms wrapped around me from behind. I struggled, but his hold on me was so constricting that I couldn't breathe. I tried to scream, but nothing came out. I woke up just as I felt something sharp come into contact with the back of my neck.

Sunday morning I awoke feeling like my face had been inflated. The girl staring back at me in the mirror had definitely not had a good night. Besides sleeping through a marathon of nightmares, I had cried more in the previous twenty-four hours than I had since my mom died, and my face showed it. My eyelids were so puffy, I looked like a boxer in the tenth round, and I wasn't winning.

I would have gone down to the kitchen and sliced up a cucumber to put on my eyes, but I had never bothered buying cucumbers. I always thought of them as incidental vegetables, nothing you could eat as a meal or a snack. You couldn't disguise their flavor with peanut butter like you could with celery. They were just there, waiting to be chopped up into a salad. Blech. So, since I was bereft of cucumbers, I soaked a washcloth in icy-cold water and laid it across my face.

The cold sting reminded me of when I played in the snow when I was little. I remembered my mom helping me build a snow fort once. It was when we lived in Kansas City, before Mom and I moved to Hawaii. I must have been four or five years old. My mom had wrapped me up like a mummy in winter gear, but my cheeks still peeked out between my hat and scarf. It didn't take long before my stinging face forced me to abandon my snow fort for the comfort of central heat and a cup of cocoa.

I peeled the washcloth off and looked in the mirror. My attempt at depuffing my face was to no avail. I went back to the bedroom and flopped onto the bed, pulling the covers over my face. It was one of those days when the oxygen being sucked into my lungs was too harsh, and breathing the recycled air from under my sheets was comforting. The extra carbon dioxide lulled me into semiconsciousness. I didn't want to be alert. I didn't want to think. I decided to remain wrapped in my cocoon and allow the day to dissolve around me.

Just when I was beginning to convince myself that I could stay there forever, the phone rang. I could count on my fingers how many times I'd heard the phone ring since we had moved to Ramsey. It rang a second time, and

I determined it was probably a wrong number. I quickly turned over in my mind the possibility it could be Ken. Then I wondered if I wanted to talk to him. I knew I did not want to talk to brainwashed, tattooed, fanatic Ken, but I did want to speak to my sweet Ken, with whom I had spent so many wonderful moments before last night. I jumped out of bed and flew down the stairs, grabbing the phone on the fourth ring.

"Hello?" I panted.

"Um. Is this Genny?"

"Yes." I could tell it wasn't Ken and instantly became disinterested.

"It's Reg."

"Reg!" I said too enthusiastically. Suddenly, I didn't care if it was Ken. It was comforting to know there was someone else in the world who wanted to talk to me. Someone who understood me and was not in a cult.

"Are you still wanting to go to the cinema with us today?"

I had completely forgotten about our plans. While they ruined my recluse-for-a-day idea, I knew it would be good for me to get out of the house with someone other than Ken.

"Of course." I thought I could hear Reg exhale in relief. "What time does it start, again?"

"Two o'clock. See you there?"

"Can't wait." I paused. "Hey, Reg?"

"Yes?"

"Thanks for calling to remind me."

"Um…no problem. See you."

"Bye."

I hung up and looked at the clock. It was already one o'clock! *What am I going to do about my face?* I thought in a panic. I jogged back upstairs to the bathroom and dug out my bag of makeup. I turned on the little portable radio that was on the bathroom counter when we moved into the house and dumped my meager selection of makeup out next to it. *Why didn't I buy more makeup from Susan at the department store?* My foundation was so old that it had turned orange and separated. It had gone unused since I bought it to wear for a Teens in Science awards ceremony when I was fifteen.

I sighed and raked it all into the garbage, except for the new concealer. *Do I put this on now, or should I do more cold compresses?* Hoping for a miracle, I rewet the washcloth with cold water and buried my face in it.

"Another power fluctuation yesterday has authorities baffled," a woman's voice announced from the radio.

"Thomas Avery from the Manx Electricity Authority had this to say about the outages."

A man's voice came through now. "While all the fluctuations have been brief, and we are referring to them as fluctuations rather than outages, we are concerned about the inconveniences they can cause our population. We're currently working on determining the cause and correcting the problem."

I turned off the radio and went to get dressed, but as I did, I found myself thinking about the power fluctuations. The sporadic nature of them and the fact that the power simply dipped and then came back on made me think there was some kind of drain on the electricity, like something being turned on briefly that required a tremendous amount of energy.

I ran down the stairs and out the front door, dutifully locking it behind me. With every step I took, the idea of going out that afternoon was becoming more and more ridiculous. I should have told Reg I'd gotten sick or something, but I didn't have the heart to let him down. Before I reached the movie theater, I detoured to examine my face in a shop window. I looked acceptable. I pulled my lank hair forward to help hide any remaining inflammation in my face. I presumed they wouldn't notice. Most boys don't notice things like that. I knew Ken would have, though.

Before I continued on, I searched the street behind me in the reflection for any tattooed men, or Keepers, as I had found out they called themselves. No one looked suspicious, so I went on to the theater.

Reg, Jim, and Ted were trying hard to stand casually near the box office and act like they weren't looking for me. Of course, Reg was the one who broke.

"Genny! Over here!" Reg called too loudly for the space between us.

"Hey," I said, smiling broadly. Like being met by a faithful dog after a bad day, it was hard not feeling warmed by a greeting from someone clearly thrilled to see me.

"I went ahead and bought your ticket. I wanted to make sure you got a seat."

I looked around the parking lot. With only a handful of cars, I was pretty sure we hadn't been in danger of that happening. Jim and Ted, arms folded and looking out at nothing in particular, pretended not to listen.

"Thanks!" I said, digging some money out of my pocket.

"No, you don't have to—"

"Reg, it's only fair. It was really thoughtful of you, but I get to pay for myself," I said decisively, handing the money to Reg. "Besides, you need money for popcorn, right? I'm assuming you eat popcorn at the movies on the Isle of Man?" I laughed.

"I think that's a universal movie-watching requisite."

Reg walked a little too closely by my side as we went in, with Jim and Ted in tow. I knew he wished we were a couple, and I wondered if by walking next to me, he was pretending it was true. After we all got popcorn and drinks, we filed into the darkened theater and sat, with me sandwiched between Reg and Jim or Ted. I knew Ken and I weren't together anymore, but I felt awkward being so physically close to another boy, even if it was poor Reg.

"So, how's Ken?" Reg asked, quickly shoving a handful of popcorn into his mouth.

"Um, all right, I guess." *Had he heard what happened last night? News does travel fast on an island.* I leaned back to check his neck for any tattoos I may have previously missed. Pasty white and tattoo-free.

"You don't sound too sure of yourself," he said, toeing someone else's spilled popcorn around on the floor.

I sighed, not knowing how much to say. I wasn't sure how much of Ken's secret society was public knowledge.

"It's been a weird twenty-four hours," I said.

"You didn't go to one of *their* gatherings, did you?" His disbelieving eyes met mine.

"Y-y-yeah," I stammered. *How did he know?* Jim and Ted snapped their heads around, and all three stared at me like I was an alien.

"Did they have magic wands?" Jim or Ted laughed, elbowing the other.

"Did they sprinkle fairy dust on you?" Ted or Jim chimed in.

"Shut up, guys!" Reg spat, turning red. Jim and Ted slunk down in their seats like rebuked children and ate their popcorn. Reg turned to me and whispered quietly, "What did they do?"

"They didn't hurt me. It was just a little creepy. They all had those tattoos on their necks, and then Ken…" I trailed off, remembering.

"Ken didn't get the mark, did he?"

"No, but only because I was there. I think if I hadn't started screaming, he would have."

"Screaming?" Reg's eyes widened.

"I kind of freaked out," I admitted. "How do you know about them?"

"You can't grow up on the island and not know about them. I mean, all your life you see these people with the marks on their necks. It's hard to miss. Everyone knows about them, but very few Manx are one of them. They act harmless, but the power they still have on the island makes them dangerous, in my opinion."

"They're not harmless," I said, trying not to remember the day my mom died.

"Genny, I think they actually believe in those old Manx fairy tales. As far as I'm concerned, anyone who bases his actions on fairy tales is dangerous."

The lights dimmed, and the trailers started. The static noise of cars crashing, tires squealing, machine guns firing, and sentimental love songs all wove together like a dream, until suddenly, the power went out, plunging the theater into complete darkness. I heard whispers around me for a moment, and then they faded as I let the inky blackness swallow me up. I felt disembodied and I found myself back at Ballaglass Glen, looking at her. The creature. *The fairy*, I admitted to myself.

She looked even more beautiful than I remembered. Her eyes were proportionately larger than a human's were, and her blue skin was luminescent. Although her limbs were as delicate as the finest tendrils of a willow, I could tell she had no worries of the elements harming her. She was part of the elements and impervious to them. She wore no clothes as such, and although her body was shaped like a female's, a pearly exoskeleton covered her torso. Her eyes looked deep into mine.

"Imogen?" I again heard her ask. I reached out my hand to touch her.

"How do you know my name?" I whispered.

"Imogen?" she repeated, just as before. I couldn't tell if this was a memory, a posttraumatic flashback, or if she were once again in front of me.

"How do you know my name?" I screamed, and a hundred eyes turned to me, glistening in the darkness.

"Genny? Are you OK?" I felt Reg touch my arm as he spoke. The movie trailers began playing again with a jerk, and for a second, the fairy's luminescent skin outshone the dumb images flashing at me in the theater. Then she dissipated in the flickering lights of the movie screen.

I struggled to take a breath and began grabbing for my inhaler. The three of them stared at me as the medicine slowly began to relax my chest.

"Yeah, I'm fine," I finally responded.

"Are you joking?" he asked, getting too close to my face. He was checking my pupil dilation. "Were you hallucinating?"

"They probably slipped her something last night," Jim or Ted volunteered.

"No! No. I'm just tired." I tried to smile reassuringly. "I'm fine. I promise."

"OK." Reg sat back in his seat, but for the rest of the movie, he would occasionally glance over to check on me.

The movie was a good distraction. I was glad I had gotten out of the house instead of succumbing to the easiness of obsessing about my problems at home. I would have been crazy by Monday. Although I let much of the movie waft past me, the basic science elements were interesting enough to grab my attention. It was much more cerebral than typical sci-fi movies are. When the romantic thread of the storyline was featured, I would drift back into thoughts of Ballaglass Glen and tattoos and Ken.

The movie ended, and we lingered in the parking lot. Jim and Ted argued about the technology behind the plot of the movie, while Reg and I awkwardly avoided the only thing on either of our minds: my talking to an invisible person in the movie theater.

"Thanks for letting me tag along," I told Reg.

"It was our pleasure…my pleasure," he added.

I flinched. I didn't want to hurt Reg, and I thought he had understood that we were buddies and that Ken and I… well, Ken and I weren't anything anymore, but regardless, that didn't make Reg and me any more than we were: just friends.

"Look," he continued, "I care about you. I mean, about what happens to you. Just stay away from him, Genny. I know Ken seems like the perfect guy, but his friends, they're really out there. They have some kind of weird hold on the island that I don't fully understand. But it goes high up. I think they even have pull with the government. I don't trust them. And since he's one of them, I don't trust him either."

I bristled at this attack on Ken. Hearing someone speak against him made me rethink my feelings. Yes, I was genuinely frightened by the events at the picnic, but did that change the Ken I knew? As upset as I was the night before, I was surprised to hear myself defending Ken.

"I don't trust them, Reg. But I trust him," I said.

Reg looked wounded.

"I'm sorry," I added.

"Yeah. Me too. Just be careful, OK?"

"Sure," I mumbled, disappointed in myself for hurting Reg. For being pulled too much by my heart and not enough by my head. I couldn't go back to Ken and try to pretend he was something different than he was, but I couldn't hate him either. I knew life would be easier for me if I could, but that wasn't going to be possible. I was doomed to be surrounded by boys who were "just friends."

Reg, Jim, Ted, and I parted ways in the parking lot. I took the long way home, weaving past the harbor, figuring that if the Keepers were tracking me, they wouldn't expect me to take the long route. The sunset was a rainbow of colors, and I sat on a bench and soaked it in. The cool breeze off the water helped to purge the emotional weight I'd labored under throughout the day. I felt unfettered as I was bathed in the golden sunlight.

I spent too long watching the boats bob gently in the water, and my comfort eventually turned to uneasiness as

I remembered the dearth of boats in Douglas Bay. That only confirmed what Reg had said about the Keepers having too much control on the island. The Keepers truly did have power if they could convince the government to enforce a law banning boats from Douglas Bay. I didn't know what was being hidden out in the Tower of Refuge, but it had to be important enough for the Keepers to ensure no one else could reach it. *But why did Ken want me to go?* I wondered. None of it made sense.

The sun dropped out of that magical little space that turns the sky into a watercolor painting. In an instant it was simply dark. I walked the rest of the way home quickly, watching for tattoos. The wind had turned bitter, and the flimsy sweater I'd worn wasn't enough to protect me from its bite. I tried to shelter my face with my hands as I walked along, but it only served to chap my hands. I was seriously regretting that I had taken the detour by the harbor.

I fought the wind all the way back to my house, and when I finally got there, a gust blew the front door out of my hands and into the wall, snapping the brittle doorstop. I got behind the door and threw my weight against it, forcing it shut, and then I slumped onto the floor, exhausted. My skin was numb from the cold. I made my way upstairs to the shower and let the hot water thaw me. Afterward I felt a little revived and decided I should make a dent in the mountainous laundry pile.

I washed and dried the first load and dragged the ironing board into the kitchen. Ironing was therapeutic for me. There was something fulfilling about having a task done so quickly. It was an instant-gratification thing, and I needed a feeling of accomplishment that day. I could make a crumpled shirt of my dad's crisp and tidy so easily, unlike my crumpled mess of a life. I took the shirt to hang up in his closet, but before I returned to the ironing board, something caught my eye.

My dad's briefcase sat slumped over, wedged between his bed and the nightstand. It was strange to see it without its permanent appendage: my father. I pulled it up onto his bed and looked over my shoulder while I fingered the lock. I tried his birthday. The lock stayed smugly shut. His mother's birthday. Nothing. Then my heart dared to hope. *My* birthday: 0-7-1-7. Again, nothing. I sighed. *It could be anything. Think. Think!* 1-0-0-3. The tumblers fell into place, and the lock clicked open. October 3, my parents' anniversary.

I reached in and carefully extracted the stack of papers like a surgeon, memorizing their order, the way they were placed against each other, every detail of their look and feel, knowing that my father would notice the slightest shift in their appearance. I was shaking. I was about to see the secrets my dad had been so careful never to let out of his grasp. *Until now.*

I began carefully leafing through the papers. I was expecting to see data and research. Top-secret experiments. With the way he'd been acting, I was half expecting to find correspondence from evil funders coercing my dad into performing unethical experiments. I read the top page.

Dear Janet,

I don't know what to do. It's been a week since you were taken from us, and I still don't know what to do. I don't know if I ever will. The simplest things in my life, getting dressed, making coffee, take every ounce of my strength.

Genny's doing no better, and I'm not in a position to help her. I can't help but blame her for your death. I know how careful you were, and that's how I know she was doing something stupid that distracted you. I'm sorry I said that. I love her and I know how much you love her, but it's just the way I feel right now.

I'm going back to work tomorrow. I realize now that all the work I've done was meaning-less. It was wasted energy. You were the only thing that ~~matters~~ mattered to me. And I will do anything it takes to get you back.

I wiped my cheeks with my sleeve so no tears would drop onto the page. *I knew he blamed me. So did I*, I thought. I flipped through the stack of papers. They were all addressed to my mom. I knew my dad had never recovered from her death, but I had no idea he was writing letters to her. I looked at a page closer to the bottom of the stack.

Dear Janet,

I may have finally found what I've been looking for! I've detected some irregular energy readings over an island in the Irish Sea. If my suspicions are correct, I believe there may be a pocket of exotic matter underneath the island.

If I can tap into that matter and harness it, I may be able to open a space-time construct. As difficult as the whole process will be scientifically, I think it will pale in comparison to accessing this highly volatile pocket without the locals interfering. I've got to come up with another reason for starting a facility on the island.

I can practically hear you now telling me to let it go, to let you go, but I can't. I will be with you again.

The page shook in my hand. I couldn't believe what I was reading. *Exotic matter? Space-time construct?* From what I had read previously, "highly volatile" was describing it mildly. Harnessing its properties would be next to impossible, and crazy. The likelihood of setting off a cataclysmic reaction would be far greater than finding a practical use for exotic matter. It was strictly theoretical that such a thing even existed, especially on the planet. If there were, however unlikely, a pocket of exotic matter somewhere on the earth, I'd have thought it should be avoided at all costs.

I was familiar with the theory that tachyons, which were a part of exotic matter, could be used to transfer matter backward in time, but it was only a crazy theory. I couldn't bring myself to believe that my dad would consider something as ridiculous as time travel. Exotic matter, tachyons, time travel: it was all completely hypothetical. It was science fiction, not science. It was completely out of character for my dad to consider such a thing. But as I pondered the man who wrote these letters, maybe it wasn't such a stretch. I read on.

Dear Janet,

I've found a man, Darius Cannell, who is interested in funding my "research." I explained to him that there is very likely a pocket of exotic matter underneath the Isle of Man, and that if I can harness the properties of this exotic matter, it may mean the end to the world energy crisis. He's also a local on the island, so he can begin the process of excavation before Genny and I arrive and assist me once I'm there. While Darius is dabbling with the possibility of alternative and unlimited energy, I will be pursuing my true work, getting back to you.

I believe I can create a wormhole and by charging the relativistic time dilation with massive amounts of electricity, control where in time the exit point will appear. I'll come for you, Janet. I will. I will stop you from dying, and we will be together again.

I ran to my laptop and looked up exotic matter. I already knew a little about it, but with the knowledge that I might be sitting on a pocket of the substance, it took on a more immediate importance in my life. Exotic matter, I read, has a negative mass, which gives it some unexpected properties. In many ways, it reacts oppositely to normal matter, like being repelled by gravity rather than attracted by it.

I sat motionless in the glow of my computer screen. I couldn't figure how my dad expected to tamper with exotic matter and not even consider the possibility of destroying the island. And then I realized: he didn't care what happened to the island or the people who lived there. Or me. Only one thing mattered to him, and that was my mom. Sacrificing everyone else was an acceptable price for him to pay.

I ran back to his bed and began shuffling through the papers. I found what I was looking for: the way in which he planned to harness the power of the exotic matter. I sat frozen, staring at the technical renderings of an electromagnetic device. With the right frequency, he could theoretically open a wormhole and make the other side whatever time he wanted. He was building a gateway to the past. I shook my head in disbelief. There was no way he could ensure the stability of the exotic matter.

"The power fluctuations," I said aloud, burying my head in my hands. Of course, he was the one causing the power fluctuations. Every time he experimented with the gateway, it was draining the power from the Isle of Man's electrical grid. I felt sick to my stomach.

At that moment, the radiator began popping as it heated up, and I jumped to my feet, scattering the papers. I ran my hand through my hair in a vain attempt to calm myself. My chest began tightening, and I fumbled to pry the inhaler out of my pocket. My dad wasn't home, but I couldn't look at the papers anymore. Not yet. I felt claustrophobic, and I had to get out of the house. I closed my eyes and began recalling the order of the papers. I banished all the emotions that were vying for control of me: fear, anger, and betrayal.

Like an automaton I assembled the papers. Next, I pulled up a mental snapshot of the papers in a stack. My fingers worked to arrange them into what I had seen, and I carefully deposited them back into the briefcase, checking to make sure the lock was on the random numbers he had dialed previously. The briefcase went back next to the bed. Like I had never touched it.

I grabbed the phone off the entry table and pulled my coat out of the closet. I watched out the window of the front door to see if my dad was pulling in. Struggling to keep the phone to my ear, I shrugged on my coat and dialed the only person who would believe me.

"Hello?" a voice asked from the other end.

"Ken?"

"Genny?"

"Can you meet me somewhere?"

"Umm…sure. I'll meet you in fifteen minutes."

"Where?"

"Our place," he said and hung up. I didn't need to ask where that was.

The cold wind ripped through my coat as if I wasn't wearing one. I pulled the knit hat out of my pocket and socked it down over my Medusa-like hair just as ice crystals began riding the wind down to the island like tiny razors. I kept my head down in a vain attempt to shield myself from nature's attack. The streets were silent but for the clicking of ice hitting the cars and house windows. The steady drumming made everything seem hollow. It was a bitter underscoring of our reason for being on the island. Hollow. All pretense.

As I turned to cut through the park, the silence returned where the ice had no percussion to strike. Out of the city's lights, everything was cloaked in darkness as the moon hid behind the wintry clouds. A dim light flickered through the giant tree's branches, which were whipping around in the same tortured frenzy as my hair.

I pushed my way through to find Ken waiting for me. He was sitting with his back against the giant trunk. He didn't say anything. He looked at me with those dark, discerning eyes that glistened in the glow from the flashlight he brought. I realized I must have looked half crazed. Maybe that was why he was silent. He was trying to figure out how to start a conversation with a crazy person in an ice storm.

"It was all a lie, Ken," I blurted out, tears suddenly streaming down my cheeks.

"What?" He rose to his feet and put his arms around me. A wave of warmth washed through me, despite the fact that he was simply one cold object encircling another. I buried my face in his shoulder and quietly sobbed.

"Why we're here," I whispered as I pulled my face up to his. "My dad's not here to work on alternative power."

Ken looked confused.

"I don't understand…"

"There's a pocket of exotic matter underneath the island." I could instantly see I had lost him. "OK, the…stuff…that black holes are made of? *That's* under the island." His eyebrows knitted together as he attempted to meld theoretical physics with his reality. "Dad's here under the guise of transforming that matter into usable and sustainable energy. But that's not why he's really here. He's going to try to use it to open up a wormhole to travel back in time."

"Time travel?" he asked in disbelief.

"He's trying to go back in time to save my mom."

"Genny—" he started.

"Look, I know this is hard for you to believe. It's hard for *me* to wrap my head around this too. But there are things you believe in that I can't understand. And, well," I stammered, "maybe we both need to step out of our comfort zones."

"OK, assuming this is all happening, what's the problem, right? I mean, aside from your dad disappearing, and no disrespect, but you never saw him anyway."

"The exotic matter is the problem. It's unpredictable and unstable, and if he's going to try to change the construct to create an opening to a wormhole, there's no telling what could happen."

Ken was silent for a moment.

"What would happen to the island?" he asked.

"Explode, implode, cause a space-time rift…There's no way of knowing. This has never been done. Maybe nothing will happen, but I think there's a possibility it could annihilate the island and everyone on it, one way or another."

"And he told you all this?" he interrupted, a little skeptical.

"No. I found the plans in his briefcase. He never leaves it behind, so when I saw it, I was curious. I was reading the papers when I started hearing things…I got scared and left. That's when I called you."

He slowly dropped his arms to his side.

"So, why did you call *me*?"

I could feel the hurt and resentment bubbling up in the space between us.

"Who else could I call?" I answered simply. "I don't have anyone else to turn to. Besides, I thought you might know what I should do." I paused, as things started to gel in my mind. "All this *would* go along with your theory about the man out in Douglas Bay, waiting to save us all."

We looked at each other, wide-eyed, realizing that our vastly different belief systems had just collided.

"We've got to stop my dad, Ken."

"You need to go see him."

"I would if I knew where my dad is or how to get there."

"Not your dad. The man in the Tower of Refuge."

A shiver rippled down my spine.

"This might be the reason he's there, what he's been waiting for," Ken said.

"You know I can't do that," I muttered, looking down. "I've only been in the water once, and I wasn't even swimming."

"Do we have time to wait?" he asked.

I didn't want to answer.

"I don't know when my dad is going to do this," I admitted, "so, no. I guess we can't wait." Tears welled up in my eyes. "I just can't go in the water, Ken."

"You have to." He hesitated for a moment, as if deciding to dare speak the next words. "It was prophesied."

"What?"

He sighed and paused once again, apparently debating what to tell me and what to keep to himself.

"You were in the prophecies, Genny. The ones that are held in the museum and can only be read by the leader of the Keepers."

My head started spinning, and I felt the same loose touch with reality I had felt at Ballaglass Glen. "How...how can you tell they were talking about me?" I laughed nervously. "It's probably some vague description of a girl—"

"It named you. Imogen Hazard. It said you would come to the Isle of Man from over the seas, and it even gave the date of your arrival. That's why there were Keepers positioned to make sure you made it safely to Ramsey. Why they're always around you, watching you, making sure you're safe. Why my mum was waiting at the tram stop to make sure you made it here safely.

"I asked her about your mum, Genny," he continued gently, "after you and I had our *talk* last night. You're right. There was a Keeper on the boat. But she didn't kill your mum. The Keeper was there to save you. You would have died too."

My mind reeled. I suddenly understood why Ken was interested in me. He was never attracted to me. I was unwittingly a part of the folklore he based his life on. It had been his job to keep me in place. In a way, maybe it made sense that the tattooed people were always present, lurking in the shadows. They were protecting me, just like Ken was, making sure I was always in the right place at the right time. And it explained the bizarre reaction toward me from everyone at the picnic. I was a legend to them. But there was one major problem.

"I'm not important, Ken. There's nothing special enough about me to warrant prophecies."

"You're more important than you can possibly realize."

I fell silent in thought and realized that not all the pieces of Ken's puzzle fit together. "If this prophecy was exact enough to mention my name and the date I arrived here, why were *you* asking *me* if we had time to wait? Didn't it mention the date of the destruction of the island?"

"I don't know. I wasn't told that," he said, a little embarrassed.

"Seems like kind of an important detail."

"I'm not the leader of the Keepers."

"Well, neither am I, because if I were," my voice rose in anger, "I think I might have divulged that little nugget."

"I can't change things for your convenience, Genny. Believe me, at this point I wish things didn't revolve around you, but they do. The prophecy says that you're the only one who can speak with *him*."

"Why does it have to be me?" I yelled.

"I don't know, Genny!" he yelled back. He ran his hand through his hair.

"I'm sorry," I muttered, touching his arm. He took me in his arms. I wasn't sure whom he was hugging anymore: Genny, the ex-girlfriend who laughed in his face about his beliefs, or Imogen Hazard, the prophesied one. It seemed pretty obvious after I thought about it, but right at that moment, I didn't care. It just felt good to be that close to him again.

"But I know one thing," Ken said. "You're not swimming."

"I can't live with myself knowing that my cowardice will cause the deaths of thousands," I cried.

"There's got to be another way to do this," he said. "Some way to get you out to the Tower of Refuge that wouldn't attract attention…"

"Couldn't the Keepers just tell the government they can retract the ban on boats in Douglas Bay? The Keepers are the ones who started it all, right?"

"There isn't enough time. It would be months of meetings before the government could change that law."

I could hear him talking, but I wasn't listening anymore. I was busy willing myself to go into the sea, steeling my nerves.

"Genny, listen to me." My wandering gaze snapped back to his. "I promise I won't let anything happen to you."

I believed him. I knew he wouldn't let anything happen to the prophesied one.

"All right," I said, "but we need to go soon."

"What about tomorrow night?" he asked.

"Do we have time to get everything ready?"

"We'll see," he wondered aloud.

"Will your parents be all right with this?"

"Are you joking? I'm sure Mum will wish you were taking her with you instead of me," he said with a little laugh, but I didn't join in on the joke.

Ken walked me back to my empty house and hugged me on the doorstep, the way a good friend would. I went inside and got ready for bed mechanically, trying not to think where I'd be the next night or what I'd be doing. There was no use fighting it. It was prophesied. So I decided not to fight my fate, which was apparently sealed. I would stop trying to plan my life and start riding the current like a kite rides the wind, not knowing exactly where I was going to end up.

Refuge

I was too nervous to eat, but had nowhere else to go besides the lunchroom at noon on Monday. I looked for Ken to no avail. I hadn't seen him all morning, so I didn't know why I expected to see him at lunch. His absence made my stomach knot. *Surely he didn't desert me*, I found myself wondering. I knew in my heart that if I could depend on one thing, it was Ken being true to his beliefs; and at that point, he believed that my father could very possibly destroy his home. While that fact should have assured me that Ken wouldn't let me down, there was still the nagging feeling that his nerves might prevail over his faith.

I bought an egg salad sandwich that I had every intention of throwing away untouched and looked over the tables to find somewhere to sit. There were my faithful few: Reg, Jim, and Ted. They even had an empty seat.

"Hi, guys," I said, taking my seat and tossing the sandwich carelessly onto the table.

"Genny!" Reg welcomed me like he hadn't seen me in years. Watching a movie with them the day before seemed like a lifetime ago to me too. Jim and Ted nodded at me coolly. I was surprised they could do anything coolly. "Really glad you made it to the movie yesterday. You feeling better?"

I hadn't really thought about how I felt. "Yeah," I guessed. "Hey, can we talk privately?" I whispered to Reg. Jim and Ted peered over at us.

"Sure," Reg said and gathered his lunch into a little, brown paper bag. We both stood and headed toward the cafeteria door.

"Are you going to eat this?" Jim or Ted called after me, holding the egg salad sandwich up in the air.

"It's all yours," I called back. The door closed behind us, and all the meaningless conversations that thickened the air of the cafeteria were shut out.

"What's up?" Reg asked, his eyes full of concern. As if ready for an embrace, he put his lunch bag on the floor. I knew I was about to lose a friend, and it broke my heart. He truly cared about me in a completely selfless way. He was beautifully transparent, and I loved him for that. As a dear, dear friend.

"I know how you feel about Ken and his—"

"Yeah, that they're crazy?" he blurted. The concern in his eyes was washed away in a sea of anger at the mention of Ken's name.

"I think something is going to happen to the island in the next few days. Something bad. I...I just want you to be careful. Stay away from the coastlines. I don't want anything to happen to you."

"Is this something that Ken told you about? One of their stupid fairy tales?" He sneered when he said "Ken."

"It's something I figured out for myself."

"Right. Whatever. He's got you so blinded in their fantasy world of mysticism and fairies that you're not thinking straight. You're smarter than that, Genny." Those last few words cut. He hit me in my weak spot. I was not stupid. Nor was I gullible.

"I can't tell you everything," I said, thinking of my dad, whom I still wanted to protect despite the danger he posed. "Just, please take care of yourself. You mean a lot to me."

"Don't lie to me, Genny. Ken is the only thing that matters to you, and he's got you so brainwashed, that's never going to change."

"That's not true, Reg," I pleaded.

Reg was done talking. He grabbed his lunch bag off the floor and strode back into the cafeteria, letting the door slam loudly behind him. I didn't follow him. I had no friends in there, and thanks to Jim or Ted, I was guessing I had no lunch at that point, either.

I didn't have anywhere to go until my next class, so I roamed up and down the halls of the school until I saw the lounge for final-year students. I pushed the door open and saw it was empty. I felt like I had walked into a refrigerator, and I remembered Ken saying on my first day that the cold kept the students away in the winter months. It was nice to find a quiet place when my mind was so full of chattering worries. I went in and continued out the other side onto the patio. I hadn't been out there since my first day. That seemed so very long ago.

The patio overlooked a little garden that was tended by students in an agriculture class. There were even a few animals off in a little field behind the school. Among them was a strange-looking little pig, covered in spiky hairs almost as thick as quills. While the other animals basked lazily, huddled together for warmth, he stood quite purposefully alone and examined me from a distance. The pig's gaze was undeniably pointed at me, and I squirmed uncomfortably. Suddenly, I remembered I had seen it before. There was a crystal miniature of a similar pig in the hotel lobby in Douglas the day I arrived.

"Imogen Hazard?" a deep voice asked from behind me.

I recognized that baritone voice instantly.

"Oh, Mr. Moore," I replied, happy to be diverted from my staring contest with the pig. "I didn't see you."

He hobbled over to the railing and leaned against it next to me.

"The lounge is a bit nippy in the winter. Not many students are warm-blooded enough to brave it until the spring. That's handy for me, though. The only vending machines in the school are in this lounge, so I get them all to myself all winter. Shhh…don't tell anyone, but," he whispered, leaning in, "I have a bit of a weakness for chocolate."

I giggled. "I like to think of chocolate as a strength rather than a weakness."

"How beautifully put," he said, stroking his beard thoughtfully.

"How are you?" I asked, genuinely concerned for him.

A little smile shone from under his grizzled beard. "Very thoughtful of you to ask." He chuckled. "I suppose I'm as well as can be expected." He nodded toward his walking stick. "The question is, how are *you*?"

"I'm OK. I guess I've got a lot on my mind," I confided.

"You always have a lot on your mind, don't you?" he asked.

"Well, yes, I guess I do."

"I'm proud of our students," he said, nodding to the fields. "I think they've done a fantastic job with our little farm."

"That reminds me, what kind of a pig do we keep here? I've never seen one quite like it."

"No pigs, Genny. We have two cows, a handful of sheep, and a horse."

"But," I interrupted, pointing toward the field. To my shock, the pig was no longer there. "That's funny. I saw a pig down in the field just a minute ago. At least I think it was a pig. It was covered in long, spiky hair."

"There's an old Manx legend that describes a pig like that. It's supposed to be good luck. Well," he said, looking past me into the field, "I don't see one now. Maybe you're just weak from lack of food. You didn't eat lunch today, did you?"

I shook my head.

"You probably just need some chocolate then," he said, snapping a piece of his chocolate bar off and handing it to me. "There. You'll be right as rain in few minutes."

I took a bite. "Thank you, Mr. Moore," I said, and he began making his way off the patio.

"Don't worry, Genny," he said, not looking back. "Whatever it is that's bothering you enough to skip lunch, it will work out. It always does."

"Thank you, sir," I replied and turned to look back at the field. There was still no pig. The bell sounded, and I snapped back into my daily routine.

There had still been no sign of Ken, and I was getting worried as I sat next to an empty desk in English class. Moments later Ken slid into his seat as the bell rang. He had a smug smile on his face. As Mr. Creer began his lecture, I expected Ken to lean over and say something to me. Anything. But he didn't. It was as if I weren't there. I supposed the only reason I was a part of his life at all at that moment was because I was the key to the Keepers fulfilling their destiny. That was the only reason I'd ever been a part of his life.

How could I have been so foolish as to think that the handsome, popular star of the swim team would want to be with me? How could I have believed that his fondness for me was genuine? Maybe I *was* as gullible as Reg accused me of being. Ken was nothing more than a plant by his clan. He had fulfilled his purpose in keeping me in line, right down to trying to teach me to swim. The trouble was, they hadn't anticipated how quickly the big event was going to follow my arrival on the island.

The final bell had rung when Ken finally looked at me while stuffing his book into his backpack.

"I've got it all taken care of," he said, grinning.

"Good," I replied, knowing I would hear the details without asking.

"All this time, I was worried about trying to teach you how to swim," he whispered, pulling me into the hallway. "It totally threw me when you told me you couldn't. All I could think of was that if we can't take a boat, you *have* to swim. But," he said even more quietly, "I've come up with an alternative. Meet me at the electric tram station as soon as you can, and we'll go."

"I'll be there in an hour, hour and a half."

"As long as you're there by six thirty. That's the last tram to Douglas. See you then," he said and bounced down the hallway.

I walked quickly home. It didn't seem logical to be putting on a swimming suit in late November. My pasty skin glowed in the bathroom light. I shuddered and quickly layered a sweater and jeans overtop. I looked at my face in the mirror. It was the reflection of someone who knew she was heading to the gallows; there was unmistakable fear behind her eyes. I leaned closer and tried to rub the concern away. I smiled a little at the ridiculous girl staring back at me, and the more I smiled, the more I could see my mom, smiling back. I had never been one to spend too much time in front of a mirror, and maybe that's why I had never really noticed it before, but I could see my mom so clearly—in my eyes, my smile.

"I love you, Mom," I whispered to the mirror. In my bedroom I dumped my schoolbooks out of my backpack and stuffed it full of whatever I could think of that might be useful. I went downstairs and paused at the door. I looked at a house that was never a home and sighed, wondering if I'd ever see it again. Then I banished thoughts that were not useful.

Put on coat. Woolly scarf. Lock door. Put keys under the mat.

The tram had beaten me to the station but it was waiting patiently for me, as if it knew it had to. Ken wasn't difficult to spot; he was the only one with a surfboard. A hole was drilled through the narrow end of the board, with a lightweight rope strung through it.

"Going to catch some waves?" I tried to joke, but I knew exactly what the large floatation device's purpose was. He put his hand on my cheek, and his touch cut through my sarcasm.

"Wetsuits are in my backpack. You lie on the surfboard. I'll pull you. You don't have to swim. It's so obvious. I don't know why I had never thought of it before. I'm a good enough swimmer that I can swim for both of us. Well, what do you think?" he asked, still cradling my face while he wiped a lone tear away with his thumb. "I need to know you can do this, or we don't go. Prophecy or no."

"Yes. I can do it," I said, hoping, but not positive, that I could. Ken smiled and took my hand to lead me onto the tram.

"Last call," the driver called out. He gave an inquisitive look at the surfboard, but didn't ask any questions. Ken seated me at the far end of the carriage and wedged the surfboard between the back of our seat and the carriage wall. Once he thought it was secure, he sat down next to me, and I couldn't help but look back at it.

"Here," I said, unwrapping the scarf from around my neck. "The board will tip when we hit that curve going into Laxey. If you loop this around the board and tie it to the coat hook, that should be enough to hold it." I handed him the scarf.

"How many times have you made the trip?" He shook his head in disbelief. "How can you remember a curve going into Laxey well enough to know it's going to tip the surfboard?" he asked as he stood and began following my instructions.

"I don't know," I said with a tired smile.

"You only memorized the angles of turns on a tram route you've been on just a few times," he added, sitting back down. The tram eased forward, and as we left town, the windows became inky black, and the harsh lighting of the tram allowed for only a sallow reflection of the inside of the carriage. We were alone.

"Do you realize how special you are?" he asked, looking genuinely curious.

"I guess I've always known I was unusual. But no, I've never felt special."

"You are. You're special enough to see a light in the Tower of Refuge when no one else has."

"Or maybe just unusual enough," I corrected him.

Maybe, I wondered, *there was something special about me that I didn't understand yet.* Maybe I had spent so much time trying to understand science that I had never tried to understand myself. Maybe I was afraid to try. Maybe I just hadn't happened yet. Maybe I was a maybe, waiting to be.

I paused, considering whether to share all my secrets with Ken, namely the fairy. Surely he of all people would believe me, so it wasn't that I was worried he would laugh at me and think I was crazy. I just felt like saying something out loud would give substance to a thought. A body to a ghost. I felt like if I spoke the words, the fairy would become real. Like God speaking the world into existence, my fantasy would be born into the real world. And I didn't want to deal with the reality of fairies. Wouldn't their existence force me to reconsider everything I held to be true? But then, did I really think that if I kept silent, the fairy would no longer exist?

"Ken, the light in the Tower of Refuge isn't all I've seen. I didn't want to tell you before…I didn't know *how* to tell you." Ken sat patiently, not wanting to interrupt me. "I saw something in Ballaglass Glen. Something strange."

"Really? I didn't see anything out of the ordinary."

"You had walked ahead. I wasn't sure what it was that I saw. At first, I thought it was an insect. But then…"

"What do you think it was?"

"I think it was a"—the word stuck in my throat—"a fairy." I watched as he bridled his reaction. I'm sure anyone other than Ken would have laughed at what was surely a joke, but instead he furrowed his brow and looked worryingly at me.

"What makes you think that?"

"It was a tiny, flying humanoid. What else would you call it?" I asked, genuinely curious.

"I guess fairy is as good a term as 'flying humanoid.'"

I could see he was struggling to contain his excitement as he realized that I was serious.

"Have you ever seen one?"

"No."

I couldn't tell if he was embarrassed that he had to answer in the negative or if he was embarrassed for me because I had confessed something so odd.

"You're the first person I've ever known to say she had seen one."

"Not even your mom?"

He shook his head.

"Great," I moaned. *Why couldn't it have chosen someone else to fly up to and start a conversation?*

"Could it talk? Did it say anything?"

"No," I lied without hesitation. It was one thing to admit seeing her. It was another to divulge what she said.

"This is amazing! Why didn't you tell me before now?"

"I think I was trying to pretend it didn't happen."

"Fairies don't exactly go along with your theories, huh?" He had the same pitying expression a mother would have when her child broke his toy after she told him not to throw it over the banister.

"No. No, they don't," I said. "My life in general has been pretty well upended since I went to Ballaglass Glen."

"I'm sorry."

"You told me not to go. You were right. You don't have anything to be sorry for."

"I'm sorry for everything that happened. I'm sorry you came, and I'm sorry you left."

The tram arrived at its final destination at about eight o'clock. Heavy rain clouds obscured the stars and moon, and darkness covered Douglas like a wet blanket. The dark skies would have been a comforting cover as we took up our illegal mission, were it not for the rising winds blustering angrily off the sea. The weather reminded me of my first night in Douglas when I went to save the man on the cliff. Ken and I walked along the boardwalk, looking out at the rising waves that we were about to brave. The weather was making this expedition into the bay all the more foreboding.

"It's too early to start out," Ken said, glancing at his watch. "Let's get something to eat."

Food was the last thing on my mind. The way my stomach was twisting, I couldn't see how there was any room for food. Ken took some bags of crisps, as I had learned to call chips, out of his backpack, and we made our way to a glassed-in shelter on the boardwalk. Some boys in a park behind us were making an embarrassing attempt at parkour, and right as we walked up, one of them rammed full speed into a picnic table, taking the brunt of the impact with his chest. I couldn't help but giggle; fortunately, the glass prevented them from hearing me.

Ken and I watched them in silence for an hour or more, slowly munching our crisps. The boys were a welcome diversion. I guessed they too were taking advantage of the darkness to do things unseen. Unlike us, they weren't stupid enough to do it in a storm, though. The boys ran off as thunder started to sound, like Cinderella taking her cue from the clock striking twelve.

After another fifteen minutes, the store windows were dark, and no one was to be seen.

"All right. Let's go," Ken said, helping me to my feet. He grabbed the surfboard, and we crossed the empty road to the beach side. We descended the first set of stairs we came to from the sidewalk onto the sand below.

"On the plus side," Ken said, seeming to read my mind as he shifted the weight of the surfboard under his arm, "police aren't going to be patrolling tonight."

"Right. They'd have to be crazy to be out in this weather." We looked at each other and let out a nervous laugh. A bolt of lightning crackled through the sky to connect with the southeastern part of the island with a deafening crash. There was no more laughing, nervous or not, after that. We reached the point closest to the Tower of Refuge, and Ken stopped.

"You can go behind that set of stairs and change into your wetsuit." Ken was ever the gentleman. A row of stone stairways placed along the beach led from the promenade to the shore, and created little walls. He pulled a black, rubbery suit out of his backpack and handed it to me. "I'll change on this side."

I nervously looked around. While the skies were sizzling with electricity, I didn't want to be out of Ken's reach, even for a moment.

"Don't worry," he said. "I know it might look a little scary, but the weather is proving to be our strongest ally. Like we said, no one will be out on a night like tonight."

On the far side of the wall, I stripped down to my swim-suit and tugged the wetsuit on overtop.

"What do we do with our bags?" I asked as I shoved my clothes into my backpack, not bothering to fold them. A part of me was assuming I'd be wearing the wetsuit for the rest of my life, which wouldn't last that much longer.

"I guess leaving them here is as good a place as any," he said from the other side. "Are you ready?"

"Yes," I replied, walking over to his side of the steps. I sank as I saw his swimmer's physique poured into the wetsuit. I knew I had more important things to think about, but I still felt decidedly inadequate next to him.

"It's going to be a bit of a painful walk, but we better leave our shoes here as well." I hadn't thought of our shoes being washed out in the surf. I pried the heels loose with the opposite toes and kicked them off.

"All right. Let's go."

He hefted the surfboard under his arm, and we began to tread carefully out onto the rocks and broken-shell-studded sand toward the water. I breathed a sigh of relief when we reached the spongy, black seaweed that carpeted the outermost part of the beach. The cold, damp seaweed seemed to lick the wounds the jagged shells had made. We finally reached the edge of the water, and he placed the surfboard on the surface in front of us.

"I'm sorry," I said.

"Why?" He took my hand.

"Because I can't swim, and you're going to risk your life because I'm such a…failure." I fought back tears.

"Genny, you're not a failure at anything. Everybody needs help sometimes. You're just too stubborn to admit it. About swimming. About literature. Your life will get a lot easier when you can realize your own weaknesses and allow others' strengths to pull you through. Speaking of pull, are you ready?"

I looked out at the Tower of Refuge, silhouetted against the dark sky. A surge of water swallowed my feet and dejectedly rolled back out.

"Yes, I'm ready." We waded out into the icy water until we were waist deep. Ken held the surfboard steady while I hoisted myself up on it.

"OK," he said, patting me on the back. "Hang on and enjoy the ride." Just as he finished speaking, another violent streak of lightning hit nearby, shaking the island. I smiled nervously back at Ken and laid my head down on the cold board, closing my eyes as tightly as I could.

I could feel the difference between when Ken was still walking through the water and when he was forced to swim. As he swam, the board underneath me would surge forward and pause, surge forward and pause…I gripped the sides of the board, the icy water biting at my fingertips.

I couldn't tell how long we had been out in the water, but it was already feeling like forever. The waves grew angrier the farther out we went, perhaps at our boldness for encroaching where no one had dared trespass for a very long time. Rain pelted down on us, but the wetsuit provided some insulation from the cold. When a much larger wave crashed down, I forgot my body as my head was doused with frigid seawater. I panicked and released my hold, gasping for air. My numb fingers could no longer feel the board underneath me, and I flailed, searching in vain to grab onto something.

"Genny!" I heard Ken call through the pounding rain. I tried to answer, but only drew in a breath full of salt water. Coughing, I opened my eyes to nothingness, waves occasionally dipping to allow a view of darkness behind a sheet of relentless rain. I was forced under again and assumed that was the last thing I would see. I flailed my arms in vain, fighting the water pulling me in so many directions that I couldn't tell which way was up.

So much for prophecies, I thought grimly, giving in to the numbing coldness of the water. It was then that I might have felt an arm around my waist, hoisting me up above the surface of the water. It was hard to tell, since I couldn't really feel anything at that point. I was pretty sure I was horizontal, lying across what I could only imagine was the surfboard.

I opened my eyes and saw everything illuminated clearly in a bright-blue light. We were close enough that Ken was walking waist deep in the water, still pulling the board on which I lay. His back was bowed in fatigue. I couldn't keep my eyes open. Once the board had scraped up on the sand far enough to ensure it couldn't be washed back out into the bay, I heard a heavy thud. I tried to remember what it was that Ken had brought and just dropped onto the wet sand.

I lay coughing and gasping for breath on the tiny stretch of sand. The harsh wind swept off the sea and lashed at my wet skin like a cat-o'-nine-tails. Every breath stung as the cold air filled my salt-scoured lungs. Finally, I opened my burning eyes and through the tangles of my hair saw Ken collapsed beside me. *He* was the thud I had heard. There was no doubt in my mind he had saved my life.

"Well," he panted, "I hope this is worth it, because I don't see how we're getting back." I looked back and realized he was right. The distant lights of Douglas seemed impossibly far away. Then my view fell to the cold sand beneath me, which glowed aqua blue. I lifted my head to look at the castle and the blue light emanating from its small, glassless windows. Ken and I lay motionless, mesmerized by the strangeness of the scene. I had half expected the light to be accompanied by a mechanical hum, but the only sounds we heard were the waves washing up.

We looked at each other and wordlessly pulled ourselves up to our feet. Adrenaline pumped through my body, overriding the debilitating fatigue that I should have been experiencing. The sand crunched under our feet as we walked toward the weather-beaten wooden door to the castle. It was a strange feeling, being only steps away from solving a mystery that had been so central to our relationship. All of our planning and dreaming and talking about the Tower of Refuge would be over once we opened the door. Ken hesitated with his hand on the handle.

"Are you sure you shouldn't wait here?" he asked.

"What?"

"I was just thinking, it may be safer if you waited here." He wouldn't look me in the eyes. He seemed transfixed on some point behind me in the middle distance.

"I didn't come all this way to wait outside!" I couldn't disguise the anger in my voice.

"I'm not saying you shouldn't come in at all. Just maybe let me check it out first."

"Unbelievable."

He released the door handle and hesitatingly took my hand, finally daring to look at me. "I…I don't think I could take it if anything happened to you. It's bad enough that

I feel like we're closing this chapter of our…friendship, but what if you got hurt somehow? I couldn't live if…" He gently brushed away the wet hair that was still clinging to my face and cradled my chin in his hand.

"What? I cannot figure you out, Ken!"

His hand dropped away from me.

"I have tried so hard to interpret your actions and figure out what 'we' are. Is this only a friendship to you? Because you say one thing and act like another. What exactly am I to you, Ken?" Despite being soaked, I could feel the fire burning behind my eyes. "I don't know what I am to you."

"Everything," he said simply. "You're everything to me, Genny."

"Then who is 'Genny' to you? Buddy? Girlfriend? Chosen One?" I couldn't control my voice, which was growing louder by the word until finally I was yelling.

"You! The girl standing in front of me! The beautiful, intelligent, exasperating girl in front of me!" he said, his voice growing louder to match my volume.

Unable to respond, I turned from him and looked out at the stretch of water between us and the lights of Douglas.

"I'm sorry," he said. "I hoped you felt the same way about me."

My mind was spinning. One surreal experience on top of another was beginning to make me doubt the reality of anything that was happening to me anymore. I looked back into his worried, intense eyes.

"We've needed to talk about things, Ken." A crack of thunder punctuated my thought. "But I sure didn't think we were going to discuss this here."

"We have to discuss this here and now," he said urgently, taking my hands in his. "I was taught all my life what my duty was, and that, Genny, was to take care of Imogen Hazard. Can you imagine how much I was dreading Imogen Hazard coming to the island? Knowing I was somehow destined to help this legend I'd never met carry out the all-important task of helping to save the island?"

I couldn't tell if it was the rain or if his eyes had become suddenly moist.

"But there you were that day," he continued softly, "standing at your locker, and everything changed. I didn't even remember what my duty was anymore. I fell for you the moment I saw you, and all I wanted was to be with you. That was why I started hiding things from you. I was keeping everything about the Keepers away from you because I saw how frightened you were. Because I selfishly didn't want to lose you."

He gently let go of my hands, and I felt colder than I'd ever felt in my life. Even the inches between us were too far for me to be away from him.

"And now that you know I'm one of them, I understand that you can't feel the same way about me. But nothing can change how I feel for you. I can't help but love you, Genny."

A sob burst out of me, and he wrapped me up in his arms. I knew one thing for sure. There was no longer a "me," only a "we." And we were real. My life had irrevocably intertwined with Ken's, and nothing on the other side of the door was going to change that.

"I love you, Ken. I love you," I cried. "You can't lose me. I won't let you."

He kissed my cheek quickly and I felt my face flush. "I'm yours forever, Genny. We were meant to be together because of *us*. Not because of what you are or what I have to do. Not because of the things happening around us. Never doubt that again. Just promise me that you won't let anything happen to you."

"Just as long as you promise me the same."

"Deal."

This time I took the door handle and pulled with all my weight while he stood close behind me. The harsh conditions had caused the wooden door to swell against the stone, making it creep open only centimeters at a time. The blue light wasn't as blinding as I expected. There was a strange quality to it. It wasn't flat like man-made light. It had an organic quality and seemed to wrap around the opening between the door and the wall and illuminate my hand from the inside.

I stepped inside the room and warmed instantly. The drastic temperature change made me disoriented, and I stared at the incandescent blue stones in the floor to steady myself. I was sure I was hallucinating, but it looked like there were tiny scribbles of writing covering the stones.

"You have no idea how long I've been waiting for you."

The voice I heard was not Ken's. I looked up and tried to focus on the source of the voice as the floor seemed to shift beneath me. Ken took hold of my shoulders from behind to steady me. We were in a large, stone room, and in the center, sitting cross-legged on a table, was a boy of about thirteen. Incredibly, it was he who lit up the room like a blue sun in a dark little universe. His radiant blue skin blazed a fluidic glow even through his simple clothes. His head was smooth like a polished stone. Despite the fact we had evidently just barged into his home, he looked completely nonplussed.

"I'm sorry?" I muttered, stepping backward into Ken.

The boy cocked his head to one side and smiled a little.

"We haven't had guests in a very, very long time," he said quietly.

"Oh…it's a bit off the beaten path, isn't it?" I said and instantly regretted it.

He giggled nonetheless. "My name is Mannix."

"I'm Genny, and this is Ken." I gestured backward.

"Kendreague," Ken corrected. "Hello."

Something beyond the boy's blue skin demanded respect. Every word he had spoken, the look on his face, even his name, carried with them an understood gravitas. He was so careful and graceful in his subtle movements that I wasn't sure he was a human.

"You've risked your lives coming here tonight. Why?"

"We came for your help," I answered.

"I don't appear to be in a situation where I can help anyone out here. Wouldn't you agree?"

"Not from what I've heard," I said, "and I might just be the whole reason you're here."

"Are you planning to destroy my island?" he asked, cocking his head.

"No, but my father might be."

"There are legends about who you are," Ken interjected. "What you are. We thought you could do something to stop him."

Mannix straightened his head and looked at Ken for some time.

"And what if the legends hadn't been true, Genny?" Mannix asked, looking at me rather than Ken, who shifted uncomfortably behind me. Neither of us answered. "What if you had gotten here and discovered nothing more than an empty room?"

"If the legends hadn't been true, then I would have put my hopes in a fairy tale, and we'd all be lost."

"Well, it seems some fairy tales are true. The impossible has become possible tonight, hasn't it, Genny?" he said, his eyes seeing right through to the hidden places of my heart. I had to look away.

For the first time, I took in the room itself. There were stacks upon stacks of books. Hundreds. They appeared to be arranged in piles according to subject matter. Science. Mathematics. Literature. Sheet music. As I had thought before, writing covered much of the floor and also the walls.

"I've had a lot of time on my hands," Mannix said, noticing where my eyes were drawn. He nimbly slid off the table and walked slowly toward us, the entire room shifting as its light source moved. As shadows elongated or disappeared, different parts of the room became engulfed in darkness or illuminated. It was then that I saw we were not alone.

Again, he noticed my shocked gaze.

"That's my keeper," he said, gesturing toward a woman standing silent as a mannequin in the furthermost, darkened part of the room. *Is it a coincidence that the group to which Ken and his family belong is also called the Keepers?* I wondered.

"I'm taking Genny to the cellar," he told the woman. She said nothing, and I couldn't make out her expression. He led me to the back of the room, where some narrow stone stairs led downward. Ken touched my arm and casually passed in front of me. I knew he wanted to encounter whatever waited below first in order to protect me. I was baffled by Ken's reactions here. How could he possibly be afraid for my safety in the presence of the one whom he himself had described as a savior? *Sometimes,* I mused, *believing and seeing are very different things.*

As we slowed near the top of the stairs, I quickly shot a glance at the woman. She appeared to be in her twenties or thirties and was dressed in plain, homemade-looking clothes similar to Mannix's. Her long hair was twisted into a bun that revealed the edge of the red triskelion tattoo on her neck. As Mannix's glow illuminated the stairwell ahead, I noticed a teardrop fall down her cheek before she and the rest of the room were enveloped in darkness.

"We won't hurt him," I called out to her, afraid to stop moving and be left in darkness.

"*Cha noddym surral y pian,*" she answered hollowly. I could tell by her echo that she hadn't moved from where I had seen her.

"*Cair eab ceau neu-hastey ad,*" Mannix replied.

"*S'cummey. Ad nel fockle dy Ghaelg 'sy veal echey.*"

"*Agh t'eh,*" he said, as if he were reminding her of something.

We were halfway down the stairs when Ken stopped abruptly, holding me back behind him as though he were physically shielding me.

"Wait. What exactly is in the cellar?"

"An explanation," Mannix stated as he continued to walk lightly down the stairs. "Coming?" Although I couldn't see him past Ken, I heard Mannix stop when he didn't hear our comparatively clumsy footsteps behind him. "You didn't come this far to turn away now, did you?"

"What did she mean by 'I cannot bear the pain'?" Ken asked, panic seeping into his voice.

"It was a bit...ominous, wasn't it?" Mannix asked rhetorically. I still couldn't see him ahead of Ken. "My keeper and I are a bit at odds with each other sometimes. I consider her a pessimist. She sees herself as a pragmatic realist. It boils down to seeing a glass half full or half empty. You can reduce everything in life down to numbers and equations, but in the end, some things defy all the laws of reason. Reason would tell you *not* to follow the glowing, blue boy into the darkness. But, Genny, you said you wouldn't hurt me. I have faith you're not here to do that. Do you have that same faith in me?"

Ken turned to look at me, a little perturbed that he had been left out of the conversation despite physically placing himself between us.

"Yes," I said.

"Kendreague, if you would be so kind, please remain behind with my keeper. I think you would assuage some of her fears if you stayed behind."

"I'm not leaving Genny," he stated.

"You have my word she'll be fine. It needs to be this way, Ken."

"It's all right," I told Ken as I put my hand on his shoulder. "Really. I trust him. Don't you?"

He brushed his fingertips softly against my cheek. I could see the misgiving in his eyes, but we both somehow knew that Mannix was right; this was the way it needed to be.

"Of course I do," he said a little unconvincingly. "I'll be listening for you. Call out if you need me." We looked at each other for a moment longer, and his hand fell from my face. He walked up the stairs into the darkness.

"Come along," Mannix said and continued his descent. It wasn't until Ken left me alone in the darkness that I saw the all-too-familiar symbol glowing in front of me. The same symbol I had carved into the ground and scribbled on graph paper and etched into the bench at the swim meet was emblazoned at the base of Mannix's skull, illuminating my path ahead. Somehow, I was connected to this boy.

"Who did your tattoo?" I asked.

"It's a birthmark," he responded, not turning back. "Is it familiar to you?"

"No," I answered too quickly.

"It's a Celtic knot. It means balance. Do you have balance in your life?"

What does balance have to do with me? I wondered. What was special about the times when I had unconsciously drawn the knot? Under the tree, at the Indian restaurant, at the swim meet. I had been reading or remembering literature each time the Celtic knot had bubbled out of me like a chemical reaction. *Could that be the balance? Allowing myself to use the left side of my brain? To release my dogged grip on the objective and embrace the subjective?* I thought about the wholeness I'd felt each of those times, for only a moment, before I would pull myself back into the comfort of logic and reason. I realized I wanted that feeling again. That I needed it.

On the back of Mannix's head, the symbol for balance illuminated the way in front of me.

"I'm getting there," I finally replied.

"Good. Life's a journey. Not a destination."

As we neared the bottom, I noticed Mannix's blue light reflecting off the surface of a pool at the foot of the stairs. My foot splashed into about four inches of water. With my next step, the water was almost up to my knees. On a normal day, I would have begun to panic at that water level, but especially after our recent harrowing journey to the tower, my bronchioles started to spasm.

"I…can't…" I stammered.

"It's time to see why I'm here," he said, three feet in front of me and chest deep in water. "Walk over to me."

I slowly waded to his side, my breath becoming quicker and shallower as the water crept higher up my body. I tried to trust him, but my heart was pounding. I couldn't fathom a reason to be trudging deeper and deeper through a water-logged cellar.

Mannix closed his eyes and held his hands out in front of him as if he was about to push something forward. His blue aura became brighter and the edges of its radius more defined as the pool began swirling viciously around us, and the water level slowly began to drop. Outside our bubble, the water rose to the ceiling, and the bubble became completely submerged.

"Let's go for a walk." He made his way down the sloped floor that I couldn't see just moments before. The seaweed squished around my feet as we continued downward, and as the edge of the bubble that surrounded us reached a wall, I noticed an archway that had previously been underwater. As we passed through the arch, I stopped to put my hand on the wall. The stones were completely dry, but the algae clinging to them glistened with seawater.

"Interesting, isn't it?" he noted. "This force field that I generate seems to be impermeable only to water. Organics inside the sphere retain their moisture and the moisture clinging to them, but inorganics become dry." He patted the wall. "I've had these powers all my life, but I'm still discovering little nuances to them all the time."

He led us down the steep incline onto the floor of Douglas Bay. The farther we descended, the more claustrophobic I became. The reality of the sheer amount of water that could crush down on top of us made my asthma near crippling.

"We're going to run out of oxygen," I gasped.

He looked hard at me, and his gaze traveled down to my chest. Almost imperceptibly, his fingers flickered toward me, and I instantly felt my chest relax. I took a deep breath, not quite believing what had just happened.

"What did you just do to me?"

"I just opened things up for you," he replied as though he were informing me of the weather. "You do have asthma, right?"

I didn't respond. I was too busy breathing.

"Sorry, but I didn't heal you. Just a temporary fix. And not to worry," he continued, gesturing to the bubble around us. "The oxygen won't run out. As far as I can tell, this shield is semipermeable. It allows oxygen in and carbon dioxide and other waste out. We could stay here forever. Not that we will," he added, with a laugh. "I've spent a good portion of my life out here. This is where I come to think."

I was in shock as I felt my lungs expanding and contracting more easily than I had ever felt in my life. I considered asking him about the powers he had, but that had to wait, as I couldn't believe my own eyes.

I stared out at the alien world around me. I was mesmerized by a scene that had never been viewed by human eyes, at least not in this way—unencumbered by a mask or an oxygen tank. Above us, the flashes of lightning caught the crests of waves rolling in from the Irish Sea. The lightning undulated above, and the moon, beginning to peek out from the clouds, appeared to spasm through the rippling water.

The glowing bubble that cocooned us illuminated the living waters outside. Seaweed swayed in the water like a wheat field on a breezy day, but it fell cold and limp once inside our sphere as we continued to walk. On the other side of the bubble, the current quickly swept the seaweed upright, as if nothing had interrupted its dance. Startled, a school of little fish forked around us on either side when they approached the all-but-invisible wall. In front of us was a long, low rock that made a perfect bench.

"Let's sit."

I couldn't sit. I was too awestruck. He sat cross-legged on the rock, not facing the sea that must have been tiresome to him, but facing me. I was about to ask the most obvious of questions, but I was distracted by a green glow out in the water. It was a seahorse, or so it seemed. It had wings—delicate, like a butterfly's—that fluttered in the water's currents.

"I've seen that before," I said, hypnotized. "It's just like the one I saw in Cerdwyn's shop. I thought it was ridiculous back then. I didn't know anything like it really existed."

"Some things take their shape from faith. They exist solely because people believe they do. Others, like that seahorse, exist whether you, Genny, know or believe they do."

"Which one are you?" I asked, looking back at him.

He giggled.

"I'm one of the more tangible creatures of this earth. It doesn't matter if you believe in me. I'll still be here."

"Are you a human?" I asked bluntly, as I finally sat down next to Mannix on the dry stone. This time he laughed until he shook, but the walls of the protective bubble didn't budge.

"Yes."

"Are you the one from the legends? The one who's supposed to save the world?"

"Yes," he said, looking down. "I suppose so. It just depends on whether or not the world is going to need saving. That's where you come into the equation." He flashed a look up at me with eyes that next to his brilliant-blue skin were coal black.

"What? How can I stop him?"

He paused. "Why did you come to the Isle of Man?"

"I didn't *want* to come here! I came here because of my dad."

"I know your father's purpose in coming here. But you have a purpose too. How do you feel about your father's... experiment?"

"How do you know about that? I'm not even supposed to know what my dad's doing." I looked into his black eyes. "What else do you know?"

"Enough. Your father made a deal with the Manx government to conduct a study into alternative energy. He informed them about the energy reading he had detected deep underground, but neglected to explain to them exactly what it is. Truthfully, even he doesn't know what he's dealing with, Genny. But I think you're aware of most of this."

I nodded.

"Two years ago, while still in America, he commissioned a small team to begin drilling," Mannix said.

"I thought the Keepers influenced the government. Why would they let him begin drilling if they could prevent it?"

"They did have a heavy say in our government at one time, but they have little pull with it now. A modern government has no need for antiquated throwbacks like the Keepers. I believe that was how they worded it. The government still maintains the law forbidding boats in Douglas Bay, as much to keep with quaint history for tourism's sake as to appease the Keepers, but that's about all it will do for us now. The Manx government is no different from any other. When it was propositioned for the project by your father's funders, it was offered more money than it could have ever imagined coming to the Isle of Man. Enough to complete any projects it wanted. It was impossible for officials to turn it down. And everything the Keepers warned them about was nothing more to them than fairy tales."

"Who are my dad's funders?"

"I don't know *everything*, Genny," he said, smiling through the sadness in his eyes.

"But you do know that all of our lives hang in the balance."

"As well as you do. It's no coincidence I'm here, waiting all my life with the ability to hold back water while a man recklessly tampers with a natural mystery only miles away." He leaned toward me, and I saw fear in his previously placid eyes. "I believe I exist to save the people of this island from what your father is about to do. *That's* my purpose. But it's *your* purpose to try to stop him before he causes this disaster. It is your destiny."

"I told you, he won't listen to me. I thought you could do something to stop him. Use your magic. At least talk to him yourself. He's a lot more likely to believe someone with glowing blue skin than he is me."

"Have you ever read in the Bible about Lazarus and the rich man?" he posed.

I shook my head.

"Both men died," he said, folding his hands in his lap and looking out beyond our bubble and into the seething life of the ocean. "Lazarus went to heaven; the rich, man to hell. The rich man asked Abraham to send Lazarus to his five brothers, to warn them of the torment that awaited them if they did not repent. 'They have Moses and the prophets,' Abraham replied. 'Let them hear them.' The rich man countered, 'Nay, father Abraham, but if one went unto them from the dead, they will repent.' And Abraham said to him, 'If they hear not Moses and the prophets, neither will they be persuaded, though one rose from the dead.'

"You see, Genny? Your father will listen to you, and he'll either believe you, or he won't. You could bring the boy with glowing blue skin, or even raise the dead and bring them along too, but it won't make a difference in whether or not he believes and in what he chooses to do. Just like the rich man's brothers, he will have all the information he needs from you, if you can be bold enough to talk to him."

I buried my head in my hands. "I don't know why I even came here. I could have saved Ken and myself a trip. Not to mention that we could have just died out there in the bay."

"There was a zero percent chance you could have died."

I was about to ask how he could possibly know that, but he went on. "And you, Genny, came here for more than help. You came in the name of science. You came to prove that the fairy tale was *not* true. But I am. I'm real, and some legends and myths and fairy tales are very much true. And this fact can give you the strength to do what you need to do.

"The fact is," he continued, "you would not have confronted your father without seeing me first. If you hadn't come here, you'd be sitting in your room right now, playing your violin, obsessing about how your dad won't listen to you, wondering in all your brilliance, but still not knowing, how you and Ken will work out. Consider me your reality check. You know now that I exist, which means your worst fears about your father are about to come true."

"But doesn't the very fact that you're here mean you know I'm going to fail?"

"The future is always in flux. If you don't do your part to make the present right, then it is guaranteed that we truly have no hope for the future."

I felt like my brain was about to explode. I hadn't told Ken, but I thought "my part" was to risk my life coming to see Mannix. Maybe Mannix was right, and this trip was more than a detour, but that only meant the hardest part wasn't over; I had to convince my dad to stop what he had worked for years to accomplish, his reunion with the woman I took from him.

"Your father is drilling on the far side of Snaefell Summit. He's not far from making contact with the...what do you call it? Exotic matter? You need to hurry, Genny. You need to stop him."

"All right. I'll go. I hope I can accomplish what you think I can. And I hope that afterward, you can go and live a life outside of the Tower of Refuge and find another destiny for yourself."

"I haven't been stuck here forever, but thank you. It would be nice to exist in some kind of normality." He nimbly hopped up from his seat, and our bubble of protection moved along with us as we walked back to the tower's underwater entrance.

"I'll wait down here, and you can get Ken, if you'd like. I can walk you both back to the shore, and you can avoid the rest of the storm."

I breathed a sigh of relief. I couldn't believe I was happier to be underwater than on top of it, but it was much safer underneath, sheltered from the raging winds and tearing rain. I went up the stairs, still dimly lit by Mannix's aura below. As I rounded the corner into the main room, I could see the silhouettes of Ken and the woman by the lightning flashes in the window.

"Mannix is going to walk us back to the shore," I said, instantly realizing how ridiculous I must have sounded. "I'll explain on the way downstairs," I added. To my surprise, Ken hugged the woman before walking over to me.

Once we were out of earshot, I whispered, "What was *that* all about?"

"We share a bond. All Keepers do," he added.

We walked along in silence for most of the way back. It seemed to me that Ken was more interested in Mannix than he was in the experience of walking along the bed of Douglas Bay in a force field. Instead of being riveted to the underwater world outside the bubble like I was, I would catch Ken staring at the boy. I supposed I shouldn't have expected otherwise. I couldn't imagine coming face to face with the object of my faith, having it confirmed before my very eyes.

Mannix stopped finally, and with a gentle flex of his fingers, the bubble extended out of the water onto the dry land.

"This is where we must part ways," he said.

Even though I had never met him before, I felt strangely emotional about leaving him. I wanted to see him again, and I wasn't sure if I ever would.

"Thank you," I said. I refused to say good-bye. It sounded much too final.

"No problem. It's nice to get out." He laughed, nodding to the endless water surrounding us.

"No, thank you for everything. Everything you've said to me…everything you might do for us all."

He didn't respond. How could he? There was no way to respond to a thank you for sacrificing any and all hope of a normal life.

Ken reached out to shake hands with Mannix. Despite the wide smile spreading across his face, tears streamed down Mannix's cheeks as he grasped Ken's hands.

"It's been an honor to meet you," Ken said.

"The honor is mine." They parted, and Ken took my hand. We tentatively walked to the wall of the bubble and looked back one last time at Mannix. He didn't look like a savior or hero to me. He looked like a teenager. Aside from the bald head and blue skin, it might as well have been Ken or me standing there. It didn't seem fair that this boy had lived his young life carrying a burden of this weight.

I closed my eyes and braced myself as I walked through the force field. I could briefly hear a low hum as I passed through it, and on the other side, the crashing waves were deafening. I hadn't realized how quiet it was in the bubble. The wind sounded like a freight train to my desensitized ears.

"My dad's on the far side of Snaefell," I yelled over the wind without stopping to discuss what we had seen. There would be plenty of time for that later.

"Right. The first tram back to Ramsey will be in about half an hour," he said, glancing at his swimmer's watch. We reached the bags we had abandoned at the wall of the beach and wordlessly went to our separate sides of the stairs. At least the rain had stopped, so my bare skin wouldn't be pelted as I changed back into my clothes.

Being alone for a moment, my focus melted, and my mind ping-ponged between all the surreal things that fought to be the most unbelievable: nearly drowning; a blue boy; walking underwater; and an impending confrontation with my father, who suddenly resembled a comic-book super villain. By the time I was dressed and had slung my bag onto my shoulder, I resolved not to think of anything but the task at hand: stopping my father.

The skies were beginning to lighten as we walked back to the tram station. It was as if the dawn had halted the storm, and the wind, embarrassed in the spotlight to have caused such a fuss, petered quickly out to nothing. The stillness was startling after experiencing the full wrath of nature. Ken held my hand tightly, and I wondered if he was bracing for the storm to return. Maybe he was preparing for a storm of a different kind.

The Day of Change

The tram driver milled around the outside of the tram. He clearly wasn't expecting anyone on the first tram out. We flashed our return-trip ticket stub at him as we stepped up into the tram. The driver looked dubious. Two teenagers spending the night in Douglas and returning on the first tram back *had* to have been up to no good, he surely thought, but said nothing. We sat down without a word; it was too quiet to talk. The driver walked to the door of our carriage to listen nonchalantly, and once he realized he would hear nothing of our sordid night in Douglas, he walked back to the front of the tram. At precisely five o'clock, the tram jerked forward, and we were on our way.

"How do we get to Snaefell?" I asked.

"We'll get off in Laxey. The tram from there will be the quickest way to Snaefell. Once we get to the peak, I guess we'll just have to hike around until we find his laboratory."

"Wait, I thought you said the tram from Laxey to Snaefell wasn't in operation because of line work."

"Well, that's not entirely true. It isn't in operation, but it's not because of line work. The Manx government quietly shut it down. Whoever's funding your dad's research is making sure the island is well compensated. In return, the government is ensuring complete security by cutting off all access to Snaefell, by tram or road."

"They don't even realize they've been rolling out a red carpet for the man who could destroy them all," I mused aloud. "After being decommissioned for so long, won't it be kind of obvious that a tram is going up the mountain? Besides, who's going to drive it? Don't tell me you are." I was beginning to wonder if there was anything Ken couldn't do.

"No." He chuckled. "I can't drive a tram." He suddenly grew solemn, and was lost in thought for a moment. "You don't need to worry about anything. I'll make sure you get there. You need to take care of the rest."

It didn't take me long to drift off to sleep. Crazy dreams played in my head about fairies and seahorses and a glowing, blue boy. When I awoke as the tram halted in Laxey, I was shocked that forty-five minutes had passed so quickly. I felt hopelessly groggy gathering up my backpack until the cold air slapped my face as I stepped off the tram. The tram driver watched us curiously before starting the tram back up to roll off to the right, toward the Laxey Wheel and eventually to its destination of Ramsey.

Ken led me over a second set of tracks that in the distance curved to the left. Beside it stood a covered shed, the size of a tramcar. The long night was taking its toll on me, and my feet dragged as we walked through the still-sleeping Laxey high street.

Ken pulled me into a narrow, cobblestoned alleyway that might have been a little creepy were it not for the potted flowers that hung over most of the doorways. Of course, he stopped at the worn door without flowers at the end of the alleyway and knocked. I could hear movement within, and when the door opened, a skinny, black cat shot out and ran down the alleyway into the early morning sunlight of the high street.

"Who's there?" a rough voice asked from within.

"Kendreague Creer. I have Imogen Hazard with me."

After a pause, the door opened. We walked into what looked like an old lady's tattered living room. Doilies littered the little tables that were scattered haphazardly around the room, almost as if they existed solely to carry the lacework. The black cat shot back through the door and pounced onto the worn, floral-print sofa just as the door clicked shut. We were left with the weak light that glowed from a little lamp with a stained, fringed lampshade.

"Why is she here?" a deep voice asked from the shadowed area at the front door. The voice had a heavy Manx accent. A shadowed figure moved into the dim light. I froze as the tattooed man from the Douglas tram station stepped into view and sat down next to the cat. He stroked his pet, which purred like a motor and curled up next to him.

I glanced over at the heavy wooden door and wondered if I could heave it open and escape before I was caught. But then I remembered Ken was there, and he didn't appear to be worried in the least. The man turned a wooden chair, which was also placed randomly, to face the sofa and motioned for me to take a seat. He relaxed on the sofa, and I hesitantly sat and faced the man who had struck fear in me ever since I arrived on the Isle of Man.

"We need you to take us to Snaefell Summit," Ken stated, pulling a chair aside mine and sitting.

"I can't say I'm surprised," he said, running his fingers along the textured surface of a doily on the table. "Your mum told me awhile back the time may be near. I'm prepared to risk my life to do what needs to be done." He turned his blue eyes to me. "What are you prepared to do?"

I swallowed and thought about the question. I'd thought not too long before that risking my life out on Douglas Bay would be enough, but now I knew the answer. I looked into the face of the man who had haunted me.

"Whatever needs to be done."

"Good," the man said, slapping his legs as he left his cat on the sofa and crossed the room. He came back with a familiar black leather bag. I shrank in my chair as he set the bag on a table and unzipped a large outside pocket. I had spent a lot of time imagining the horrible instruments of torture that lay inside. Instead, he pulled out a massive ring of keys. I straightened up and wondered if either of them had noticed my reaction.

"When do we go?" he asked, grasping the keys tightly in his calloused hands.

"As soon as possible, John. We have reason to believe the event may be close at hand," Ken said.

Emotion welled up in John's eyes, and he shut them tightly to prevent tears from rolling down his cheeks. It was a paradox to see a man who looked that menacing with tears fringing his eyelashes. He inhaled and hardened himself into the man I remembered.

Opening his piercing blue eyes, he said, "My bag's all I need. Ready to go?" John twirled the key ring round and round on his index finger. It was as if the keys comforted him somehow.

"Yeah," Ken said, standing, and I quickly followed.

John gave his cat one last stroke on the head and went to open the front door for us. I had forgotten how dark the interior of the house was until the harsh sunlight poured in. I squinted as we walked into the alleyway that had been dark when we arrived at the house. Once we were all out, John spun the key ring until he landed on the right key, and locked his door.

"Why do you have so many keys?" I asked him.

"Will you take care of Coal for me?" John asked Ken, looking straight ahead as we strode quickly forward. I didn't think John was ignoring my question. He seemed so lost in thought that I was sure he hadn't heard me.

"I may not need to, John," Ken said, looking up at him. After a pause, he added, "But if needs be, I will."

"I appreciate it," he replied.

We retraced our steps to the tram stop. John very gently placed his bag at the door of the shed, which housed the two trams for Snaefell that had lain dormant for so many months. From behind the overgrown grass that hedged the shed, John pulled out a crowbar. Normally, I would have panicked at the thought of aiding a breaking and entering, but my fear for the fate of the Isle of Man outweighed my fear of breaking the law, so I only looked around to ensure that no one would stop us from our mission. It didn't take much for John to break in. His arms were solid, and one quick push cracked the wood holding the lock.

"They took my shed key," he explained, "but they forgot to take my ignition key."

I nodded.

Inside, the early morning sunlight streamed through little spaces between the old wooden roof boards and caught the spider webs that decorated the interior. I was so busy dodging webs that I stumbled over the track that ran to the end of the shed. As Ken steadied me, John once again laid his bag on the ground, and pulled his keys out of his pocket.

There appeared to be at least fifty keys on the ring, but he unlocked the driver door with the first key he settled on. He then went to the back of the single-car tram and opened the rear passenger door for us. I ran my hand down the side of the wooden car as I walked, and left a moat in the dust on the side. "Snaefell Mountain Railway" was painted along the bottom of the tram.

"Shouldn't we ride up front with you?" Ken asked.

John chuckled to himself.

"Old habits die hard. Here I am breaking into a tram shed and stealing a tram, and I was worried about breaking a rule prohibiting passengers from entering the driver's section. Be my guest, if you'd like. I'd actually enjoy the company today."

He held the driver door open for us. Ken scooted to the end, and John lumbered in after me and closed his door, sandwiching me between the two of them. It was difficult for me to get over the fear I had harbored for John. He looked exactly as I had remembered him from Douglas and all the subsequent nightmares. He leaned forward to start the engine, and the red tattoo on his neck flashed at me like a warning sign.

Despite what I had recently learned about the Keepers, I couldn't shake the "fight or flight" reflex I had every time

I saw the tattoo. I tried to move closer to Ken, but there was nowhere to go. I didn't understand why we couldn't have ridden in the back. The solitude would have given us a few moments to collect our thoughts before…I didn't even want to think about what came next.

The tram slid forward noisily on the track and pushed the splintered wooden doors of the shed open. They creaked shut behind us as the tram trundled forward. I still didn't see anyone about in town, so maybe our mission would be covert.

"As you can see, the key with the black bow is the ignition of the tram," John began out of nowhere. I now noticed he had colored the bows of the keys with markers to make every key a different shade. "The entry doors key has a yellow bow."

I found myself wondering if he was going to go through every key on that blasted key ring. *How can I possibly concentrate with him blathering on about keys?* I wondered. The lack of sleep had left my nerves fraught, and my patience, which had never been one of my virtues, was waning. *At least*, I thought, *his rambling is curing me of my fear of him.*

"I've never used the red key before. It opens the vault underneath the Manx History Museum where all the prophecies on the original manuscripts are kept."

"You've never seen the prophecies?" I asked.

"Only the leader of the Keepers has access to the prophecies," he said, never taking his eyes off the tracks that lay ahead. "My mum was the leader for thirty years. I always went to the vault with her when I was growing up, and even as a man. But I knew my place. I waited outside. Never dared to ask if I could go in with her. Those words weren't for these eyes." His eyes became moist. "I haven't been back since she passed on. That's when the leadership was passed to Cerdwyn. Couldn't have gone to anyone more worthy."

"Your mother was an amazing woman," Ken told him. "A woman of great faith."

"That she was. How much time I spent in her later years, listening to her quote portions of the prophecies, all the while she was knitting those little doilies." John laughed in spite of himself. "I kept telling her, 'I think you've made enough, Mum. You can't put a bloody cup of tea down anywhere in the house without hitting a doily. How many doilies does a house need?' And she'd say, 'You're *supposed* to put your teacup on a doily! Besides, a house doesn't need *any* doilies, but a home can't have enough.' I haven't been able to make myself get rid of a doily since."

John's eyes flitted briefly over to Ken. "It seems both our mums were women of great faith. And they carried many of the same burdens. No way to live a life, is't?"

"No, but it's the only life any of us have known," Ken said quietly.

The tram climbed higher. Looking out Ken's window, the Laxey Wheel was looking more like a toy miniature now. Seeing the big red wheel in the distance below, nestled in the lush greenery with heather surrounding the track, I felt a little like a child looking down at a model I had just built. It was too pretty and perfect to be real. The scene made my worries feel a little further away. Maybe fear shrinks in the face of beauty.

"The Laxey Wheel was built back in mining days," John announced, rather like a tour guide. "Her name is Lady Isabella. She was built back in 1854 to pump water from the mine shafts. She's the largest working waterwheel in the world," he added proudly.

"She's lovely," I said, stretching in front of Ken to catch a final glimpse of the wheel before it slipped out of view in Ken's window. Ahead, the trees became sparse on the stripped landscape. Mining had left its scar on the island.

Ken gently put his hand on my back while I still leaned over his lap to look out the window.

"The navy-blue key unlocks the front door of my house," John started again. His voice sounded strange. Was he trembling? "That's an important one, because you'll need that to get Coal."

I was trying to straighten back up to see if John was all right, but I never got a chance. The sound is what I remember next. It was like the crash of a restaurant full of waiters all dropping their trays of drinks at the same time. The glass shards blew in from the front window, spraying our faces. John pushed me farther down, forcing my head to fall into Ken's lap. Ken instinctively bent over me, covering my head with his chest. The side of my face stung like it had been rubbed with sandpaper.

It was dark underneath Ken's chest, but I could just see John in the space between Ken's left shoulder and his head with my left eye. John was clutching his chest with his left hand, his blood-speckled right hand still on the controls of the tram. Another bout of shots ripped through the tram, and Ken huddled tighter over me, closing my view.

"John!" Ken screamed.

"Not far to the top," John gurgled. "You'll make it."

"What's happening?" I cried. No one answered. "Who's doing this?"

"You'll make it just fine. White, Ken…White…"

The tram shifted as if it were rounding a wide corner, and the shots stopped. I imagined we were out of range of whoever was shooting at us, but for how long? *They'd already be mobilizing*, I thought. *How much time would we have to find my dad before they caught up to us?* And from what I had seen a few moments before, John would need immediate medical attention. The tram jerked to a stop.

"Genny, we've got to go," Ken said, reaching past me to take the key out of the ignition. He shoved the key ring into his pocket and pushed his door open. I hadn't realized I was shaking until Ken helped me sit upright. He jumped out the door and reached back for my hand.

"John?" I reached back and put my hand on his shoulder. His jacket was sticky. The black leather had camouflaged what I couldn't see. My palm was covered in blood.

"He's gone, Genny."

"How do you know?" I screamed. "We might be able to save him!"

"I just know. And he did too. We have to go now, Genny, or we'll be next." I took Ken's hand, and he pulled me out onto the ground. My wobbling ankles made the ground feel like it was shaking. I held tight to his arm as he pulled me along. I couldn't manage to hold my head up, so I watched my tears fall to the ground as we jogged ahead. Alien-looking slate formations jutted out of the sparse grass, and I felt like I might as well be running on the moon.

I looked up and saw we were heading toward a tiny white building that had the words "Welcome to Snaefell Summit—2,036 Feet High" painted along the top. The door was unlocked, and Ken quickly led me inside. It looked like it once was used as a little café, but that was years before. Dust covered an old, rudimentary cash register and the counter on which it rested.

We were only in that room for a second before Ken pulled me through to the kitchen area and into what must have been a pantry. He instantly knelt in the back corner and pried the linoleum off the floor. Underneath was a little door with a lock. Ken pulled the key ring out his pocket and quickly found the white key. He forced it into the old lock and pulled the door open. Inside was a modern-looking single switch. He looked at his watch.

"Eleven fifty-six," he read. "We made it." At that moment, his watch rang an alarm as it turned 11:57.

"Hold on," he said and flipped the switch. An instant later a deafening explosion outside made me fall to the ground. Bits of plaster rained down on us, and the few dusty jelly jars that remained on the shelves vibrated, threatening to shimmy off the edge. The shaking finally stopped, and the ground grew still. Ken turned and put his arms around me.

"It's safe now. No one can hurt you."

"What just happened?" I stammered.

"John's bag. It was full of explosives. We knew the shooter would go to the tram to look for you. And we knew when. That's why I had to—"

"Kill him?"

"It was either him or you, Genny, and he wouldn't have hesitated. Neither could I." Ken tried to steady his voice, but the fear-fed adrenaline made it impossible.

"Who was it?"

"I don't know. I only knew the time and the place of the attack." He paused, allowing the flood of information to penetrate and trickle into my mind.

"John knew he was going to die?" My voice shook uncontrollably.

"The future is always in flux, Genny. But yes, he knew it would very probably happen."

I tried to swallow my anger. Anger at Ken for letting a friend die. Anger at John for valuing his own life so little. *There had to be another way.*

"We've got to go," Ken said. "Can you move?" I nodded, and he gently pulled me up. We walked back through the kitchen and into the dining area, where the windows had shattered. The glass crunched under our feet as we walked.

Outside, black smoke, the color of burning oil and metal and bodies, billowed around the bend where we had left the tramcar. Even at that distance, I could feel the heat from the explosion on my face. We paused for only a moment, and we headed on toward the other side of the summit. The sky was warming to an azure blue, the same color as the sea. The sun was unseasonably warm. It would have been a beautiful day, holding the hand of the one I loved, were it not for what the day had held.

I wondered if there were days, special days, through which all the threads of the universe ran. In life, you live thousands of days of mediocrity and tediousness and boredom and nothingness, and then you hit the one when everything changes. I wondered if they were the same days for everyone universally. The days of change.

We walked for about an hour in a westerly direction, away from the sea and toward the interior of the island. We could have made much better time were we not so exhausted. My feet dragged along, occasionally catching on the random shards of shale that protruded from the ground like blades. Ken was always there to catch me. I couldn't understand why he was faring so much better; he hadn't had any more sleep than I had.

"Thank you," I said, interrupting the silence.

"What for?"

"For doing all of this."

"Genny," he said, stopping. "There's something you need to understand. There are two different things going on here. I started off doing this to save my home and my people. It's what I was raised to do. Born to do, in a way. What I never realized was the girl I was going to be helping was you." He brushed my cheek. "I never knew I was going to fall in love with you." He took both my hands in his. "I grew up hearing about Imogen who would 'come from afar' and help to save the island. I never imagined you. So brave. So beautiful. I love you, Genny, not the Imogen in the prophecies. I love *you*."

I looked into the eyes of the only person in the world who could see past my intellect, and see just me.

"And now, I think I'm fulfilling all of the things I've been called on to do, not out of duty, but just so that at the end of it all, I can be with you," he said.

I had tried in vain to cut off my feelings so long ago, the day my mother died. I had tried to make it so I couldn't feel the sadness anymore. The trouble is that when you cut off one emotion, you dismember them all. I hadn't felt anything positive since then either: contentment, joy, love…

"I tried so hard not to love you, Ken," I said finally, "but I couldn't help it." I smiled into his brown eyes. "I love you, Ken. I always will. You've stolen my heart."

"I promise you, when this is all over, I will never let you go, Genny. Ever."

He kissed me, and for a moment, the world seemed to stop spinning, and the fear that had held me for so long disappeared like fog when the morning sun hits. Ken was my sun. And I didn't care what was going to happen anymore, as long as I had him with me. We held each other tightly, and all I could think of was Ken and his lips pressed to mine. Logic didn't matter. That was the old Genny. Everything was going to be fine. No matter what.

The End

We started walking again, and I soon wondered if Ken had paused to talk because he knew what was about to come into view. Down below us, nestled in the dark valley, was a small lake with a cheap-looking metal building beside it, garishly marring the landscape. The building looked like it was made of aluminum, and I wondered how my dad had kept warm on the cold nights we'd had that autumn. Why I should care about him at that point, I didn't know, but I was overwhelmed with pity for him. I also realized why he had come home so rarely. This place was so secluded, it would take hours to get back to Ramsey. It was no wonder the locals were completely clueless to its existence.

"That lake looks strange," Ken commented. He was right. It had an odd luminescence to it. Not like it was lit from within, but more like the water was of a slightly denser makeup than usual and reflected light in an almost imperceptibly different way.

We began our slow descent into the valley. The surrounding peaks obscured the sunlight, and a chilling wind swirled around the cone-shaped space. It was difficult to gain a foothold on the steep slope. The constant shade made the spongy ground and the shards of shale slippery. Ken and I held on to each other for support, even though if one of us started to slide, the other would be pulled along and would tumble to the bottom too.

"What are you going to say to him?" Ken asked.

"I don't know yet. I guess I'll know what to say when I see him. That's what I'm counting on, anyway."

"You're smart, Genny. You'll know what to say."

I may be smart, but I've never been too brilliant at communicating with my dad, I thought.

We had finally reached the bottom of the valley. The peaks reached so high on all sides that I felt like we were in a giant bucket. It was a dark and hopeless place, and I fought to prevent that feeling from taking hold of me. Instead of going directly to the building, we were both wordlessly drawn to the lake. The water was as strange up close as I had observed at the top.

"Ken, do you have John's key ring?"

He quickly pulled it out of his pocket and handed it to me. I took one of the keys and knelt down, dipping a key into the lake, careful not to let the liquid touch my skin.

"That's not water, is it?" Ken asked.

"I think it is," I said, watching the strangely mutated water roll slowly down the key like an expectant blob of mercury. "It's just not…normal water. Maybe it has something to do with the exotic matter being so close. It looks like this valley goes below sea level. I bet its proximity to the energy is altering the makeup of the water. Weird stuff, huh?"

"Is that how'd you describe it scientifically?" Ken laughed. "You're loosening up."

"'Loosening up' happens once you're shot at," I replied, trying to be funny, but instead I instantly thought of John and wished I hadn't said it. I sounded flippant, even to myself. "Sorry," I muttered and stood up. I couldn't let emotions get to me now: embarrassment, sadness, fear… I knew now was the time to steel myself, like John had done. I began walking to the building, and Ken quickly followed.

"Look, I've been thinking," Ken started, taking my hand. "I know this sounds strange after I tried to talk you out of going into the Tower of Refuge, but I don't think I should go in there with you."

"I'd like you to be with me," I said after awhile.

"Genny, your dad's never even seen me before. It's going to be hard enough for him to see you walking in uninvited, but you walking in with some guy he's never seen might freak him out. I think you should go in alone, but I'll be waiting right outside…if you need me."

"I never knew I needed anyone until I met you. But you're right."

He kissed my cheek, and we walked together to the door. As we neared the building, I saw that the exterior was not as flimsy as I'd thought. It was reinforced steel.

"Oh no," Ken moaned. The lock on the door had an electronic number pad. Without hesitating, I pushed the numbers 1-0-0-3, and the lock released.

"You're incredible," he said, smiling, and kissed me again on the cheek. "Good luck."

I smiled and heaved the metal door open. I hesitantly stepped inside and waited, allowing my eyes to adjust to the darkness. As I could begin to discern, I saw a long concrete corridor stretched out in front of me, sloping down and barely lit by a few flickering fluorescent lights affixed to the ceiling. I quietly shut the door behind me and followed the corridor to a small landing, where it turned sharply to continue down in the opposite direction. There, the concrete surfaces of the floor, walls, and ceiling ended, and it was simply a tunnel dug out of the earth. At that point, the fluorescent lighting ended too. I edged my way forward onto the soft soil.

It appeared there was a turn up ahead, because I could see a dim light shining from around the corner. I allowed the light to guide me until I rounded the bend. Lying on the ground was a light bulb with no socket or cord attached. Yet it shone as if it were screwed into a lamp that was plugged into an electrical outlet. I gently reached down and picked it up. It continued to shine in my hand, but it was hot, like a lit bulb should be, and I quickly put it back on the ground. I stooped down and marveled at it, amazed by the sight. *The air down here must carry a current that can operate electrical appliances—including light bulbs.*

Then I saw that with no concrete to barricade them, little rivulets of water were making their way downward along the ground. The water had the same metallic-liquid qualities as the lake had. Over and over again, I turned at the landings to go down farther still. The deeper I descended, the more moisture I noticed oozing out of the soil.

The tunnel meandered left and right, seemingly haphazardly, but always down. Sporadic lit light bulbs lying on the ground illuminated the way. I paused at each one to take a closer look. Finally, from beyond another bend in the tunnel, a bright-blue light glowed. The similarity between this blue light and the blue glow that emanated from Mannix was unmistakable, undulating, and alive.

This must be the source of his power, I realized. *The exotic matter. He doesn't just derive his power from the island. He is part of the island. The Isle of Man. Mannix.* Suddenly, the weight of my encounter with Mannix was crushing down upon me. *No wonder Ken was so reverent. Mannix was beyond a legend. He was the island incarnate.*

I stopped at the edge of the opening and peeked around the corner. Mesmerized, I walked forward into a large, natural cave. The billowing blue light I had become so familiar with glowed out of a giant pit in the center. Little else about the contents of this cave was natural anymore, though. Computers and hardware unrecognizable to even me lined the walls. I could only imagine how long it had taken to move everything down the winding path I had just walked.

In front of the pit stood a ring roughly seven feet in diameter. Cables hung from it and were attached to the various computers. The cables littered the floor of the cave like a clumsily made spider's web. Draped into the pit were two massive cables that were swallowed up by the blinding blue light. I knew immediately what this contraption was: the space-time construct I had read about in my dad's letters. He was trying to harness the power of the exotic matter—control it—and in so doing, control the exit point of a wormhole he was creating. He was attempting time travel.

"What are you doing here?" I heard my dad ask from right behind me.

"Dad!" I was unable to repress the strident tone in my voice as I whirled around.

"How did you find this place?" he asked, taking hold of my arm and pulling me close to him. My face was inches from his. He was drawn, and his paleness was accentuated by the blue glow. His cheekbones were sharp under his loose skin, and the bones in his arms and hands were too prominent. He was like a walking skeleton. I barely recognized him.

"I—I—" I stammered. I couldn't think of an answer as to how I could have accidentally happened upon this very carefully hidden lab. "I remember you said—"

"I never told you anything about this place. Are you alone?" His eyes darted wildly, searching behind me to see if I had brought anyone else. Ken was right to stay outside. There was no telling what my dad would have done if he'd seen Ken. His grip tightened on my arm, his bony fingers pressing into my muscle.

"Dad, you're hurting me!" I tried to wiggle my arm free. He let go and shook his head as though he suddenly realized he had been hurting his own flesh and blood. His eyes lost focus, and he was clearly dazed. His body began to sway, and I realized he was about to pass out.

"Dad!" I screamed and reached out to steady him.

"Imogen?" he asked, as though I were an apparition. His voice had softened in that instant.

"Yes, Dad. It's me, Imogen. Please. We need to talk." I was trembling so badly, I could barely form the words.

I wasn't sure if I was trembling from fear of the eminent catastrophe or fear of my dad's reaction after I begged him to stop this madness. Both options seemed like they would end tragically.

"Genny?" He was still having trouble focusing on me.

"Dad, I've come here because I know what you're trying to do. I miss Mom too, but this could kill us all. You've got to stop this."

He stepped back from me toward the pit. The closer he stumbled toward the raw exotic matter, the more sharply his wandering eyes focused on me and hardened like cold steel.

"There is no stopping, Genny."

"Dad, you could kill thousands of people. Maybe destroy the whole island. You don't know what you're dealing with."

"And you think you do?" he spat. He laughed like a villain from an old movie.

"No. No one understands exotic matter. I don't, and neither do you. But I do know one thing: you can't trade the world for one person."

"Yes. Yes, I can," he said matter-of-factly. "Because no matter what happens to this plane of reality, I won't be here. I'll be with Janet." Something about the way he called my mom Janet made me wonder if he had forgotten I was his daughter.

"Maybe, Dad. If you don't blink out of existence. And even if you did make it back to save her, look what you would have sacrificed."

"I would have sacrificed nothing. With Janet alive, I'd never need to come to the Isle of Man. This," he said, gesturing widely, "will never happen."

"You would have sacrificed me!" Tears burst from my eyes and rolled down my cheeks. "Don't you see that? Forget about everyone else, then. But you're willing to let me die?" I cried.

"You're waiting on the other side too, Genny." I could tell he was losing his focus again.

"What about the me right here in front of you?"

"You're on the other side," he repeated and stumbled toward the ring.

"So are you, Dad," I realized. "Did you forget? There will be two of you if you go back. What are you going to do about that?"

"I'll take care of him," he said coldly.

"What do you mean? You're not planning to kill the other you, are you?" I laughed in disbelief.

"I said I'll take care of it!" he bellowed. "Darius!"

A man in a white lab coat ran out from an opening in the cave behind a wall of computers.

"What's going on, Dr. Hazard?" he asked. He was clearly shocked to see another person in the laboratory.

"Get her out of here! She's going to ruin everything. Your funding, my work…it will all be wasted, Darius! We must save our precious alternative energy." Dad's face was contorted with rage, and his sallow skin blazed red even in the blue glow that surrounded us. He was almost unrecognizable as the man I knew as my father.

The man named Darius came up behind me and pulled my arms together in a hold behind my back. I kicked at him, trying desperately to free myself. He didn't look strong, but he quickly overpowered me and began dragging me toward the tunnel.

"I love you, Dad. If you do this, you'll kill me! Please don't kill me," I begged. "Please don't kill me."

Darius turned his head to look at my dad, and I went limp when I saw the red mark on his neck. It was the mark of the Keepers, but marred almost beyond recognition. Thick, raised scars cut through the triskelion. The scars looked old, so I could only imagine that years before, someone had tried to claw it out of existence. I shuddered, and when I did, he whipped my body around the corner into the tunnel.

Before my eyes could readjust to the darkness, I heard a grunt as the air was knocked out of him. His hands fell away from my wrists, and his body flew against the wall with a thud. I suddenly felt another hand on mine. I turned. Ken had followed me down and waited in the tunnel.

"Quick," I said to him. "There's still time."

Ken and I ran back into the laboratory. My dad was standing at the ring, peering into the gaping hole. Dad turned, looked at me, and pressed a button on a control he removed from his pocket. The giant ring that stood in front of him began spinning violently and sucked the blue light into a swirling vortex behind it. The dark room pulsed an icy blue as though it were lit by a strobe light; the equipment rattled and clattered and gradually began vibrating its way around the floor like possessed machinery.

"Dad! Stop! You don't know what you're doing. It's the exotic matter. You've been exposed to it for too long. It's changed you!"

"Who are you?" he demanded, walking briskly toward us. "This is a restricted area!"

"It's me, Dad. Genny. Imogen. Remember? I'm your daughter. I'm Janet's daughter."

"Janet," he whispered. "I remember now. That's why I'm here. You will not stop me from being with her. Nothing can."

Without warning, he turned from me and charged toward the vortex.

"No!" I screamed as my dad threw himself through the ring.

I watched helplessly as the blue light of the vortex swallowed my dad. A massive surge of radiation crashed outward like a wave caused by a boulder dropped into a pond. For a split second, I thought I saw tiny figures surging up from the opening in the ground, weaving their way through the blue light. The force of the blast ripped Ken's body away from mine, but I could feel his grip tight on my hand for a second longer before that, too, was wrenched from me.

Golden sunlight played on my eyelids, and I lay still, listening to the waves crash. I didn't remember falling asleep outside. Snapshots of a bizarre nightmare began popping into my consciousness. *What in the world did I eat to deserve that?* I smiled to myself. The sun blinded me when I opened my eyes, so I closed them and tried to sit up. The back of my head throbbed like I had been clubbed. I reached up to rub it and jerked my hand away from the giant goose egg. *Where am I?* I wondered.

A salty breeze blew on my face as I sat up, and rough pebbles dug into the palms of my hands as I pressed into the ground. I was able to pry my eyes open just enough to see the sea. I was on a beach, very close to the shoreline. The waves lapping up were only just out of reach. I looked around and saw a strange little castle out in the sea. I couldn't remember how I ended up there; at that moment, I couldn't remember much of anything at all. To the northwest I could see a pillar of black smoke rising from a mountain. Snaefell Summit, I recalled. I had seen that smoke before. That exact smoke.

Everything that had happened came crashing down on me. Or, judging by the height of the smoke, everything that was *about* to happen. We had been blasted back in time. The smoke was thickening in the sky, and that meant the tram explosion that Ken had set off happened earlier. But it was about an hour after the explosion had happened that my dad...*Oh no! I didn't stop him*, I realized.

Somewhere near the top of Snaefell Summit, there was another me who didn't know that yet. She was still laboring under the delusion that she could say the right thing and fix everything. That she could save the Isle of Man. With only an hour to go until my dad threw himself into the vortex, I didn't even have enough time to reach Snaefell Summit to try again.

Ken? Where's Ken, I wondered, feeling a lump rise in my throat. I wheeled around, scanning the beach for him. Off in the distance, I could just make out something lying on the beach. I tried to run, but only stumbled along, dragging my feet through the rocky sand. It was Ken, I saw as I approached the heap lying in the black, oily seaweed. Surf washed up on his face, but he lay motionless.

"Ken? Ken!" I began shrieking and crying uncontrollably. Surely, in an effort to save everyone, I hadn't lost the only thing that mattered to me. I wrenched him out of the water's reach. "Ken, please…"

He finally tried to take a breath, coughing and spewing salt water from his mouth.

"Where are we?" he sputtered.

"Douglas Bay. We've gone about an hour back in time." He looked at me, speechless for a moment. "I couldn't stop him, Ken. Something happened when my dad jumped into the pocket of exotic matter. I don't know what happened to the island, but you and I were blasted an hour back in time. We've got to warn Mannix."

"The tide's come in since we were here earlier, and I don't have a surfboard this time. How do we get there?"

"There," I said, pointing to a blue, glowing dome just visible under the water's surface about twenty feet out into the bay.

"He's been waiting for us," Ken said in amazement.

"That means he already knew I'd fail," I hissed.

We waded out into the water. Normally, I would have begun to panic as soon as the water hit my knees, but I was too angry to notice. I strode farther and farther out, not caring if Ken was even with me. Right before my head would have submerged, I ducked down and found myself back in Mannix's protective bubble. He *had* been waiting for us.

"You knew. You knew all along I'd fail, but you sent me off anyway," I spat out as soon as I saw him. Mannix, who once had looked like an ethereal boy-priest, at that moment seemed like nothing more than an immature prankster with more power than he knew how to handle. "Ha-ha. Very funny. Well, I guess you didn't realize that because of your little joke, a man died today. He gave his life for me, and *that* was because of you," I said, shoving my finger at his face.

"Genny!" Ken gasped.

I didn't care if I was being disrespectful to his beloved idol.

"It's all right," Mannix said to Ken. "Are you finished, Genny?"

"No, I'm not. This whole thing was an exercise in futility. I feel like an idiot, just stupidly following along and doing what you said, when you knew all along it wouldn't work."

"I knew the outcome was inevitable," he said quietly. "But I knew you had to go through it, so you could start to become the person you need to be."

"What?" I was incredulous. How could he even pretend to know me? To know what I was and wasn't capable of? "I was just fine the way I was! Just fine!"

"You had to grow. You have a lot you must do very soon, and you weren't ready. Most of the time, people can grow and evolve at their own pace and in their own time. But time is a luxury we couldn't afford."

"Couldn't afford? We couldn't afford to lose John," I countered, not being able to hold the angry tears in any longer.

"John knew he was giving his life for this."

"For *what*? We didn't accomplish anything! And how does everyone know the future around here but me?"

"Mannix?" Ken interrupted, looking at his watch. "It's almost time."

Mannix exhaled slowly like a sad, deflating balloon.

"I know." With that, Mannix knelt on the dry earth beneath him. "Please, give me the strength to do what must be done," he prayed quietly.

I looked up as if I'd see someone or something, but of course, all I saw was water. Then to my shock, Mannix began walking toward the beach instead of away from it and back to the safety and anonymity of the Tower of Refuge. The protective bubble moved along with him, staying centered on him like an umbrella.

Ken took my hand, and we followed behind. Mannix's usual perfect posture buckled while the sunlight grew brighter and brighter as the layer of water above us thinned. His footsteps were heavy as the weight of the world seemed to be upon his shoulders. He stooped for a moment, like a broken man, and wiped his eyes. I forgot my animosity and my feeling of betrayal as I saw the edge of the bubble and the air outside meet. Water dripped down the concave surface of our little dome as Mannix led us out into the open.

Once completely out of the water, a small break appeared in the bubble and spread, reducing the bubble down to the ground and then to nothingness. Mannix shivered in the slight breeze, and I marveled that even feeling the wind on his face would be a new experience for him. He squinted in the sunlight that must have been unbearably bright to his eyes.

A few people, who happened to be passing on the boardwalk, stopped, stunned. Mannix looked up at them and straightened into his usual erect stance, as though he realized his moment of weakness must necessarily be over. Somehow, even barefoot, he slowly and nimbly trod over the sharp stones that carpeted the beach and made his way to the steps.

Of all the unbelievable events of the last few months, this was somehow the most surreal: seeing Mannix ascend the steps and stand on the boardwalk of Douglas Bay. We followed after him, and Ken kept us close, despite the growing crowd.

A few witnesses whispered into cell phones, while others were snapping pictures. People streamed into the street from the beachfront tourist shops and down the roads that fed into the beach drive, where traffic had halted. Within minutes, it looked like half of Douglas had crowded onto the boardwalk. Curiosity and disbelief drove them there. Like me, these people were not part of the privileged few who knew the prophecies. They were not Keepers. They were as ignorant of the future as I was.

The lit storefront signs suddenly all went dark in unison. The power on the island had gone out. I thought of the power fluctuations of the previous months and knew that on the other side of Snaefell Summit, my dad had just started the ring. I remembered it spinning faster and faster and the vortex appearing before my eyes.

Mannix, like I imagined Moses at the Red Sea, raised his hands upward in front of him. With an audible sizzle of energy, a dome-shaped force field spread across the sky, incasing the island in a giant version of the bubble in which I had walked across the floor of Douglas Bay. Not a sound came from the throngs of people, not a gasp or a shriek of terror. It was too surreal to understand, much less to fear.

But the silence didn't last long. Almost as if the island were waiting for the force field to be complete, the ground heaved beneath us. My dad had given himself to the vortex, and the pocket of exotic matter that the island had been resting on since time began had imploded. There was nothing beneath us now but empty space, and the Isle of Man began to sink into the sea.

All the people who had been so quiet before were now screaming and running. I held tight to Ken so we wouldn't be separated. Over Ken's shoulder, I saw in the distance a blue beam shoot up like a geyser. The rush of energy writhed from within, and although I was too far away to see the details, I remembered what I had seen in the laboratory before being jolted back in time: tiny figures being helplessly swept along by the current.

Ken and I stood quietly next to Mannix, watching the waves of water swallow the island up. I couldn't believe how calm I was watching the water crashing down around me—just like it did to my mother, in a way—but I was inside the bubble, dry and protected. Up above us, only a small circle of sky was visible at the top of the force field, and I silently said my good-bye to sky and sun. Bubbles rushed over the surface of our dome as the island continued to plummet farther and farther down.

It didn't take long for any vestiges of sunlight to be obscured by the water above us. Although the blue glow from the dome afforded plenty of light inside, the darkness of the world around us was suddenly overwhelming. I looked at the face of my beloved Ken bathed in the blue living light and realized I'd never see it any other way again. It was all my fault. Sure, Mannix knew I wouldn't succeed in stopping my dad, but was there any way I *could* have stopped him if I had done something different? Maybe...

My thoughts returned to the present when I felt the island sinking faster and faster. There was no telling how deep we were at that point. No search-and-rescue mission would ever be able to get this deep. *What about supplies,* I thought in a panic. *How have I never thought of that before? Food? Fresh water?* My thoughts became as claustrophobic as the thought of living my life in a bubble. I wanted to ask Mannix, but I didn't dare disturb him. I consoled myself by remembering that Mannix knew the future and that no step of preparedness would have escaped his notice.

Most of the crowd had disappeared to take refuge, leaving only a few of us who gathered around Mannix. We were pilgrims, venturing into a new world. The criers, the screamers, the panickers, they had all run to hide. Only the brave remained. I looked at the few dozen faces around me, illuminated in blue. I wasn't surprised when I noticed the tattoos on each one of their necks, the red ink muted into a mellow purple by the blue glow. It didn't look so scary to me anymore. "'Whichever way you throw us, we will stand,'" the taxi driver told me at the airport on the day I arrived on the Isle of Man. And here we stood, staring bravely into the darkness as we plunged to the newly created depths of the sea.

The island finally rested, and I no longer felt like I was in a dropping elevator. I tentatively took a step forward. The group that remained wordlessly began descending the steps onto what was once a beach, but now was merely a strip of rough sand and rocks that led to the Tower of Refuge and then the wall of the dome. It was strange that the rocks felt the same under my feet. *Why wouldn't they?* I corrected myself, but still I marveled that everything within our protective dome was unchanged.

At its center peak, the dome looked to be about one hundred meters high. It slowly dropped in height to seal us in along the circumference of the island. Minute flashes of white light sparked periodically in random places on its surface, like little surges of electricity. Ken was—the island was—our *world* was bathed in its blue light.

As we neared the wall of the dome, I could just make out some fish, illuminated by the glow, darting away from the surface. I suddenly felt like we were in an enormous, upturned fishbowl where we were the fish and the fish were the amused people, looking in at us who were dumb to the world outside. Beyond that, the sea was an inkwell of blackness.

I couldn't imagine how this had affected the sea around us, these helpless creatures being sucked downward along with us to depths they should never have experienced. The bottom had fallen out of the sea. While we were protected inside, I wondered how their bodies would adjust to the new pressure at this depth. And this depth would prevent any hope of escape for us. I remembered reading that a small submarine had once reached the Marianas Trench, thought to be the deepest point in the ocean. The water pressure at that depth was over one thousand atmospheres.

It was hard to tell exactly how deep we were. When the pocket of exotic matter had been disturbed, it created a sinkhole that appeared to have obliterated the floor of the Irish Sea. The island simply sank along with the seabed. We didn't have the supplies necessary on the island to manufacture a means to get someone to the surface. Our only hope was that surface dwellers might find us, and they could physically reach us.

Mannix, exhausted to the point of collapse, had walked back to the Tower of Refuge, with a Keeper on each side for support. I was worried about him; he looked so weak, but the Keepers cautioned me not to speak to him until he had had time to recover. I couldn't forget; Mannix's job was far from done.

Within the hour Cerdwyn and thirty or more Keepers arrived in Douglas on the tram. I couldn't believe it, but an hour after the Isle of Man dropped off the face of the map, the electric tram was running. That was thanks to Mannix, who constantly provided a current that ran through the air to power all electrical devices, and Stanley, a prepared Keeper who was a tram driver by trade. He had waited all his life for this, so since it happened on his shift, the tram only missed one run, and that was while the island was actually falling.

Unbelievably, the island stayed perfectly intact during the sinking process. It very well could have fallen at an angle, crumbling the landmass into bits, but it didn't. It was as if a magician had pulled the tablecloth out from under a set table. Everything was still in its place. For the island, that included an undisturbed tram track.

As the people of Douglas made their way out of their homes, they were drawn out of curiosity and awe to the wall, where Keepers were gathering to counsel and inform people of what had happened and what the next steps for the island would be. A group of Keepers was sent to each town to do the same. It pays to be organized, and they had had hundreds of years to ready themselves.

Cerdwyn ran across the beach toward us, her long skirt skimming the rough rocks. She grabbed Ken and hugged her son like they had been apart for years. Ken smiled at me sheepishly, still locked in his mother's embrace.

"I'm all right, Mum. I'm all right," Ken assured her.

"I knew you would be, my pet," she said, ruffling his hair before he could. Then she turned to me.

"Oh, my dear Genny," she said, seizing me in the same fashion. Being wrapped in her warmth and the softness of her sweaters made me relax to the point of collapse. I needed a mom right now, even if it wasn't my own. I felt like a swaddled baby in her arms.

"I don't understand, Cerdwyn," I confided quietly in her ear. "I don't understand."

"My brilliant girl," she whispered, "we can't understand everything." Kissing me on the cheek, she added, "Nobody can. Not even you." She released me, and Ken put his arm around me. "I was told that he wishes to see me," she told us, motioning to the Tower. I hadn't noticed before that the same two Keepers who had escorted Mannix back to the Tower of Refuge now accompanied her. Ken and I began walking with her, but the two Keepers stopped us.

"I'm sorry, but he has asked to see Cerdwyn alone."

"We must do as he wishes," Cerdwyn said, engulfing us both in a giant hug. "I'll be back soon." She released us and walked the remainder of the way to the tower with the two Keepers.

Masses of Keepers were busy grouping people together farther along, but Ken and I were alone where we stood. Normal citizens, dumb to what had happened, wandered in a daze along the boardwalk above, unknowingly waiting to be led by a Keeper. I imagined it was like that all around the small island. People wandering. People leading. I supposed it would only be so long before life would continue like it did before. Nothing, no matter how catastrophic, can stop life from happening.

"How are you doing?" Ken asked.

"I don't know. Fine, I guess. How about you?"

"Fine." We both giggled at the stupid conversation, but I guessed "fine" was as good as anyone could be after her world ended. We stood looking at the dome that walled us in. It shimmered like electrified glass, if such a thing could exist. I remembered a dream I had in which I was encircled by a slithering blue web, and I wondered what Mannix's blue dome would look like under a microscope. I thought I might just know already.

We stood for a moment more, staring at the impossible. I had learned that anything was possible.

"I love you," Ken said.

"I love you too," I replied. He grabbed me and kissed me. It was as if all the stress and responsibility that we had carried for so long had transformed into passion. I stopped analyzing and hypothesizing, and the only thought in my head, if you could call it a thought, was heat. I ran my hands through his hair, as I had longed to do every time

I watched him scruff it up in frustration. He was mine, and I was his.

"Marry me," he whispered, his lips still on mine.

"OK," I whispered back without a second of hesitation. He pulled back a little, which confused me. He smiled when he saw the look on my face.

"Sorry," he said, chuckling. "I didn't think you'd say yes. It's not really your MO to act impulsively. I thought I'd have to work on you for a while." He pulled me hard back into his arms.

"Life will never be the same." I paused and looked down at the small rocks I had trod across barefoot on the way to the Tower of Refuge. The rocks were now bathed in the constantly fluctuating blue hue of the dome. "And I realized I don't want to be the same either. All I want now is you." We kissed again. "So yes, I want to marry you. And the sooner, the better."

Ken kissed me good-bye at the Ramsey tram station, and we held each other for a long time. He knew that once again, what I needed to do, I needed to do alone. He wanted to go back to his house to pack up some things anyway, he said. He'd meet me at my house afterward. I knew I needed to do the same, but the thought of going back to my house was almost too much. I couldn't deal with seeing my dad's coffee cup, his jacket hanging in the closet, the briefcase—knowing now they belonged to a monster. I couldn't breathe the air from that place and not think I was somehow taking in his evil and making it a part of me.

As though he could read my mind, Ken said gently, "It wasn't him, you know. That man—he wasn't your dad. That stuff changed him. You need to remember him the way he used to be."

I let go of the image of him, crazed and possessed, flinging himself into the blue glow coming from the pit. Maybe it really had been too late for him. Maybe he was more exotic matter than human by that point.

"I know. It wasn't him."

The blue glow illuminated the familiar streets of Ramsey, making the scene like a topsy-turvy dream—it was like being home, but the rooms were in the wrong places. I pulled a scrap of paper out of my pocket and double-checked the address, even though I was certain I had remembered it correctly. Anything to delay the inevitable. I slowly walked up the steps to the front door, wondering what exactly I was going to say. I had had the whole tram ride back to rehearse, but all I could do was stare out the window at the familiar that wasn't quite right.

I knocked on the door. After some rustling inside, the curtain was pulled back a little, and then the door opened. Instead of inviting me in, Reg stepped quickly out, shutting the door behind him. I opened my mouth to speak, but nothing came out.

"Why are you here?" he asked, his voice harsh.

I was taken aback. I had assumed all would be forgiven and forgotten between us. I thought that since all I had warned him about had come to pass, he would be sorry for the way he had treated me that day in the cafeteria.

"What do you want, Genny?"

"I need your help, Reg. Everyone does. We're a good team, and I think we should work together to help the island. After all, we know how to make a generator." I smiled.

How could I ask him the next part? What could I say? I was beginning to think my idea was stupid, but who else could I go to? Beside Ken, Reg was my best friend.

"And…I came to ask you to be my man of honor at my wedding," I stammered.

"I won't be able to make it," he replied quickly. "I've got a funeral to get ready for."

"Who died?" I asked, forgetting the reason I had come.

"Jim, Genny. Jim's gone."

"What! What happened?"

"Jim and Ted had skipped school to go to Port Saint Mary's so Jim could learn to surf before he went on a weekend. He didn't want Jocelyn to see him surf before he got better. Ted says Jim was out too far from the shore when the"—he struggled for the word—"force field went up and trapped him on the outside. When the island began to sink, the downward current pulled him under." Reg wedged his fingers underneath his glasses to wipe away a tear.

If I had stopped my dad, Jim would still be alive. I pulled out my inhaler and took a puff.

"I'm so sorry," I managed to say. After hearing so many people fumble over their condolences to me after my mom died, I would have thought I'd know what to say to a friend who'd lost someone, but I didn't. I stood dumb.

"Is it true what they're saying about your dad? That he was responsible for all this?"

I only nodded.

Reg took off his glasses and rubbed his red, tired eyes. "Did you know?"

I nodded. "That's why I tried to warn you." The words coming out of my mouth seemed so insignificant, so hollow. I knew what he was thinking. That I never should have moved to the island. He was right, of course, but I knew better than anyone that you can't turn back the clock. At least, not successfully.

"Well, I've got things to do," Reg said, stepping back into his house. "See you around."

"Yeah," I said, unable to disguise the sadness in my voice, "see you."

"Oh yeah. Congratulations," he said as he shut the door.

I was alone on his front doorstep, and even though the climate on the island would be a constant seventy-two degrees from then on, I felt cold. Ken meant the world to me, but I never wanted to lose Reg. You shouldn't have to lose your friend because of the one you love.

I left and started back to my house, hoping that somehow Ken would beat me there. I had to get my violin, and we still had another stop to make.

The door creaked open, and Ken and I tiptoed into the darkness, leaving all our things out in the alleyway. I don't know why we were being so quiet. Was it out of respect for the dead, or because we couldn't believe John wasn't going to be sitting on the sofa, rubbing his calloused hand gently over a doily on the end table? Everything was exactly as we had left it. I touched the back of the wooden chair where I had sat shrinking away from the poor man who was so willing to give his life for his beliefs, for me.

"We'd better shut the door so Coal can't get out," Ken whispered. I switched the lamp on, the fringe from the shade tickling my wrist as I slid my hand away. "Remember, the last time we were here, he didn't stay." Ken crossed the room to shut the front door. Before he could reach it, a black furry bullet shot across the floor and into the alleyway. Ken groaned, running his hand through his thick, black hair.

"He didn't stay, but he came back," I reminded him. I passed by Ken and pushed the door closed until it was only slightly ajar. Blue light gently billowed through the opening like smoke wafting in, but instead of being thick and murky, it was pure and cleansing. That would take some getting used to.

"All we can do is wait." I sat on the chair as I had before. Ken sat tentatively on the edge of his chair, his elbows resting on his knees.

"We can sit on the sofa, you know," he said, nodding to the place where John had sat only the day before. It seemed like a lifetime ago.

"Doesn't seem right." I stared straight ahead at the sofa, remembering everything I could about John, but deleting all the scary aspects.

I heard Ken slide back into his chair and relax. "I know what you mean," he said with a sigh.

"Tell me about John's mom," I said, admiring the quantity of the handmade doilies that were strewn around the little room.

"She was the leader of the Keepers before my mom. She was leader for, wow, forty years or so."

"John said she and your mom carried many of the same burdens. I'm beginning to see what he meant. I can't imagine living your life knowing a catastrophe is going to happen. It's like knowing the date of your death. I think I'd rather not know the future. Ignorance is bliss, right?"

"You have no idea," he mused, and the door creaked open, allowing a larger swath of blue light to swirl into the room. Coal tentatively put one paw over the threshold. Then another. His head poked through, and his nose twitched at the smell of strangers. But the hope of food won out over wariness, and he trotted over and rubbed against Ken's legs and then mine. I reached down and scratched between his ears, and he twisted his head back and forth gratefully.

"I'm afraid you're going on a little trip, Coal," Ken said. "We'll be your mummy and daddy now."

"Ugh," I groaned. "Don't tell him that. He'll never go with us."

"Don't be silly." Ken reached down to pick up Coal. As he lifted the cat, Coal's back feet stayed on the ground for longer than they should have, making his body appear to stretch to double its original length. Ken finally gathered Coal up into a squirming bundle and clutched him tightly to his chest.

"You'd be a fantastic mother," he told me with a goofy grin on his face.

"How?" I scoffed. "I didn't have an example for most of my life." A snapshot of my mom appeared in my head and even that was yellowing with age. I forced myself to remember her laugh, her touch, and then too many memories began flooding back. A picnic in the park. Our talks as she drove me to school. The day she died.

"You didn't have her for as long as you should have, but in that short amount of time, she helped to make you who you are."

I stroked Coal's black fur and quickly pulled my hand away. "You get a bath tonight, mister."

"Cats bathe themselves, don't they?"

"Apparently not well enough. He smells like leftover fry oil. I'm giving him a bath as soon as we get back."

"See." Ken smiled again. "I told you you'd be a good mother."

"Ugh." I sighed and turned the lamp off, following Ken and the blue trail of light out the front door.

"Can you lock up?" Ken said while struggling to hold Coal, who had given up and gone limp. "The keys are in my pocket."

In fact, only a few of the keys were in his jeans pocket. The rest of the fifty or so keys swung off the bracelet-sized metal key ring that hung next to his hip. I slid the keys out and found the key with a navy-blue bow.

"What will happen to the house?" I asked as I locked the door.

"I guess it will stay just like this. Full of doilies, but empty of people."

"Seems like a waste."

"It's not like people are going to be moving to the island. Besides, that place is like a shrine to the Keepers."

"It's still sad," I commented and wedged the key ring back into his pocket.

"Look around you, Genny. I think we're going to have sadder things to deal with than an empty house."

I frowned as we reached the high street. I looked up, wishing desperately to be assured by a hopeful golden sun, but instead there was only the blue dome above us, holding back tons of water from crushing us. Our sky now had a ceiling, and although it gave us life, it also gave us boundaries.

"We have some things to be happy about, right?"

"We have us to be happy about, Genny." He kissed me quickly, and we made our way to the tram that would take us to Douglas.

The Beginning

Ballaglass Glen was different in many ways. The light no longer streamed down in shafts that trembled in a way that defied the laws of science. The aura from our protective dome filtered through the leafy canopy of the glen and circled around objects, caressing them and moving on. I was endlessly fascinated by the properties of this light from the first time I saw it pouring out of the Tower of Refuge.

Another reason the glen looked different that day was because it had been painstakingly adorned for a wedding.

Cerdwyn had gathered vines and covered the handrails of the footbridge that crossed the stream. To my surprise, the stream, fed from a source deep within the earth and exiting out North Barrule, still ran through the rocky valley. In the vines she had woven hundreds of little bluebells that grew in the area. That, coupled with the blue glow, lent the glen the same cool, crystalline wonder of an early-December morning after a heavy snow.

Although I had been in the glen all morning, Cerdwyn shooed me up the steps toward the tramline to get dressed and to stay hidden so no one would see me in my wedding dress. As I ascended the steps, I noticed a hollowed-out place to the left, where Cerdwyn had pushed brush out of the way to create a makeshift dressing room. The dress was hanging on a branch. As I reached for it, a voice from behind startled me.

"My mum told me to be your lady-in-waiting today." I turned to see Celine, but she refused to make eye contact with me. "I thought you'd rather be alone, but Mum doesn't know our...history, and I thought it would be easier to be obedient than to go into everything with her," she said, staring at the dress as she spoke. She waited for me to say something, but when I didn't, she continued. "I'm sorry, for what it's worth. I never hated you. I hated everything that came along with you. It's not your fault, I guess."

I didn't really know what to say. It was a halfhearted apology at best, and she was right. I didn't want someone who, despite her protest, clearly hated me to help me prepare for the most important day of my life. It was strange that after all that had happened, I would consider a silly ceremony as *the* most important day of my life, but it was. And Celine was right; I didn't want her there, but I understood why she couldn't say no to her mom. I wouldn't say no to Cerdwyn either.

"Fine," I said. She turned her head as I undressed, and she slipped the dress off the hanger. She was careful to keep the hem off the ground as I stepped into it.

I left all the elaborate dresses for the other girls on the island to fight over in the coming years. There would be no more factory-made dresses on the Isle of Man. The last ones shipped to the island would be snapped up while new, and passed down for many generations. This dress was simple, like me, right down to my bare feet. But I thought its simplicity made it beautiful. I wondered if that's the way Ken felt about me. Celine zipped me up, and I faced her.

"Thank you," I said, and her eyes finally met mine, but only for a moment.

"You're welcome. I'll go tell them you're ready." She turned to leave, but I stopped her.

"Celine, we're about to be"—I tried not to choke on the word—"sisters-in-law. I know how upset you were that Ken left your best friend for me, but we need to let the past go, right? I mean, I forgive you for how you treated me."

She looked blankly at me. "My mother will kill me if I ruin your wedding day, so let's just drop the subject for now. But I'll put your fears to rest. I didn't care if Ken and Karyn broke up."

"So, why do you hate me?" I blurted.

"I just said I don't hate you." The familiar acid tone returned to her voice.

"You said you hated everything that came along with me. What came along with me?"

"Forget I said anything." The anger sizzled in her voice. Any pretense at niceties was gone. "Forget I apologized. Congratulations. You got Ken."

She left me alone in my little room. *What a wedding day,* I thought glumly as I decided against sitting down on the ground in my white dress. *If she wasn't upset about Karyn, then what's the problem? What does she think I'm going to do to Ken?* I didn't have a sibling, so I began to wonder if maybe I didn't have the capacity to understand what she was going through: her twin brother marrying so young. And to a "comeover."

She doesn't have to love me, I assured myself, *because Ken does.*

The Beginning

I heard violins begin playing below in the glen, so I stepped out and made my way down the steps. I was sure my dress was white when I left the store with it, but now it was a beautiful, patterned, iridescent blue that changed every time I moved, mirroring the shadows of the leaves in the trees.

I thought of how I'd always heard of wedding-day jitters. Maybe it was because of our unique situation, but I certainly didn't have any. Marrying Ken was the most natural step I could hypothesize. Our wedding was a decision that married emotions with logic. I wasn't giddy with excitement like I imagined so many girls are when they're getting married. I wondered if the horror of what had happened and the fear of the unknown had extinguished the emotional highs and lows in every inhabitant of the Isle of Man, at least for a while.

Cerdwyn and Ken waited for me on the footbridge. He smiled at me. It wasn't the cocky grin that always made me melt at school or when we were studying under our tree, but a smile of contentment. I had been perfectly calm up until that point, but my heart began galloping at the sight of him. I was embarrassed by the smile that spread too widely across my face. I didn't remember ever smiling so big, but maybe that's because I had never been so happy. I laughed at myself, realizing that true love could conquer fear.

He took my hand at the edge of the bridge and led me to Cerdwyn. The same bluebells that adorned the glen were woven into her hair, making her look like a queen of the fairies. The long, heavy skirts and sweaters she usually wore had been replaced with a flowing, blue and green silk dress. She raised her hands toward the sky, even though the sky was far beyond our sight. When she did, the pendant hidden beneath her neckline was pulled out. In silver that shone blue in the light was the Celtic knot I knew like the back of my hand. A part of me. A part of Mannix.

"Family. Friends. Brothers and sisters who thrive in the rays of our blue sun, we are gathered here in this, the most magical place of our mystical homeland, to unite these two people, Imogen and Kendreague, in marriage. Let them be our Adam and Eve, the harbinger of continuing life on our Isle of Man. But we are no longer an island, but part of the sea. So let us call our home by our former name: *Mannin. Arrane ashoonagh dy Vannin*: O land of our birth. We may not live in Eden, my brothers and sisters, but we live in a new world. Our separation from the surface world does not mean we are unimportant. We are still part of this planet, even though they cannot see us. They will think we are dead, but we are as alive as they are. We are as vital as they are. We are as important as they are."

Cerdwyn, lost in her thoughts, looked into my eyes and seemed to remember where she was. "But I digress." She smiled.

"Kendreague, do you take Imogen to be your wife, your life partner, your confidante, the love of your life?" she asked.

"I do," he said, gently squeezing my hand.

"And do you, Imogen, take Kendreague to be your husband, your life partner, your confidant, the love of your life?"

"I do," I replied without hesitation. How could I not? I knew there could never be anyone else for me but Ken. Ken was my everything: my best friend, my love, the closest thing I had to family. Our lives had already been fused together by fate. All I was doing with a ceremony was making it legal.

"Then I now pronounce you husband and wife," Cerdwyn announced, barely able to contain her glee. By the time she said, "You may kiss the bride," we were already locked in an embrace, our lips searing each other. We giggled as we pulled apart, and hand in hand, we walked off the footbridge and proceeded to a clearing where a man and a woman stood on either side of a large, flat stone. Each had a black leather case on the ground, exactly like John's case, and a red cloth was laid out in front of the stone. The congregation chattered a little as they hastened to join us, eager to get a spot close to the front. Cerdwyn stood before the stone and addressed the crowd.

"It is indeed an honor to have two souls present themselves for this dedication ceremony. I believe it must be a first to have two become one, and in the same day, both join the clan of the Keepers. I cannot imagine there is one in our midst who could say aught against either of these," she said, smiling. I glanced over at Celine, who thankfully kept her mouth shut. What could she have said, anyway? *Genny shouldn't be a Keeper because I hate her?*

Cerdwyn smiled at us and continued.

"Kendreague and Imogen, do you both swear to take whatever means necessary to protect Mannin, and all of her inhabitants? Even if it means sacrificing one of your lives for another?"

"We do," Ken and I replied in unison.

"Then you are hereby known as Keepers. You may receive the marks."

A sudden rumble shook the ground. Everyone looked around in fear, wondering if this was the final death throes of the island. I knew immediately the tremor signaled an instability in the exotic matter. But the earth beneath us stilled and the crowd again focused on Ken and me.

Ken and I knelt next to each other on the cloth and turning our faces to the right, laid our heads on the bare stone. The woman next to me knelt below my right shoulder and removed the tattoo gun from her case.

"This will hurt a bit," she whispered, "but you'll do just fine. Just concentrate on something else."

The stone felt surprisingly smooth and warm under my face, comforting; I wondered if it was only in comparison to the metal just coming into contact with the back of my neck. Like a mouse being toyed with by a cat, I felt the first sharp, almost playful scratch. *Am I bleeding yet?* I imagined a trickle of crimson blazing a trail down the side of my neck that may or may not actually have been there. *Wasn't this destined to happen?* In a way, everything since my flight to the Isle of Man was leading up to this. Somewhere along the way, I lost my hold on logic, because if I had been paying attention, I would have realized that this was always the logical conclusion.

My eyes began watering from the sting. I didn't want to cry. I couldn't let them see me cry. I had to be brave. *This isn't the end*, I assured myself. *It's a new beginning*

Concentrate on something else, I reminded myself. I looked out into the congregation as she began to drag the vibrating needle against the skin on my neck. Most of the people who were staring at me were smiling broadly, hardly able to contain their excitement. I blinked the tears from my eyes and once again, Celine was right in my line of vision. She wasn't scowling at me, though, like I was so used to seeing. She was looking instead at Ken, her sad eyes full of worry. I closed my eyes. I was exhausted trying to understand the mind of Celine. She was much more complicated than any equation. I wished she could have stood on Ken's side with her mother so I wouldn't have to look at her.

The pain of the tattoo brought about a strange clarity of thought. I was suddenly awestruck at the significance of what I was doing. The symbol I had feared was being etched onto my body, becoming a part of me, along with the beliefs I had mocked and the nation to which I was alien. The side of my neck stung like a sunburn, and I imagined the cool water of the brook that tripped through the glen running over my tender skin and cooling the burn. My vows to

Ken and my vows to the Keepers, the two most ridiculous thoughts I could have dreamed up a few months ago, were the most natural decisions for me to make that day.

"All finished," the woman whispered to me. Ken squeezed my hand and helped me to my feet. I stood on my tiptoes to peer over Ken's shoulder at his tattoo. His skin was puffy and looked as tender as mine felt, but the triskelion was easy to detect.

"*Quocunque jeceris stabit*," Cerdwyn announced grandly. "Whithersoever you throw it, it will stand!" A cheer exploded from the crowd, and they threw blue, sparkly confetti up into the air. Again, I wondered how much longer extravagances like confetti would be available to the people of our land. I could only imagine how Spartan our existence would become, but then again, at least we were alive.

Ken kissed me, scooping his hand around my waist and pulling me into his arms. I threw my head back, laughing. The sparkles danced around on the gentle air currents that circulated in our bubble, some swirling up high into the canopy of branches. I wondered what it would feel like to be so free that I could ride the wind like those little sparkles. After a lifetime of burden, that moment was the closest I had ever gotten.

"I love you more than the sun can shine," he whispered into my ear. "I love you more because you are mine."

"T.E. Brown?" I asked.

"Kendreague Creer. I just made it up."

"Show-off," I said, laughing.

Whatever the future held, I knew I'd have Ken at my side, and with that knowledge, I could face anything. The Isle of Man was like the new Atlantis: apart, but protected; alone, but comforted by our own; hit hard, but stronger than ever. *Quocunque jeceris stabit.* We had been thrown, but we would stand.

Appendix

Manx – English Translations

Page 15: *Shamyr as yn oaie eck er y baie.* Room that looks on the bay.

Dy ve shickyr. Of course.

Page 25: *Cha nel fys aym c'raad ta mee.* I don't know where I am.

T'ou balley. You are home.

Page 26: *Shoh hooin ee.* Here she comes.

Ish t'ayn. It is she.

Page 154: *Cadjoor y fadyraght.* Just like the prophecy.

Page 164: *Hooar mee ee.* I found her.

Bee er dty hwoaie. Careful now!

Gow kiarail! Watch your step!

Page 195: *Shee dy row hiu.* Peace be unto you.
Nar jarrood. T'ou balley. Never forget. You are home.
*S'treih mooar lhiam dy jarroo shegin dhyt jean reesht eh,
Imogen.* I am very sorry indeed that you must do it
over again, Imogen.

Page 206: *T'eh ny arreyder.* He is a Keeper.

Page 274: *Cha noddym surral y pian.* I cannot bear the pain.
Cair eab ceau neu-hastey ad. Just try to ignore them.
S'cummey. Ad nel fockle dy Ghaelg 'sy veal echey. It
doesn't matter. She doesn't know a word of Manx.
Agh t'eh. But he does.

Dear reader,

Please take a moment to rate and/or review Blue Sun on GoodReads.com or Amazon.com.

Many thanks,
Tracy Abrey

ACKNOWLEDGEMENTS

Thanks to my husband, David, for his support and his suggestion of the Isle of Man for the island setting of *Blue Sun*. Thanks to my children, Tommy and Sophie, for being so supportive of Mommy being an author. Thanks to my parents for always believing in me. Thank you to God for allowing me to write and gifting me with a story to tell.

Thanks to my beta-reader buddies: Stacy Burbidge, Stacy Fogarty, and Spring Simpson. I would have given up many times over were it not for you three. Thanks also to Andrew Ross, photographer, and Nathan Swearengin, graphic design artist, for their part in making *Blue Sun* look great.

Thanks to www.mannin.info for a great English-to-Manx online dictionary. I couldn't have written Manx dialogue without this super website.

A most special thanks to Tommy for begging me to tell him stories on the way home from school when he was little. One of those stories was the seed from which the *Blue Sun* saga grew.

Tracy Abrey has been passionate about writing since stating in her second grade "school days" book that when she grew up she wanted to write books. Earning a BA in English Literature and French from Houston Baptist University and having taught high school English as she pursued her MA in English Literature at DePaul University, her childhood passion has morphed into a career focused on young adult urban fantasy. Abrey has lived in Canada, France, and England and currently resides in the US with her husband and two children.

CPSIA information can be obtained at www.ICGtesting.com
Printed in the USA
LVOW05s1932301014

411282LV00015B/328/P